HP   †

WESTERN ISLES LIBRARIES

Readers are requested to take great care of the item while in their possession, and to point out any defects that they may notice in them to the librarian.

This item should be returned on or before the latest date stamped below, but an extension of the period of loan may be granted when desired.

Date of return	Date of return	Date of return
T. 31.8.18	NOB 17/7/19	
27 SEP 2018	16 SEP 2019	
19 OCT 2018	17 OCT 2019	
24 NOV 2018	13 JAN 2020	
3/1/19	17 FEB 2020	
Sy. 3.1.19	LT 18/02/20	
- 8 FEB 2019	15 OCT 2020	
- 2 MAR 2019	U.I.M.	
14 MAR 2019	Cy. 25.11.20	
29 MAR 2019	Sy. W. 8. 21	
- 3 MAY 2019		
- 3 MAY 2019		
- 8 MAY 2019		
22 JUN 2019		

WITHDRAWN

'A fierce and poignant novel, about superstitions and everything they conceal. For the last few chapters I was holding my breath' Beth Underdown, author of THE WITCHFINDER'S SISTER

'A dark, mesmerising tale. This is a raw, unflinching portrait of nineteenth century Skye: brutal, bleak and beautiful. There is so much here to love – the beautiful prose, the sense of place, the exploration of the power of stories to warn and to comfort. But above all, this is a powerful, unputdownable story that had me turning the pages deep into the night. A beautiful and eerie page-turner' Antonia Senior, author of TREASON'S DAUGHTER

'A deliciously Gothic read, Mazzola entwines sinister fairy tales with the dark side of Victorian history. Daphne Du Maurier fans will be hugging this to their chests' Laura Purcell, author of THE SILENT COMPANIONS

'A beautifully written, and spellbinding story which takes us back to the nineteenth century Isle of Skye, capturing the atmosphere, mystery – and menace – of an impoverished and divided island community . . . [an] extraordinary thriller' Mary Chamberlain, author of THE DRESSMAKER OF DACHAU

'I have rarely encountered such a creepy and unsettling story. With echoes of *The Wicker Man*, the remote and desolate setting adds to the sense of threat but also gives it a timeless quality, like the folkloric stories it evokes' Elizabeth Fremantle, author of THE GIRL IN THE GLASS TOWER

'A captivating, haunting mystery that will keep you turning the pages through mist and sea spray' Elisabeth Gifford, author of THE GOOD DOCTOR OF WARSAW

'Anna Mazzola expertly weaves a chilling web of menace and intrigue that utterly ensnared and beguiled me. Beautifully written and compelling' Rowan Coleman, author of THE SUMMER OF IMPOSSIBLE THINGS

'Paints a beautiful but sinister picture of an isolated island community . . . wonderfully dark, atmospheric and utterly captivating' Katherine Clements, author of THE COFFIN PATH

'Stunning writing, steeped in folklore, brooding landscapes and whispering villagers, and a chilling mystery cloaked with a dark and creepy atmosphere' Amanda Jennings, author of IN HER WAKE

'A stunningly unique tale. Intensely creepy and pulsating with atmosphere. A dark and deadly treat' Angela Clarke, author of TRUST ME

'Such a beautiful, atmospheric book' Sarah Day, author of MUSSOLINI'S ISLAND

'A hauntingly beautiful story of loss in all its forms' Catherine Hokin, author of BLOOD AND ROSES

'Darkly gothic and soaked in atmosphere' Rachel Rhys, author of DANGEROUS CROSSING

'A beautifully written, meticulously researched, atmospheric book that draws you into a brooding world of folklore and social conflict' Adam Hamdy, author of PENDULUM

'Laced with murder, mystery and folklore . . . drenched in stormy Scottish atmosphere' Jason Hewitt, author of THE DYNAMITE ROOM

'[A] chilling Victorian story of corruption and abuse. Anna Mazzola brings the landscape to vivid life' Essie Fox, author of THE LAST DAYS OF LEDA GREY

'As provocative as it is evocative, and Anna Mazzola's enticing blend of historical record and gothic unease offers unpredictable insights into the nature of story-telling and power alike' Lydia Syson, author of MR PEACOCK'S POSSESSIONS

The
Story
Keeper

ANNA MAZZOLA

WESTERN ISLES LIBRARIES		
34134010134457		
Bertrams	24/07/2018	
		£18.99

WITHDRAWN

TINDER
PRESS

Copyright © 2018 The Short Storyteller Limited

The right of Anna Mazzola to be identified as the Author of
the Work has been asserted by her in accordance with the
Copyright, Designs and Patents Act 1988.

First published in Great Britain in 2018 by Tinder Press
An imprint of HEADLINE PUBLISHING GROUP

1

Apart from any use permitted under UK copyright law, this publication
may only be reproduced, stored, or transmitted, in any form, or by any means,
with prior permission in writing of the publishers or, in the case of
reprographic production, in accordance with the terms of licences
issued by the Copyright Licensing Agency.

All characters in this publication are fictitious and any resemblance
to real persons, living or dead, is purely coincidental.

Cataloguing in Publication Data is available from the British Library

Hardback ISBN 978 1 4722 3478 0
Trade paperback ISBN 978 1 4722 3479 7

Typeset in Aldine 401 BT by Avon DataSet Ltd, Bidford-on-Avon, Warwickshire

Printed and bound in Great Britain by Clays Ltd, Elcograf S.p.A.

Headline's policy is to use papers that are natural, renewable and recyclable
products and made from wood grown in well-managed forests and other
controlled sources. The logging and manufacturing processes are expected
to conform to the environmental regulations of the country of origin.

MIX
Paper from
responsible sources
FSC® C104740

HEADLINE PUBLISHING GROUP
An Hachette UK Company
Carmelite House
50 Victoria Embankment
London EC4Y 0DZ

www.tinderpress.co.uk
www.headline.co.uk
www.hachette.co.uk

For my mother, Elizabeth, who introduced me
to the evil fairies when I was very young

Author's Note

In this book I have made use of some Scottish clan names, but these are not intended to indicate any real person. This is a work of fiction. However, the descriptions of the Clearances in Boreraig and Suisnish were informed by the historical accounts. Those events really happened and are still imprinted upon the land and on the collective memory.

All the verse epigraphs come from the poem 'Kilmeny', by James Hogg, which was published in 1813.

Many years ago, far away to the west, there lived a young girl with skin so pale that they called her Bainne – milk. Her lips were as red as blood, and her eyes as dark as the peats that they used to make fire. Her mother and father did not think her beautiful, however. They thought her strange and shameful, for she did not play like the other children in the village, nor speak as they did. They often beat her and locked her away in a dark cupboard where unknown things crept. So many hours did she spend alone in the darkness that Bainne began to dream of being taken to another world – a kinder world where she might be accepted. Where she might be loved.

Part One

Chapter 1

September 1857

Shrieking split the leaden sky and Audrey looked up to see a host of birds, their wings ink-black against the grey.

'Storm coming, d'you see? They know the wind's changing.' The man gestured upwards, but his eyes were on Audrey. 'They feel it long before we can tell.'

Audrey nodded, but did not reply, for she was too tired now for conversation. It had already taken them an hour from Kyleakin and she was wet through with the fine rain and the spray from the sea, her carpet bag and its contents soaked. All around, she heard the monotone of the men singing a Gaelic lament as they rowed: a low, insistent sound, like the washing of the waves against the little boat. Behind her, an old woman in a sodden bonnet was grumbling over her damaged possessions – a bag of meal and a basket of paper roses. Apart from the man, the only other passenger was a girl in blue who sat hunched forward at the stern of the boat, her face bone-pale, her eyes squeezed shut, her narrow shoulders tensed as though in pain. Audrey watched her, wanting to help but suspecting she wished to be left alone.

'Is it far you've travelled?' the man persisted, chewing the tobacco in his cheek.

'From London.' She glanced briefly at him and then away. Three days it had taken her: first the overnight train to Glasgow, then a steamer to Oban and a boat to Kyleakin. She who had never travelled alone in her life.

The man continued to watch her out of the corner of his eye. After a minute or so, he said, 'It's fair cut off, Skye. Not much goes in. Those that can, leave.' He pushed back his hat. 'Strange place for a young lady from London to be visiting this time of year.'

Audrey looked towards the emerald water as it seethed into the darkness. She could have given him many reasons: this is the island my mother loved. This is the island where my mother died. I have come here because I needed to get away.

'I am expected there,' she said.

The girl was leaning forward now, over the side of the boat, clutching a poor bit of fabric about her shoulders. Audrey watched to see if anyone would offer to help. She, after all, was a stranger, a Sassenach. But no one moved.

She forced herself to rise, her body aching with cold and cramp, and moved alongside the girl. She spoke quietly. 'Can I help? Are you ill?'

The girl, when she turned to her, seemed startled, dark eyes shining. Audrey removed a small silver flask from her cloak, uncorked it and held it out. 'It's brandy and water. It might do you good.'

'That's kind of you, miss, but no.' She spoke with the soft Highland English Audrey had heard in Oban.

Cold water sprayed across the boat as they reached rougher waves, and the girl shook violently. Audrey removed her own shawl and wrapped it around her thin shoulders, over her damp blue dress.

The girl smiled then, her lips ghost-pale. 'It's just the sea, that's all it is. I never liked the sea.'

There was no conversation for the remainder of the journey, only the raging of the rising winds, the rush of the water, the slap of the oars. They passed numerous caverns, echoing arches hollowed out by the waves, and the Isle of Pabay, flat and barren. As the autumn dusk descended, the coastline withdrew into formless gloom. Then came lights, a pier and, further off, a line of trees with the turret of a house rising above it, like some enchanted castle spiralling into the sky. Beyond the house and the pier loomed the red hills, their outlines vague and ominous in the growing dark.

The boat drew up to a pier and Audrey saw a few figures standing, arms folded, waiting for the vessel to come in. A boatman in the stern tossed a coiled heaving line ashore and two men on the pier seized it to haul them in. Others moved forward to help bring the boat alongside the landing jetty, and there was laughter from some of the men: a surprising sound after the quietness of the journey. Audrey should have been exhausted, but the chill of the night air and the strangeness of the place made her mind keen, her senses sharp. The air smelt of salt, seaweed, woodsmoke.

The boatmen helped the women to disembark, Audrey first, then the girl, who removed Audrey's shawl, folded it and handed it back. 'Thank you, miss, for your kindness.'

Audrey smiled. 'I only hope you feel well soon.'

The girl nodded, turned and walked up the pier, her movements awkward and slow.

'You've someone to meet you, have you?' It was the man with the tobacco.

'Yes,' Audrey said quickly. 'Yes, I'm sure they're sending someone.'

She had no idea, in fact, whether anyone would come to greet her. The letter had simply given her the address and instructions on where to catch the boat.

The man looked at her curiously. 'Someone from the big house, is it now?'

Audrey met his gaze. 'The big house?'

'Lanerly Hall.'

'Yes, Lanerly. I'm here at Miss Buchanan's invitation.'

'That so?' And then, when she did not respond: 'Well, all the best to you, miss.'

He walked up the pier together with the other men. Audrey was alone in the falling rain. She picked up her bags and started in the direction of the village.

'Miss Hart?'

The voice seemed to emanate from the darkness. As she

looked more closely, Audrey saw a figure in outline. A tall, broad-shouldered man stepped forward. 'You're Audrey Hart, are you?'

A flare from a torch lit his face momentarily: his white forehead and dark brows. There was a severity about him that made Audrey shrink back, but he reached forward and took hold of her bag. For a moment, she froze, unsure whether to release it, and there was a brief, awkward tussle, ending in the man's favour.

'I'm Murdo Maclean,' he said, as if she should know. 'I'm the factor for the Buchanan estate.'

He began to walk with her bags in the opposite direction, away from the village, and up a path that ran along the sea ledge. Audrey rushed to try to catch up with him, her wet skirts clinging to her legs. In the near-darkness, she stumbled over stones, once turning her ankle and holding in the pain. The man walked briskly past a gate and a sign that read, 'PRIVATE LAND', then past a large stone outhouse, and onwards to a house where lights flickered in an upstairs room. Audrey gazed up at it, hoping to see some friendly face within.

'That isn't Lanerly, if that's what you're thinking,' Murdo said. 'It's Corry House, where I live.'

'I see.' Audrey winced at the pain in her ankle. 'Very pretty.'

Murdo continued on the path, which ran now along the shore. The wind pulled at Audrey's hair, the rain stung her face. At the edge of the land they reached two stone gate piers topped with griffins, marking the entrance to a long gravel drive. As they walked along it, the dark shape of the mansion rose out of the gloom before them, a wide, imposing grey-stone building, two flights of steps running up to the door. This must be the house she had seen from the boat, but at this distance it seemed not so much a house as a fortress: the turret appearing to swell into the darkness. There was something oddly familiar about it too, like a picture in a storybook she had read as a child.

Murdo must have caught her expression in the torchlight. 'Not what you were expecting, eh? Takes a bit of getting used to.'

He set down one of her bags before the door and lifted the scallop-shaped knocker. Eventually there came the sound of footsteps and the great oak door was opened a crack.

'You might show us a warmer welcome, Effy,' Murdo growled.

The door was opened further, revealing a young woman with a snub nose and a frilled white cap. She looked at Audrey appraisingly, taking in her wet skirts and sodden hat. Her manner was so unlike that of the servants at home that Audrey wondered for a moment whether this might be the daughter of the house. Murdo, however, more or less pushed the girl out of the way as he walked through with the bags, and she dropped at last into a grudging curtsey.

'There's a fire lit in the kitchen,' she said abruptly, moving in front of Murdo and leading them through a wide, dimly lit hallway to a whitewashed door. Beyond was the kitchen, an immense room with a flagged floor. Hams and game birds hung from the ceiling, a fire blazed in the grate of the arched fireplace, and the warm air was rich with the scent of oats baking.

The maid pulled a worn horsehair-seated chair towards the fire and gestured to Audrey to sit in it. 'You'd best be getting out of those things or you'll catch your death. It's rightly cold for September.'

Audrey was grateful to take the weight off her sore ankle. 'All my possessions are wet through. Perhaps your mistress . . . ?'

The maid stared at her for a moment, running her eyes over her. Whatever she saw, she found it inadequate. 'There's clothes as belonged to her niece. I'll fetch you some. Mr Maclean, there's tea brewing, or you can pour yourself a dram. Mairi,' she added sharply, 'make yourself useful.'

Something stirred in the corner of the room. What Audrey had taken to be a bundle of clothing on a chair was in fact a young girl, who had evidently been asleep, her legs tucked up under her. She rubbed her eyes, untangled her limbs and walked over to the stove.

Murdo took up a bottle and poured himself a thick measure of whisky, knocking it back in two gulps. He refilled his tumbler and sat on a chair to Audrey's right, placing his feet on the fender. 'You're here to collect fairy stories for Miss Buchanan, then.'

This seemed more of a statement than a question.

'Well, I'm here to be interviewed for the position of her

assistant, but I may not be quite what Miss Buchanan is looking for.'

Murdo stared at her for a moment. 'I'd wager you're exactly what she's looking for.'

There was something unpleasant in his tone and Audrey made no response. They sat for a minute or so, not speaking, the only sounds the crackling of the fire and the rattle of china cups as the girl brought over a tray. Audrey was pleased to see that it held a plate of cakes. She had eaten nothing since a meat pie at an inn many hours earlier. She took one of the cakes in her hand and bit into it; it crumbled against her tongue – oats, honey, currants. The girl poured her a cup of tea. She was dark-haired, sharp-chinned, almost elfin. Mairi, Effy had called her. *Mah-ree*. She could not have been more than fifteen years old.

After a few minutes, Effy returned, some clothing over her arm and a lamp in her hand. 'I've lit a fire in your room, miss. If you'll follow me.'

Audrey stood, ready to leave. 'Well, goodbye, Mr Maclean.'

Murdo glanced at her but made no move to get up. His eyes were back on the fire when he said, 'I'd wish you luck with your interview for the position, Miss Hart, but you might not thank me for it.'

Audrey followed Effy along a hallway and up a spiral staircase, the lamplight glowing yellow against the ornate wallpaper. They came upon another hallway, dark-panelled, with several doorways along it, each painted a different colour. Effy opened a door to her right. 'The Green Chintz Room,' she announced.

It was a fair-sized room with myrtle-green walls and heavy damask curtains over lace. A small fire had been lit, but the room was still cold, and Audrey, in her wet dress, shivered.

Effy placed the dry clothing on a chair near the fireplace. 'These are some things of the mistress's niece. A nightgown and shawl, and a dress and undergarments for the morning. I reckon they'll fit you fair enough, you being so small.'

Audrey ignored this. 'And the niece? She won't mind?'

Effy gave her a look. 'I shouldn't think so.'

A bed draped with a green chintz canopy and embroidered blankets stood in the centre of the room, and on a small desk, an oil lamp flared. There was a damp and slightly sour smell to the place. It had the feel of a room that had been neglected for years.

'There's water in the jug,' Effy pointed at the marble-topped washstand, 'but I'll bring you fresh in the morn.' She made to leave.

'Will I see Miss Buchanan in the morning?' Audrey asked.

Effy fixed her with a slightly contemptuous look. 'I should say so. That's why you're here, isn't it?'

She gave her reluctant curtsey again and left, shutting the door behind her.

★

Audrey dressed herself in the nightgown, a strange outmoded thing made of linen, with long frilled sleeves. She shrugged the shawl around her shoulders and drew another chair up to the fire. From her case she removed a rich brown leather book, its gold-edged pages damp from the journey. It was the folklore journal that her mother had taken with her from place to place, writing down the stories and songs she heard. Audrey opened the book at the section where the Skye tales began. Marking the page was a newspaper clipping, the small black-bordered box she had first come across three weeks ago: *Lady folklorist seeks assistant. Gaelic- and English-speaking, quick-witted, level-headed. Wages moderate. Immediate start.*

For maybe the tenth time, she unfolded and read the letter Miss Buchanan had sent, inviting her to visit Skye to discuss the position. Her sentences were clipped and to the point, giving little away. It was impossible to know what kind of woman she would be, or what she would make of Audrey. What was certain was that if she did not offer Audrey the position, her situation would be precarious. She had used almost all of her savings for the journey over, and she had nowhere else to go, no one else to ask.

She closed the journal, moved over to the window and pushed back the curtains. At first, she could see only her own dark reflection, but, pressing her face to the cold glass, she saw that the view was of Broadford Bay – the full expanse of it, slate-grey and broken through with moving lines of white. She could hear the sullen murmur of the waves, breaking on the dark rocks. To her right was the black outline of the pier where her boat had drawn in and, nearby, the wavering light of a torch. Surely it could not be another boat: it was too late and the sea too strong.

Audrey was too weary now to wonder. Her earlier exhilaration was gone and she was so tired she could not even bring herself to brush and plait her salt-matted hair. She mumbled a quick prayer, then climbed beneath the chilly sheets and drew her knees up to her chest. Despite her exhaustion, the cold kept her from sleep and for some time she lay awake, shivering, imagining what her father and stepmother would be doing now – now that they knew she was gone.

She had not told them of her correspondence with Miss Buchanan. She knew what they would think. For a young woman of her standing to seek a position would suggest to the outside world that she needed money, or, worse, that she sought intellectual fulfilment. It would confirm to society that she was unusual, unmarriageable, odd. Her father might have wanted her out of the way, but in a church, volunteering, or in a back parlour, sewing, not damaging his medical practice with her curious ways.

Audrey had told no one of her plans. She had prepared for her trip alone. She had left a note saying only that she was leaving London to become a folklorist's assistant; that she hoped they would understand and wished them well. She had quit the house before dawn and made her own way, unchaperoned, to this distant island. Her father would not allow her to return to his house, not after everything else.

'You are my daughter and you will do as I ask,' he had said. 'You will withdraw your comments, and you will explain that you are sorry – that you made a mistake.'

'I did not make a mistake, Father, and I did not speak of it lightly. I will not brush this aside simply because it inconveniences you.'

'It is you I am trying to protect, Audrey.'

'I do not need protecting. I am twenty-four.'

'With everything ahead of you.'

With nothing ahead of me, she had thought. You and Dorothea have made sure of that. I am like a child lost in the woods, not knowing which path to follow or which course to pursue, because everything I have done and said, everything I am, has been deemed wrong.

But she could not bring herself to say any of that. There was little point. Instead, she had packed her few books and clothes into a travelling case and left the house that was never a home. She was alone now. Well, so be it. In many ways she had been alone for years. She listened to the wash of the waves in the bay, to the spatter of rain on the windows, and the opening and closing of doors downstairs, and eventually she slid like a boat into a shallow, disturbed sleep.

Some time later, there came a shout. Audrey sat bolt upright in bed, alert, listening for more. There was nothing, however: no noise save for the ceaseless rain and the wind battering at the casements. It must have been the call of a vixen. Or perhaps, asleep, her mind had turned the shrieking of the wind into something more human. Uneasy, her thoughts confused, she ran her fingers over the ruby ring she wore on her right hand: her mother's ring, the ring that, as a child, she had believed would protect her. She pulled the covers up to her ears. The sound did not come again.

Chapter 2

Never, since the banquet of time,
Found I a virgin in her prime,
Till late this bonnie maiden I saw
As spotless as the morning snaw:
Full twenty years she has lived as free
As the spirits that sojourn in this countrye:
I have brought her away frae the snares of men,
That sin or death she never may ken.

'Kilmeny', by James Hogg, 1813

I t was the birds that woke her, their liquid voices trickling into her dreams. Audrey became aware of a watery light filling the room and of a chill to the air. The fire had died during the night and, when she ventured beyond the covers, she found that the room was now cold as a tomb. She dressed quickly in the grey dress Effy had left and splashed icy water from the jug onto her face and hands. There was a knock at her door.

'Yes?'

Effy entered, carrying a breakfast tray. In the morning light, Audrey saw that the maid was younger than she had at first thought.

'Sleep well, did you, miss?'

'Well enough. Although at one point I thought I heard a shout.'

'Maybe the deer. The red deer have come down from the hills now. Herself says you're to be joining her in the library once you've done with your breakfast.'

'Where is the library?'

'Down the stairs, through the hall and to your right, but I'll wait outside till you've eaten.'

Effy walked from the room, shutting the door behind her. Audrey eyed the jellied surface of the eggs on her breakfast tray. She thought of breakfasts at the house in London: the long dining table with its plain silver cutlery and white linen; her father's insistence that nothing should be left, nothing wasted. Well, she no longer had to live by his rules. She ignored the eggs, ate a thin slice of toast, and drank her tea standing at the window, looking down at the flat, calm, glistening sea and over to the uneven mountains of the mainland rising brown, green and russet across the bay.

When she emerged from her room, she found Effy waiting for her. The maid led her down the spiral staircase and across a hallway lined with a series of portraits in heavy gold frames. Portraits, Audrey supposed, of Miss Buchanan's ancestors. In some places the pictures had been removed, leaving dark squares upon the wall. Portrait ghosts.

They reached a wide doorway with an elaborate rococo handle made up of golden shells. Inside the room, Audrey had a brief impression of vastness – a fan-vaulted ceiling stretching high above, a chandelier dripping crystal, and books everywhere, their gold and silver spines filling three of the four walls, the shelves running right into the far corners. As they walked further in and past a Chinese fire screen, she saw seated at a table a woman in a green dress, with perfectly white hair gathered back into a high chignon. She looked up as they approached, but she did not smile. Her eyes were glass-blue. 'Miss Hart.'

'Miss Buchanan. How nice to meet you at last.'

The woman's expression did not change. 'You are not at all as I had imagined you. Please, sit down.'

Audrey lowered herself onto a wing-backed chair opposite Miss Buchanan. On the table stood a bowl of polished stones, holes in their centres: hag stones.

'Effy, you may leave us now.'

Miss Buchanan collected up the pages she had been sifting through. Her hands were wrinkled and spotted with dark blotches, the tendons standing out from the skin. 'So, you have come all this way to see me.'

'Yes.'

'It took you a long time, I think.'

'Three days.'

A pause. 'Why, then?'

'Why did it take me so long?'

'Why did you come here, Miss Hart?'

'I came in answer to your letter. Because I believe I can

fulfil the role for which you advertised.'

For the first time, the woman smiled, but her eyes remained fixed and sharp.

'But why come all this way for this position?'

Audrey looked up at a stag's head, its eyes seeming curiously alive. She had come here to make something of herself, to find herself, to find her mother. She had come here to escape.

'There are not many positions of this kind to be had.'

'No, perhaps not.' The woman sat straight-backed, waiting.

'And I believe I have the requisite skills. I speak Gaelic, as I said in my letter. Not fluently, but I learn quickly and I will improve.' Audrey could feel her heart thumping in her chest, aware that she was not answering the question she had been asked. Why come all the way here, for this?

Miss Buchanan seemed not to notice, for she moved on to her next subject. 'You said in your letter that you first collected folklore in Perthshire.'

'Yes, a long time ago. When we lived in Aberfeldy.' She told Miss Buchanan of how, as a girl, she had accompanied her mother as she visited the women in their cottages, sitting with them as they spun and baked and talked. They had welcomed her mother, those women, for they knew her to be of the same stock as them; they knew that she believed the stories just as they did. And, more than that, her mother had an easy way with them, with everyone she met. Gracious, natural, at ease with herself. Audrey had inherited certain things from her mother – the large grey-green eyes, the slight frame, the intelligence and curiosity. But she had never had the peace within herself that her mother possessed – that facet that made her so easy to love.

Miss Buchanan looked away, towards a glass display case full of strange treasures: iridescent butterflies and glossy beetles, a tray of tiny flints. 'Your mother taught you to love folklore, then.'

'Yes, she herself had grown up with the stories.' And she made them magical, infectious. 'She collected them, in fact. I have her journal. Some of the tales are from Skye.'

Miss Buchanan's eyes returned to her. 'Is that so? Well, then you must take a copy of them for me.' For a moment she was silent, looking down at her notes. 'And you said that you were part of the Association of Folklorists. What are they like? Tell me about them.'

'They were very welcoming.' Strangely welcoming, given her youth, her gender, her middling social status. 'I attended many of their meetings and their lectures. I was part of a group considering Celtic folklore.' She had listened to speeches by doctors and collectors and sometimes dared to ask questions of her own. It was the first time in her adult life that she had felt accepted. But it had not lasted long.

Miss Buchanan gave the ghost of a smile. 'You were lucky to have such an opportunity: to discuss theories with other folklorists. I can do so only in correspondence.' The smile was gone. 'You said in your letter you were teaching previously in an institution. Did that relate to folklore?'

Audrey's mouth was strangely dry. 'No. I was merely volunteering at an orphanage.'

It had been her father's idea of an acceptable pastime. He had never had any patience with stories and superstition, or with anything that could not be measured and put down in figures, and he was bemused by Audrey's involvement with the folklore association. 'It would be better to turn your energies to something else. Charitable works, perhaps. A hospital. An orphanage. In fact, now that I think of it, a college friend of mine, Samuel, is on the board of guardians at an asylum for orphan girls. I will speak to him about it next week.'

'Is that wise?' Dorothea had interjected. 'All those untutored young girls? Surely there is some other endeavour. And I doubt Samuel has the time. Viola tells me he is much occupied at the moment – she rarely sees him.'

But her father had been insistent, as he always was when he had set his mind to an idea. It was an excellent plan and he would arrange it immediately. What followed was therefore partly his fault.

'Well, what were you doing there?' Miss Buchanan asked.

'I was assisting with the girls' instruction: teaching them to read and write and to understand the first rules in arithmetic.'

Audrey saw again the vast windowless dining hall with its long wooden tables and cooked-cabbage smell; the blue-robed girls, some so small that they seemed much younger than nine, some with faces that indicated a knowledge far older than twelve. 'We give them the skills to survive,' Miss Hodge, the matron, had told her. 'We protect them,' she had whispered, 'from immorality. From falling.'

'That's all?' Miss Buchanan said.

'I taught some of them about stories too. Most had never been read to as children, you see.'

She thought then of her students: Susan, a foundling child, whose only token of her mother was an engraved coin. Cora, kept as a servant from the age of seven. Rose, who had lived out on the streets for as long as she could remember. They had only wanted to learn.

'And what are folk tales? Why do they matter?'

Audrey hesitated, thrown by the change of subject. The stories mattered to her because they were part of who her mother was, part of her childhood, part of her home. But that was not the right answer. 'A folk tale is a story that has been handed down through word of mouth. A tale that belongs to a particular people rather than to an individual.'

'Yes, but why are they important, Miss Hart?'

'Because they give us insight into the cultures from which they spring. Because . . .' She faltered, trying to remember the explanation a visiting lecturer had given.

'Folk tales are the tales of the people,' interrupted Miss Buchanan. 'Of communities.'

'Yes.'

'Every group of people have their own stories that they create to make sense of their world. Therefore, in folk stories, in fairy tales, we see the reflection of humankind:

its strength, flaws, hopes, fears. They tell us what it takes to survive. That, Miss Hart, is why the stories are important, and why they must be protected.'

Audrey swallowed, knowing she had failed in her answer to this question. 'I see.'

'I have many things preserved here,' Miss Buchanan continued, gesturing towards the glass cases. 'A selkie skin, a mummified mermaid, insects and animals associated with witchcraft and superstition.' She paused. 'These things will last, at least for a time. The stories will not.'

Audrey's gaze alighted on the empty eyes and tortured grimace of a dried cat, lying prone in one of the glass cabinets. 'Because they are no longer believed?'

Miss Buchanan shook her head sharply. 'Because they are being destroyed. Thirty or forty years ago, crofters in these parts would spend whole winter nights around the fire telling and listening to the old tales. Now, they are afraid. The clergy have condemned the practice amongst the people; the schoolmasters are beating the old traditions out of their pupils. The stories are being hidden, burnt, buried alive. At the same time, men and women depart our shores for America, Canada, Australia. The customs and the stories leave with them. The age-old cycle of telling and retelling has been broken and it falls to us to preserve the information. We must work fast.'

She spoke urgently, but her face remained pale as snow, her blue eyes fixed on Audrey's. Where had her obsession come from? Audrey wondered. There was something unhealthy about it, something cold. She flinched at the touch of something brushing at her skirts: a slender grey cat stared at her with round amber eyes.

She looked back to Miss Buchanan. 'You said in your letter that you were working with the Grimm brothers?'

'No. I said that I was in correspondence with them. My idea is to create a collection of fairy tales and folklore that works upon the model they initiated in the *Household Tales*. I want to go further than them, however. They have bent the stories to suit their reader, altering the endings to make them more palatable. What I will produce will be pure, the original language of the peasants, the true magic. This is why it's vital that whoever collects the stories does so in a way that will record the primal language and bring it back to me in a raw state. Nothing is to be added, omitted or altered. Do you understand?'

Audrey stared at her. 'Are you saying that you require me to gather the stories myself?'

Miss Buchanan looked up. 'Of course.'

Audrey closed her eyes for a moment. She had imagined that the role of assistant meant cataloguing information, researching, writing up notes, not going out to meet the crofters herself. She was no good with people, certainly not with a community who were likely to resent her very presence. It was one thing in Aberfeldy, where she had been born and raised, but here she was an interloper, a stranger. What right did she have to steal their stories?

'I had assumed that you collected the tales yourself,' she said slowly.

Miss Buchanan gave a thin-lipped smile and touched a

walking cane that was balanced against the table: the crook handle was silver, formed into the shape of a bird's head with a long curving beak.

'I'm sorry, I hadn't realised.'

Miss Buchanan waved away her apology. 'An accident, many years ago. I am confined, largely, to the house. But my mind, you see, has compensated for what my body lacked. I might not have been able to attend university, but I have read everything there is to read about folklore and anthropology. I have taught myself what no one would. For years now I have been cataloguing stories collected from all over Scotland and Ireland and dividing them into strands: the myths and legends, the water-horse stories, the changeling trope, and so on. More recently, I have been collecting the stories others bring me from the Skye crofters.'

The cat was winding its way around Miss Buchanan's legs and she reached out a hand to stroke it. 'At the moment Vinegar here is my only assistant.'

'Who, then, has brought you the Skye tales?'

'My nephew, Alec, was assisting me. He doesn't always have the right manner, however, and there are resentments amongst the crofting community that complicate matters. Besides, he is rather more occupied with his own fairy stories these days.'

'Oh yes?'

Miss Buchanan gave a tight smile. 'He creates tales for children.' She spoke the word *children* as though it were something dirty. 'Nevertheless,' she continued, 'it would be useful for you to look at the work he has already carried out. He should be here now, but he is notoriously unpunctual.' She looked at Audrey sharply. 'It's crucial that whoever is appointed is reliable and unsusceptible. Are you reliable, Miss Hart?'

Audrey nodded. 'Yes.'

'And you don't believe you are susceptible? You are not easily influenced by feelings or emotions, taken in by false claims?'

'No. I don't believe so.' Or at least not any more.

'There is nothing about you that I ought to know?'

Audrey saw darkness for a moment; heard the sound of a door closing. She shook her head. Reliable. Unsusceptible. She could do that. She would do anything that this woman asked of her if it meant she was allowed to stay here, far away from London.

Miss Buchanan looked up at the soft tread of approaching footsteps. 'About time.'

Audrey turned in her seat to see a slender man with tousled hair the colour of chestnuts, a thin nose and the dreamy look of someone who had only just awoken.

'My apologies, Aunt. I woke late. And you must be Miss Hart.'

Audrey stood up. 'Indeed I am.'

The man dipped his head and smiled. 'I do hope your journey wasn't too arduous.'

He had the same clear blue eyes as his aunt, but warmer, crinkled at the edges.

Audrey smiled back, instantly liking him. 'I arrived in a rather bedraggled state last night, I must admit, but your maid, Effy, found me some dry clothing.'

Alec Buchanan looked at Audrey's dress and his smile faded. 'Yes, I see she did.'

Miss Buchanan's mouth tightened, through irritation or impatience. 'Alec, it is important that Miss Hart masters the correct method of collecting the stories. Please show her your notebooks, the instructions I drew up, and the lists of the known storytellers. She would do well to learn from your efforts.'

'My failures, you mean.'

Miss Buchanan raised an eyebrow. 'We cannot waste more time.'

'Indeed, Aunt. So you keep saying. Miss Hart, perhaps you would come with me to my study: I can show you my collection. You'll find, however, that I haven't got very far.'

Miss Buchanan regarded Audrey closely.

'I'm sure Miss Hart understands the importance of the work she is being asked to undertake, Alec, and of succeeding in it.' The words were crisp, but despite that, Audrey felt a surge of excitement.

'You are happy, then, for me to begin the work?'

'I am eager that you commence it as soon as possible, as that is the only way I shall get the full measure of you.' She raised a hand to indicate they were dismissed. 'I will be watching your progress.'

★

'This way.' Alec ambled before Audrey, hands in pockets, through a large sitting room with a grey marble fireplace and a gilt-wood mirror embedded with shells.

Although the furniture here, as in the library, was elegant, it was, Audrey thought, the elegance of an ageing grand dame. The carpets and draperies were losing their colour, the chairs were worn and split at the seams, and the room was pervaded by a scent, not unpleasant, of old books and withered rose petals.

'It's a marvellous house,' she said. 'More shells,' she added, pointing at the gilded fretwork on the ceiling.

'Yes, shells for the sea. Lest anyone forget how close we are to it.'

'Wonderfully close.'

'Too close, in fact. Three years ago, the sea came right in during a storm and destroyed much of the lower floor. It's all shut off now, waiting for my father to find the money and inclination to repair it.'

'Does he live here too?'

They had wandered into a mock-medieval hall where silver pistols and cutlasses glinted from the walls.

'He spends most of his time in Glasgow, or in London, with my brothers, but he comes here occasionally to oversee the estate, or to chivvy me into doing it. You'll meet him soon enough.'

Stealing a look at him, Audrey wondered how old Alec was. He had a boyish frame that gave the initial impression of someone not much more than twenty, but there were fine lines around his mouth and eyes. He must, in fact, be several years older than her, in his early thirties, perhaps.

They had reached the door of his study.

'You will have to forgive the disarray.'

Alec had not lied. Papers were strewn about the study floor, and books were piled in heaps or lay open on all available surfaces. On one wall hung a large painting in which a multitude of fairies danced around red and white toadstools.

'Always those spotted toadstools,' Audrey said, staring at it.

Alec was rummaging through the chaos of his desk. '*Amanita muscaria*.' He smiled at her. 'Fly agaric. I studied botany, for all the good it did me. They grow around here, you know, so watch out for the fairies.'

Audrey looked back at the figures in the painting: a delicate blur of white and blue. 'Is it Richard Doyle?'

He laughed. 'No, it's my own work. Not nearly so good.'

'I think it very good. Miss Buchanan said that you were writing fairy stories for children. Are you illustrating them too?'

'Yes.' He looked amused. 'She doesn't think much of that. Folklore, in my aunt's view, is a very serious business.'

'Well, if she achieves what she's set out to do, she'll have gathered the first proper collection of Scottish folklore. That's quite something.'

'Yes, indeed. That's why you're here, is it?'

Audrey hesitated only for a fraction of a second. 'Yes.

I've been interested in folklore since childhood, but I haven't had the opportunity to put it to any real use for some time.'

Not since her mother died, and her world was drained of colour.

'Aren't there opportunities in London? I thought it would be full of folklore enthusiasts dragging the old stories out of the slum-dwellers.'

She gave a half-smile. 'It is, but it isn't really considered a suitable occupation for a young lady.' Or at least that was the view of her father and his wife. 'This position seemed a rare opportunity. I had at least to try.'

Alec looked at her appraisingly. 'It was a brave thing for you to do, I think. To travel all this way alone.'

'Brave or foolhardy.'

From a pile of documents Alec extracted a leather-bound notebook and brought it over to the table in the centre of the room. He fished around in his jacket and pulled out a pair of wire-rimmed spectacles, which he set on his nose. 'These are the stories I managed to record. I've tried to group them by area, but there isn't much to go on, as you'll see. I don't have the right manner with these people. They don't trust me.'

Audrey took the book from him, and while he explained how the stories should be written down, she flicked through the pages, looking at the slanting lines of handwriting: 'The Fairy Midwife of Kilmaluag', 'The Two Hunchbacks of Edinbane'.

Alec opened another book. 'My aunt prepared this list

of people who are said to be the keepers of the tales, but I'm not sure how accurate it is. They're mostly names that she's gleaned from Effy or the stable boy, or from Murdo Maclean, the factor, and at least half of them no longer live in the places listed. Many were cleared, you see, from the lands, and then moved on. Many have emigrated.'

'Yes, so I understand.' She had read the reports of starvation and desperation; of communities scattered and houses torn down.

Alec walked over to his desk and began sorting through some papers. 'I hope you will have better luck than me. My attempts to extract any story, song or custom seemed to act as a pinch of snuff does on a snail. They may take to an outsider better than they take to the son of a landowner.'

Audrey tensed. Would she always be an outsider, wherever she went?

'I was born in Scotland,' she said shortly.

Alec looked up from his papers. 'Oh yes?'

'Yes, in Aberfeldy.'

'How so?'

'That's where my parents lived. My mother was from Ullapool originally.'

The daughter of a fisherman. So lovely that a young doctor visiting from London ended up marrying well below his class and remaining in Scotland to start a practice there.

'Was it your mother who taught you Gaelic, then?' Alec asked.

'Yes, she spoke it to me when I was a child.'

Had sung it to her in her cradle. Audrey had been born

several years after her parents' marriage, the long-desired and, as it turned out, only child. Perhaps it was that which explained why she had turned out a little strange – not having any siblings to cut her down, bully her and shape her. But she remembered her early years as a time of magic: days learning Gaelic and English, evenings by the nursery fire, her mother with her foot driving the spinning wheel, telling her stories of elves and kelpies, brownies and fairies, stories that made Audrey's eyes round with fear and wonder. Because she knew they were not mere stories – they were real.

Audrey looked at Alec. 'That was a long time ago, though. I left Scotland when I was twelve. I'm not sure how much of the crofters' dialect I'll understand. Did you have an interpreter?'

'No, I managed by myself. I speak Gaelic, albeit not fluently.'

'What if I can't understand them well enough? Is she expecting . . . ?'

'Oh, you can take on an interpreter if needs be. That won't be the difficulty.' He had walked over to a shelf and removed a large book, which he opened and laid flat on the table. 'The fallen angels.' He gestured to an illustration of bird-like creatures. 'They believe, around here, you see, that fairies are the angels that were shut out of heaven but haven't yet reached hell.'

Audrey looked more closely. Their faces were not those of birds, she realised, but humans, their faces dark with misery. 'People think, then, that fairies are evil?'

'Often, yes. They can be malevolent if riled – laying curses, stealing babies, inflicting illness. A bad lot.'

Audrey stared still at the picture, at the thin outstretched arms of the fairies. On the opposite page, a gaggle of small winged creatures were dragging a man, screaming, into the sky.

'And you really think this is the stuff of stories for children?'

He smiled. 'I think children like those kind of stories the best of all.'

Audrey turned. A noise had come from outside the door, a light swishing sound. Of skirts upon the floor?

Alec, however, seemed not to have heard it. He was collecting up his books. 'Children love to be frightened. I think we all do.'

Luncheon was held in the dining room, adorned with once-majestic Ionic columns and cracked gold plasterwork. Miss Buchanan sat at one end of the long table, occasionally throwing bits of food to her cat.

'Miss Hart, I have asked Murdo to take you into Dunan to meet some of the tenants this afternoon.'

Audrey thought of Murdo Maclean stepping out of the darkness of the pier. There was something threatening about him, like a horse only part-tamed. 'That's very kind, but I'm sure I can find it myself.'

Miss Buchanan shook her head. 'No. It's some miles north of Broadford; better to go in the gig. Seek him out after lunch. He'll be at Corry Lodge.'

Audrey pressed her lips together. 'Very well.' Did Miss Buchanan know that she came across as commanding and brusque? Perhaps, confined to Lanerly, she had lost the ability to converse.

Her expression must have given her away, for Alec, who sat across from her, leant forward and whispered, 'Don't worry about Maclean. His bark is worse than his bite.'

She envisaged not a dog, but a wolf, its teeth bared, its gums red. And she thought then of Samuel. 'The perfect gentleman,' her father had told her. 'We knew one another at the Royal College and he was on the rise even then. He'll ensure you're looked after at the orphanage. Any contact of his will be treated well, I daresay.'

But in fact she did not meet him until some time after she had begun teaching. He had appeared one day at the back of the classroom, a tall man in a finely tailored suit, with sleek black hair, silver at the temples.

'Don't let me stop you, Miss Hart. I'm only here to listen.'

She had stumbled through the rest of her lesson, trying to ignore his dark-eyed stare.

'You have quite the gift,' he had said to her afterwards. 'And there was your father worrying that you would be too shy.'

He had smiled at this point and it had lifted his entire face. 'If you don't mind, though, I've a few ideas. Some things I've picked up that might assist.'

That was how it all began: a compliment. An offer to help. A trick.

★

After lunch, Audrey returned to her room and brushed the mud from the hem of her now dry skirts. She changed into her own clothes, fetched her cloak, bonnet and gloves and left Lanerly by the front door. In the daylight, she saw that the house was much shabbier than she had first supposed. The porch was harled all over with lime, and ivy had curled its dark green fingers across the front of the house. The steps were cracked in places, with weeds growing through, as though nature was trying to reclaim the place. As she reached the end of the long drive, she noticed that the two griffin statues on the gate piers were darkened with rain damage, their curved beaks mottled grey and black. Gazing at them, she had the sense again of having seen this place before, in a picture, or a dream.

She followed the main pathway along the coast to Murdo's house, the rectangular grey-stone building she had seen last night. By the gate to Corry Lodge, rosebay willow-herb grew wild, but there had been no attempt to make the place look welcoming or homely. A sharp-faced woman answered the door to her knock. 'You'll be Miss Hart, then.'

'Yes. Miss Buchanan told me to ask for Mr Maclean.'

'I'm his wife,' the woman said, then shouted: 'Murdo!'

Audrey looked about the vestibule. It seemed a cheerless place, with plain white walls and the smell of limewash and soap. A boy of perhaps eleven or twelve was crouched by a row of boots holding a brush and cloth and staring at her. She supposed they rarely saw strangers but his gaze, unwavering, made her uneasy.

After a minute or so, Murdo arrived, shrugging on a greatcoat. He nodded at her. 'Morning, Miss Hart.'

'Good morning, Mr Maclean.'

He gave the boy a smart clip about the ear. 'See will you get the horse ready. By Mary,' he murmured, fastening the buttons on his coat, 'you'd think he'd never seen a lady in all his life.'

Audrey forced a smile. 'It's kind of you to take me to Dunan.'

'*An Dùnan*,' he said, correcting her pronunciation. 'I've business there in any event.'

Murdo's wife was watching him. 'You'll not be long?'

He lifted his face to her. His brow briefly unfurrowed, he was almost handsome. 'I'll be as long as it takes,' he said.

The horse and gig made its way towards Broadford village. Although the summer was almost at an end, the path was still bursting with wild flowers: eyebright, red campion, ragwort and foxgloves, and the honeyed fragrance of sweet gale scented the air. Swallows flickered above – darts of light in the sky – and from the undergrowth a falcon rose.

Audrey listened to the trot of the horse's hooves, the creaking of the gig, the rumble of wheels, and thought of the mud-choked streets of London, the whinnying of horses and the shouts of men. How she had hated it at first, with its inescapable noise and stench and people. And the buildings towering above her, shutting out the sky.

She had wanted only to return to her home, to where

the hills grew purple with the heather in summer and white in winter, thick with snow. To the house where she had been born and raised, the house her mother had made their own.

Audrey had been ten when her mother died – her mother with her shrewd green-flecked eyes and soft touch and such a hold on life that it had seemed impossible she would ever leave it. Even now, she would sometimes be seized with sadness, remembering little gestures, sentences, the sound of her mother's voice, the way she cracked an egg against a bowl, the way she plaited Audrey's hair or kissed her forehead before she went to sleep. And she had never had anyone to share it with, that hollowing sense of sadness, that grief.

Her father had grieved too, of course, but his grief was different: silent and remote. For two years, he had largely shut himself off from the world, barely speaking to her, or to anyone, save as was required for his work. On the rare occasions she had tried to approach him, he had claimed to be too busy, too tired, too ill. Perhaps it was that she looked so much like her mother. Perhaps it was that, in other ways, she was not like her at all.

And so Audrey had taken comfort in the things she knew. She had read the books of fairy tales and folklore her mother had given her, and the gold-edged journal she had kept by her bed. She had continued the work they had begun together: taking people's stories and writing them down, accompanying the groundsman on his visits and talking with the women while he transacted his business with the men. It was a way of keeping her mother, or part of her, alive.

Then, when Audrey was twelve, her father married again. The courtship was brief, the woman young. Nineteen, slender, dark-haired and with a face like a closed flower. 'Miss Dorothea,' her father said, when he introduced them. 'I'm sure you will be the best of friends.'

But Audrey had never been much good at making friends.

Two months after her father remarried, Audrey learnt they were to leave Aberfeldy. Dorothea thought it dull. She didn't know anyone. There was no society. Moreover, it wasn't healthy or proper for Audrey to flit about the place talking to the servants, listening to their strange stories, making a nuisance of herself.

'Don't you think you're a little old to be chasing after fairies?'

Audrey had looked at Dorothea coldly. 'I'm not chasing fairies. I am going to be a folklorist.'

'Are you indeed? How does one become a folklorist?'

Audrey knew the answer to this. 'By reading and practising and studying.'

'I see. Who is going to pay for all this studying? And who is going to marry you at the end of it?' Dorothea looked at her levelly. 'You must understand your father's financial situation. We all make sacrifices.' Perhaps she had been talking about her own marriage, to a man nearly twice her age with half her wit.

'You are a very pretty girl, Audrey, or at least you would

be if you only made a little more effort with your appearance. Men do not choose a wife for her intellectual abilities, I'm afraid, but on the basis of other qualities. It's those we must work on if we are to succeed.'

Audrey had been quite sure that her father would think this nonsense. He, after all, had married a woman brighter and livelier than most of London, albeit with little education and no dowry. And surely he could have no intention of leaving their beautiful house with its garden and library and the staff whom Audrey had grown to love.

But her father had agreed with his new wife. Or perhaps he simply wished to leave the place that reminded him of the broken body of his first one. At all events, they had left Perthshire and gone to London – a city of dirt, poverty and ceaseless noise. Audrey remembered the first time she had been taken about the streets, Dorothea walking by her side pointing out things she thought her stepdaughter should find interesting: shop-window displays, coffee sellers, Gothic arches, Corinthian columns; diverting her from the things she didn't want her to see – the puddles of refuse, the rouged whores, the sunken-eyed children with outstretched arms.

'Isn't it glorious, Audrey? Do you understand what I meant now? I think you will like it here immensely.'

But she had not liked it. She had been so sick with longing for her real home that after a few weeks all her clothes had to be taken in.

Audrey looked now at Murdo's expressionless face. 'Have you worked here long?'

'Ten years.'

'Always for Lord Buchanan?'

'For him. For others.'

'Other landowners, you mean?'

'Oh yes. All landowners.'

Silence. 'Do you have any children?'

'No,' he said. 'I have no children.'

There was a bitterness to his voice and Audrey knew at once that she had said the wrong thing. Dorothea had tried to teach her the art of small talk – complimenting a woman on how she was dressed; praising a man for some clever thought – but she had never mastered it. As the gig progressed down the path, she thought of all of those parties and balls and teas: an embarrassment of stilted conversations and awkward silences. Reminders that she did not quite belong.

They were crossing a bridge now, and then the road opened out, the village before it. To the left was a neat little row of shops and a larger building – Broadford Inn. 'It's the only inn hereabouts. Decent enough. Not a place for a lady, of course.'

A lady. There it was again. Was he sneering at her?

There were only a few people about. A man sweeping the street in front of one of the shops. A woman with a straw basket. How different from the noise and colour and clutter of London.

'You won't have much need, I'd have thought, to be coming into Broadford, but I thought I'd show you the place, such as it is. That's the grocer's there, the post office, and the smithy. There's a lime kiln further down towards the shore.'

Audrey glimpsed two figures at the door of one of the buildings and felt a surge of recognition. Was that the girl from the boat? They were too far away to tell, and they did not dismount in the village. They continued west, further up the coast, past sparse fir trees and sheep-filled hills, specks of white on green.

At Dunan, Murdo stopped the gig and jumped down onto the rock-strewn road. He walked to Audrey's side and offered her his hand, rough and warm. Audrey stepped down and looked about her. A few stone cottages were scattered about the place in twos and threes, leading down to the sea. The strip of land before them was striped with lazy beds of different colours: green cereal crops of some kind, the softer tone of hay and grass.

'That one there.' Murdo pointed towards a squat little house of stones topped with rough thatch. 'That's where the Steeles bide.'

Audrey watched as blue smoke curled into the air above the house. 'Will they not think it rude my simply turning up on their doorstep?'

Murdo gave the trace of a smile. 'Leave a calling card if you like. We haven't your London niceties here, Miss Hart.'

'And you – you'll be nearby?'

'My men and I have business with a family not half a mile away. I should be back within the hour. I'll meet you here.'

He walked away towards where two men were standing waiting, their hands in their pockets, their expressions closed.

The sea air stung Audrey's cheeks as she approached the house, past a bare elder tree twisted into the shape of a gnarled hand by the prevailing wind. The ground before the house was divided into narrow strips, with the dried tops of some crop poking above the earth. A small patch of flax shuddered in the wind, and near the byre door, a sad-looking pony grazed on short tufts of grass, his legs hobbled to prevent his straying. The walls of the house were of rough unhewn stone, and from within she could hear a woman singing.

The door was open, so Audrey called: 'Good morning?'

The singing stopped. As she stepped forward into the doorway, she was hit by the stench of animal excrement and peat reek. A stained brown face appeared before her, the eyes cold blue against the dark skin, the mouth unsmiling, deep lines scored downward from the corners.

'Mrs Steele?' Audrey asked.

The woman frowned.

'My name is Miss Hart. Audrey Hart. I'm helping Miss Buchanan.'

A shake of the head. 'No English.'

Audrey smiled. 'My name is Audrey,' she said, this time in Gaelic. 'You will have to excuse my poor command of the language.'

The woman's face softened a little. '*Thig a-steach*,' she said. Come in.

Audrey ducked beneath the lintel of the low doorway. The air inside was thick with peat smoke that stung her eyes and caught, sour, at the back of her throat. A red glow came from a fire in the centre of the house, which seemed at first to comprise just one room, the floor of beaten earth. Rusty tools lined the walls, and next to the door stood a heap of peats. A lean-faced man sat on a low stool in the corner of the room, twisting twigs of heather into a rope.

'Maighstir Steele?' Audrey asked.

The man did not get up, but nodded at her. '*Fàilte.*'

The woman moved over to the fire, where a large pot hung from a thick iron chain in the centre of the ceiling, and began to poke at the peats with a pair of tongs.

As she took in her surroundings, Audrey explained who she was and why she was there. Through a rough doorway she saw a second room – a byre – from which the gentle eyes of a cow looked out. Behind the smoke and the dung there was another smell too, of damp, and she noticed that the separating wall was wet.

'I'm trying to find those who know the folk tales,' she explained.

The man continued to twist the rope; the woman poked at the peats.

'And I understand,' she continued, 'that you know some of the stories from these parts.'

'Who was it that was telling you that?' the woman asked. With her tongs, she broke the kindling peat to a flame.

Audrey hesitated. 'Miss Buchanan was informed, I don't

know who by, that you would be good people to speak to for the stories.'

Mr and Mrs Steele exchanged a look. 'No,' the woman said firmly. 'We don't know any stories.'

Audrey coughed. There were no windows in the place: the only light came from the open door and a small hole in the roof through which some of the peat smoke escaped. In the corner of the room was a box bed with a wooden frame and sheeting covering.

'Why then would she think that you did?'

The woman did not look at her. She took a horn spoon from a rude dresser standing against the wall and used it to stir something in the pot. 'The Buchanans may be thinking they know everything around here, but they don't.'

For a moment Audrey considered apologising for her mistake, bidding the couple farewell and leaving the stinking, smoke-choked house. But how would she explain her failure? And more than that, she could sense that there was something here. They were lying.

'Have you always lived on Skye?' she persisted.

'Always,' the man said. 'And we'll never be leaving. Not until they drag us into the boats. Our sons have gone, but we're not giving up our home. You can tell that to the Buchanans.'

The woman was shaking her head at him.

'I'm not here to report on you. That's not what . . .' Audrey searched for the right words. 'I first came to Skye as a young child,' she said at last.

The woman looked up. 'Oh indeed?'

'Yes, with my mother. We came every spring.' She paused. The Steeles were watching her and she knew she had to explain. 'That's part of the reason I came here. I wanted to find out why she loved the place so much. Why she kept coming back.'

She thought she understood it in part. As a young woman, her mother had obtained work here at the kelp-making, in the days before the industry died. She had often spoken of the girls she had known then, of the dancing at the ceilidhs and the stories they had told. But why seek this place out again and again? It was grand, yes, but it was a desolate sort of grandeur. Audrey's first impression of the island was of somewhere unwelcoming, traumatised, strange.

'She gathered some of the old stories and songs herself,' she said. 'She had a gift, I think. People trusted her.'

Nothing.

'So I wanted to understand the stories, you see. Not just for Miss Buchanan, but for myself.'

The man regarded her carefully.

'We used to be knowing the stories,' he said, 'but we no longer remember them.'

'I see.' A hen squawked at the floor by Audrey's feet, pecking something from the earthen floor. 'I know some people think they are harmful, the old stories.'

'It's not the old stories you need to be worrying about,' the woman said. 'It's the new ones.'

'The new ones?'

The man shook his head as if to silence his wife.

'What are the new stories?' Audrey persisted.

'There are no stories. My wife doesn't know what she says.'

'If you'd prefer, I can avoid mentioning your names. I've no wish to cause you trouble.'

'Ah, but there will be trouble.'

'Trouble from whom?'

'Them that don't want the stories told.'

'Who? The kirk?'

'The little people,' the woman said quietly.

'They punish,' the man said. 'They take.'

'What do they take?'

'They take what they want and leave the husk. Just like the landowners.'

Audrey heard something drop. She looked up to see another hen perched in the blackened rafter, stretching its wings.

The little people. Were they talking about fairies? Spirits who exacted vengeance on those who told tales? She regarded the woman's lined, peat-streaked face; her reddened eyes. 'What do you mean by new stories?'

The woman hesitated. 'I'm sorry, miss, but we can't help you.'

When Audrey did not move, the man stood up before her. 'You see our lives. They're hard enough as it is. We wish you well, miss, but there's nothing for you here.'

★

Outside, Audrey blinked in the harsh light. Knowing that Murdo would be some time yet, she walked away from the houses, down towards the water. The tide had withdrawn, exposing black rocks heaped with copper-brown dulse and dark masses of seaweed. Here and there shone pools of clear seawater in which purple blooms and orange lichens swayed.

Two small boys squatted at the water's edge, levering oysters from the rocks with sticks. They stared over at Audrey, then returned to their work. She gazed out across the shimmering expanse of the sea to where the hills of the Isle of Scalpay rose red and barren. Although Dunan was beautiful, there was something empty and half finished about the place. It did not feel like somewhere people made their homes, but a place of transition or limbo. That was how the house in Marylebone had always felt – never really home, never really hers. The front hall with its portraits of people she had never met, the bedroom with its rose-print wallpaper intended for some other girl. And she herself a small fish, out of water.

She remembered her first parlour-room visit. An old woman with a grip like a vice and an emaciated powdered face. 'What an adorable accent,' the woman had laughed. 'Do you intend to keep it?'

She had not spoken much after that.

It had been Dorothea's idea to send her to the Academy for Young Ladies. They would teach her to talk properly. Teach her to think properly. 'You will enjoy it,' her father said in response to Audrey's pleas.

It was every bit as bad as she had imagined it would be. There were eighteen other girls, all, it seemed to Audrey, pressed out of the same mould. They spoke in the same way, had the same narrow interests, and wore their hair pinned back in identical style. The daily regimen too was unchanging: early prayers, breakfast, piano lessons, ladies' crafts. The little free time they had was to be used for 'devotions' and other activities deemed suitable for young ladies. This did not include the collection of folklore or the study of Gaelic. It did not include reading novels or riding or any of the things Audrey had previously enjoyed. She felt herself gradually ironed out, or pushed inwards. More than anything, she felt entirely alone.

She seldom wrote home. When she did, she spoke only of the meals, the weather, the lessons, the prayers. Never the girls. Never the eighteen other young ladies who somehow knew that her mother had been 'a peasant', who somehow knew what to say to hurt her the most. People had told her that her grief for her mother would lessen, that time would heal all. But it did not lessen; it merely changed as she grew older and more withdrawn.

A yell pierced the air, of distress or anger. Then more shouting – men's voices. The boys heard it too, for they stopped poking at the oysters and stood up. Audrey walked quickly to the brow of the hill and saw Murdo striding towards her, a woman running after him, pulling at his arm. He pushed her away. Behind them she could see two men standing by a croft house, one bent over, hands on his knees.

'What happened?' Audrey said when Murdo was closer.

Murdo did not look at her. 'These folk don't seem to understand how it works. If they can't pay, they must leave. And if they won't leave, it'll be the law on them.'

He walked past her and went to the horse, stroking its neck.

'Where will they go?' Audrey asked. 'Where will they live?'

'That's no business of mine.' He led the horse to the gig. 'I'm only carrying out orders, Miss Hart.'

Audrey looked back at the people standing by the house. She felt a coldness about her heart as she saw two smaller figures behind the men – children.

On her return to Lanerly, Audrey went at once to her room and pulled out her mother's journal. She thumbed through the pages to find the story of which the Steeles' words had reminded her: 'They punish,' they had said. 'They take.'

And there it was, in her mother's small, curled handwriting:

Tale from Uig: Punishments from the Fairies

Two sisters lived on the island. The younger, who was with child, went out one evening to fetch water from the spring. As she walked, she heard the sound of sweet music and she followed it until she came across a grass mound where a tiny old woman in red danced in a ring round a fire with two children dressed in green and gold. She knew them for fairy people and they saw her and the old woman in red said, 'Well, now you are knowing our hiding place. You must not be letting anyone know of it or it will be the worse for you.' And the young woman said that she would not tell anyone of their home, but only watch them dancing for a little time.

However, the very next day she saw her older sister and whispered to her as soft as feathers of what she had seen the previous night. Shortly after that the younger sister had her child, but in punishment for telling the fairies' secrets her child was born without a mouth.

Beneath the story her mother had written:

L says that this is one of a number of stories from Skye in which people are punished for telling the fairies' tales. As in this story, the punishment is often visited upon the child.

Audrey read the paragraph once more, then closed the journal. She had always wondered whether 'L' was a folk-lorist from whose book her mother was quoting, or a real person whom her mother had known. Either way, the message tallied with what the Steeles had said: you did not tell of the fairies' secrets, not if you wanted to live in peace.

A flicker of blue, a turned head. Audrey was sure she had seen the girl from the boat somewhere in the crowd, but when she looked about for her, she saw only the wind- and sun-beaten faces of strangers.

There must have been a hundred people there – men, women and children who had walked from crofting townships all over Strath and Sleat to attend the Sunday service at the church at Broadford. They clustered on the road and on the pathway before the kirk, dressed in dark-blue homespun dresses and jackets, the occasional flash of colour in a bright handkerchief or scarlet shawl.

The kirk was a rectangular stone building, painted white as though to match the linen bonnets of the old wives. Audrey stood with Alec scanning the crowd. Effy, Mairi and Murdo's boy waited near the gate, Effy talking to another girl, and Murdo and his wife standing silently by the church door. The only person who was not there was Miss Buchanan.

Just before ten o'clock, the door opened and the people moved inside, shoes shuffling on stone. Alec showed Audrey to the family pews at the front of the kirk, a chill, bare room with the familiar church smell of burnt candle wicks and old bibles. A baby's cry rang out, resounding off the ceiling, and was abruptly hushed. In the silence that followed, the minister entered, dressed in a black cassock. He was a tall, raw-boned man in his late forties, his hairline receding. He was not handsome – his face was too long, his cheeks too hollow – but his expression was kindly and his voice was deep and rich.

'*Dèanaibh suidhe, ma 's e ur toil e.*' Please be seated.

Audrey glanced back at the room as she sat down,

seeking out the face of the boat girl. Instead, she saw the Steeles, the reluctant storytellers she had met the day before, scrubbed like stones in their Sunday best.

The minister began to chant in Gaelic, his voice sonorous. As his line ended, the entire congregation responded, singing the words back to him. The sound was astonishing, piercing, ringing out in the small packed church. So it went on: the minister giving a line, the people returning it, adding to the tune with their own adornments. Audrey recognised it as Psalm 91 – 'The Protection of the Most High' – but transformed into something new and alive. As the singing ended, the church reverberated with the echoes of the voices.

'Though ye have lien among the pots, yet shall ye be as the wings of a dove; that is covered with silver wings, and her feathers like gold. That is what the scripture tells us.'

Audrey glanced about her, surprised that the minister had spoken in English.

'This is to say that the people can be like the wings of the dove and rise from their squalor to be godly.'

Silence, and then the minister spoke the words again, but in Gaelic, translating, then explaining.

'The psalm is talking about the Israelites, brought low in Egypt, working in the brick kilns for Pharaoh, sleeping in hovels. Lord knows, these are tough times: you work in the fields, at the loom or at the fishing all year and yet have little to show for it. The land is scarcer, the soil is poorer. There are many here among you who have no meal, no oats, little milk. I am hearing that there are some not coming to kirk for want of shoes or proper coats. Well, let me tell you that all are welcome in God's church, shoes or no shoes, and I will never be turning away anyone who seeks refuge beneath the wings of the Lord.

'But let me tell you also that it isn't through material goods that you'll go finding grace. It's by casting off the burden of superstition. It's by raising yourself in God's purity that you will find comfort and strength. It's by renouncing the heathen songs and ways that you'll find the beauty of the Lord: the silver and gold of the doves' feathers.'

Was this, Audrey wondered, why Miss Buchanan was not here, or did she never leave Lanerly at all?

At the back of the church, the baby wailed again.

'But even those who are exalted to the highest privileges would be wise not to forget their former wretchedness. "Often in the day of prosperity were they reminded of their former adversity, to humble them, and to bring them near the Lord." We must all remember our humility.'

A rumble from the congregation. Perhaps this was a reference to the factors and the tacksmen who worked under them: the men who had forsaken their own communities for a handful of silver. Audrey glanced at Murdo, who sat further along the row behind them, but his expression remained fixed, his shoulders straight.

And then she saw the boat girl. She sat near the back of the church wearing a blue bonnet. Her eyes had been on the minister but, seeming to know she was watched, she glanced about until they rested, finally, on Audrey. She gave a slow smile of recognition.

Aware that Alec was again looking at her, Audrey turned to face the front.

'Those who have been the farthest off from God may yet be brought close by the blood of Christ; those whose hearts have been most at enmity with God may yet be reconciled; and those who have debased themselves even unto hell may yet become an honour to the cause of God. He can overlook all your past folly, all your vileness and degradation; can cover you with the robe of righteousness, and adorn you with the garments of salvation.'

Folly. Vileness. Degradation. The words jabbed into Audrey like pins. *Corrupted, Miss Hart. And therefore to be kept apart.* The bewilderment flooded through her again, and the shame.

When she looked back at the boat girl, she had her hands to her face.

'What is it?' Alec whispered. Audrey shook her head and returned her gaze to the minister.

'Yes, if thou wilt return, return unto me, saith the Lord. I will heal your backslidings, and love you freely. Though ye have lien so long among the pots, yet shall ye be as the wings of a dove covered with silver, and her feathers with yellow gold.'

After the service, people began to murmur to one another and to move out of the kirk, into the autumn sunshine.

'Alec.' The minister approached them and shook Alec's hand warmly. 'How are you, my son?'

'I'm well, I'm well. Miss Hart, meet our minister, Reverend Alastair Carlisle. Alastair, this is Miss Audrey Hart, who has some experience in gathering folklore. She has come all the way from London to help my aunt with her work.'

'Has she indeed?' The minister gave a slight frown. 'Well, welcome to you, Miss Hart. I hope Alec has been guiding you.'

'He has.' Audrey was unsure of his meaning. 'He has been most kind.'

'Alec is a good man. He often helps me with my works.'

'Oh yes?' Audrey had not thought that Alec, with his involvement with folklore, would have been an obvious friend of the minister.

'I merely help occasionally with handing out alms to the poorest,' Alec explained. 'That is why Alastair forgives me my interest in fairy tales. You must excuse me.' He turned to another, well-dressed man.

Audrey saw that Mairi, the kitchen girl, was behind them, talking to the girl from the boat. They stood close together, their expressions serious.

'So, Miss Hart,' the minister said, 'are you a believer in the old stories, or merely a collector of them?'

Audrey smiled. 'I suppose I'm merely a collector now, though I certainly believed them as a child.'

'Ah, well that is the dangerous thing. Start them young

and the stories and superstitions become something they accept, difficult to root out.'

There was some truth in that, Audrey thought. Even now, after years of being told such beliefs were sheer nonsense, she sometimes found herself muttering oaths against magpies or crows on rooftops. But these things were not dangerous.

'I would have thought that the old ways and stories provide some relief to the people in difficult times.'

'I try not to encourage these things, Miss Hart. I guide them away from the primitive ways and towards the Lord.'

Primitive ways. Audrey thought of her mother, placing a silver coin in a newborn baby's hand. Did that make her primitive, then? Backward? She remembered the stifled laughter of the other girls, the scorn of her schoolmistress: *A superstitious tone of mind, Audrey, is weak and ignorant. We'll have none of that here.*

'We all have different ways of making sense of this world,' she said quietly to the minister, 'and of coping with it.'

'That is true, Miss Hart, but I will tell you now that not all ways are good ways.' He touched her shoulder to lead her away from the bustle of people so that they could talk more privately. As he moved closer, she could smell the pomade on his hair, the staleness of his breath. 'Now you, my dear, are new to the area and don't know the history of this island. I, however, old man that I am, have been here for twelve years now, and I think it right to tell you that you'll do no good to encourage the local folk in their beliefs. They're isolated here, you see. These ideas breed and fester.'

'You're not from Skye yourself?'

He shook his head. 'No, no, I'm a Glasgow man, but I've visited many different Highland communities in my time, and I can tell you that this is the most vicious set of beliefs I've come upon.'

'Vicious?'

'Ach, it seems nonsense to you, I daresay, but these are no tales of happy fairies. No, these are dark tales. Darker practices.'

'Such as?'

'Strange things. Ungodly. But these are not matters for a lass like yourself.'

'I would very much like to know. I am not squeamish, I assure you. I'm here in order to understand and record the superstitions.' Audrey spoke quietly but firmly. 'Do you mean to do with the animals?' She had read of chickens being bled into the floors of the sick, of cattle driven through fire to purge them.

'The animals are part of it.' He shook his head. 'All I will say, Miss Hart, is that life is hard enough in this place without those stories. The folk wring a bare subsistence for themselves by ceaseless toil. There is much pain here, much sadness. You'll find that out yourself soon enough.'

The minister left her then, to walk among the throng of people who were waiting to speak with him. Audrey looked after him – at his lean frame, cloaked in black. His words had been generous enough, his voice smooth, but she had sensed a steeliness beneath it. He was not a man to be crossed.

It was past midday by the time they returned to the mansion, and the sun glinted on the windows and the high stone walls. As Audrey neared her room, she heard a noise from within – an uneven tapping. Was someone inside, cleaning, perhaps? But when she reached the door, she sensed that it was not the sound of a person moving. It was something else: a scuffling. For a few moments she stood with her hand upon the handle, summoning her courage, and then she pushed it down and opened the door.

She saw the jug first. It had been knocked over and water dripped down the side of the washstand, pooling on the floor. The nightdress she had left on her chair was now crumpled on the ground. Across the wall was a thin red streak of blood, and scattered across the floor, her bed, the table and bedside stool were feathers, black feathers. The scuffling noise had stopped as she opened the door, but now a bird darted upwards and began to fly wildly about the room, hitting itself against the walls and ceiling in its terror. It was too high for her to reach. She ran to throw open the window, then picked up her shawl and climbed atop her chair, thinking that she might coax the bird out of the room. With her movement, however, its flight grew more frenzied. She made a swift grab as it approached her but missed, and it threw itself against the opposite wall, then slid sickeningly down.

She crossed the room and bent towards the bird. It was a starling, its chest green and black, its broken wings no longer glossy, its scrawny legs curled forward in death. She could not bring herself to touch it. She knew how her mother would have interpreted this: a bird flying into a house meant a death to come. A tragedy.

A noise came from behind her and she turned sharply, but it was only Mairi, the kitchen girl, standing in the doorway.

'I heard the noise.' She stared at the bird, the fallen feathers, the pool of spilt water. 'I'll clear it up.'

'Yes, thank you.' Audrey forced an air of cheerfulness. 'I confess it gave me a bit of a scare. It must have flown down the chimney, mustn't it?'

Mairi said nothing, but crouched down and began to collect the feathers that were strewn across the floor. She was a slight girl and her dress, which had evidently been badly altered, was too wide about her narrow shoulders. Her long hair was pinned up, though strands had escaped down her neck, treacle-brown against her milk-white skin.

For a moment, Audrey watched her. 'That girl you were talking to at the kirk . . .'

'Aye.' Mairi did not turn around.

'What is her name?'

'Isbeil McKinnon.'

'She's a friend of yours?'

'She is. She works at the store in Broadford.'

Audrey hesitated. 'Is she ill? She was on the boat that brought me here.'

Mairi turned to look at her. 'The boat from the main-land?'

'From Kyleakin. She seemed unwell. I tried to help her, but there was little I could do.'

Mairi picked up Audrey's nightgown and folded it. 'Isbeil has her troubles.'

'Well, I don't mean to intrude, but if there's anything I can do . . .'

Mairi shook her head. 'No, I mean, I don't know what ails her.'

She bent down to the bird and, very carefully, lifted it in one hand.

Maybe it was the starling. Maybe it was the house with its groans and its whispers and its creaks; the ivy that tapped against the window like fingers. Either way, Audrey could not sleep. She thought of the stories her mother had told her, of blackbirds or crows that flew into houses and tapped on windows in the dead of night. Of the tragedies that followed: lost children, long illnesses, capsized boats and broken bones. Sometime in the early dawn she lit a candle and took from her travelling case the only picture of her mother that she possessed: an early daguerreotype, black and white. The candlelight flickered over her mother, standing smiling, her arm around her daughter. She wore a light-coloured dress, Audrey a dark gown, and behind them bloomed the flowers that once grew outside the back door: fuchsia, roses, peonies, chrysanthemums, reduced by the camera to grey.

Audrey had always known that her mother was beautiful. She knew this from the way people treated her: men who stared at her in cafés or at the theatre, women who cast sidelong glances as they walked past them in the street. And she must have been beautiful, or why would Audrey's father have married her? She had no money, no education, and sometimes Audrey suspected her father did not even like her. He seemed to veer between passion and coolness, perhaps even distaste. They argued often, though Audrey never knew what it was about. She heard raised voices downstairs or saw that her mother had been crying, her features blurred. One evening, when she was quite young, she had come upon her mother sitting on the back stairs, silent and pale. She had not asked her what was wrong, but simply sat next to her and rested her head against her shoulder.

Her mother had stroked her hair. 'You must always remember, Audrey, that you are special and you are strong, like the sea, like the mountains. Others will try to tell you that you must be something else, something dull. But you're my daughter and you're perfect as you are.'

Audrey gazed at the picture. The image did not sit on the surface of the metal, but appeared to float above it, as though she and her mother were still there on that day, suspended in time. How old had she been then? Ten? It was difficult to recall the months after that photograph was taken. She remembered points in time – a visit to Ullapool, a particularly vicious fight. She remembered their last trip to Skye: the journey by boat, the guest house in which they stayed. And then the day she had come downstairs to find her mother gone and unknown men talking to her father in hushed voices. She had been ill, she remembered, confined to her bed with some sickness, and everything that took place that day seemed part of the fever that had consumed her. No one would tell her what had happened, only that she was not to worry. She overheard stray words – 'inexplicable', 'fatal', 'terrible', 'fall'. She saw her father's grey, closed face and still she did not believe it, because surely the world was not that cruel.

She returned the photograph to her notebook and the notebook to her case. She extinguished the candle with her forefinger and thumb and lay down on her cold pillow. Her father had never fully explained her mother's death to her. Perhaps he had thought it was kinder that way, but the emptiness had filled her, choked and confused her. That was why she was here years later, still seeking answers. She closed her eyes and wondered, and the wonderings slid into fitful dreams – her mother falling, flailing, gone.

Chapter 3

One day, when she was twelve years old, Bainne's father took her far into the forest and told her that if she was to have anything to eat, she must sit and wait for his friend. Bainne did not know who this friend might be and was afraid, but she was even more afraid of her father, so she did as she was told. After she had been waiting for some time, a small man appeared, about the size of a house cat and clothed all in green. He beckoned to Bainne, who looked about for her father, but he was nowhere to be seen. Unsure whether this was the friend of whom he had spoken, she hesitated. At that moment, there appeared in the little man's hand an apple of pure gold and she knew then that she must follow him. So follow him she did, further and further into the forest.

After a time, they came to a rippling burn where the water flowed silver, and the little man urged Bainne to drink, which she gratefully did for she was very thirsty. Then he led her to a beautiful tree, and from its branches hung apples of glistening gold such as the one the little man was carrying. He picked one of these apples and handed it to Bainne. She found that inside the flesh was soft and sweet, and she ate it up quickly for she was very hungry.

But, as every child knows, one should never accept food or drink from a fairy, no matter how kind they might seem. For it will almost always be enchanted.

Audrey tried not to think of the bird as a bad omen, but as the bracken turned to rust and the hills grew bronze, it was as though something hovered over the island, casting a long shadow. She had arrived at harvest time, the busiest time. Throughout September, the crofters had been working the fields, using long scythes to reap the corn that had been yellowed and strengthened by the sun and rain of the past months. Everyone was there: mothers with babies strapped to their backs, wizened old men come to witness the show, tailors, shoemakers, clerks and fishermen brought back from the coast to help bring in the harvest. They worked in teams, shouting and singing, men cutting the grain, women gathering it into bundles, others binding up the sheaves and piling them in stooks until the fields were ridged with golden pyramids. The air was still and the sky a grey haze, but with heat smouldering behind it, soaking the workers in sweat as they moved along the rows, grabbing at the tough sheaves of straw until their hands were scratched and sore.

Audrey watched them at work, listening to the skirl of

the scythe blades and the shouts and song with a growing sense of unease. The crofters to whom she tried to talk were too busy or too wary to tell her of their stories. Some regarded her with curiosity, others with something that seemed like fear. More than once she heard the word *coigreach* muttered. Incomer, foreigner, unknown one. Only the old men, sitting watching the harvesting, listened to her questions, and they either claimed that they knew no tales any more, or stared at her in suspicious silence, pretending not to understand. She knew she was being shut out, for there was something behind it all, bubbling beneath the surface, like stifled laughter or suppressed rage. She had come here to understand her mother, to understand her own past, but more than ever, she knew she didn't belong.

Though she had been several times into Broadford village, even into the shop where she had been told she worked, Audrey had not seen Isbeil, the boat girl, again. She had wanted to find out how she fared, and her absence was unnerving, odd. In the dusky red evenings when the sky itself seemed aflame, the people returned to their crofts, leaving rowdy gangs of rooks and jackdaws to peck at the stubble fields. The smell of the grain stooks and the harvest fires wafted up to Audrey on the autumn breeze, making her think of the times she had sat with her mother, plaiting corn dolls and listening to her story of the harvest maiden, the woman black of hair and fair of skin who would step from a cairn and reap a whole field before the first light. The woman who left a man dead at dawn. She wanted to say to the crofters: I know these stories. I understand them. I will keep them safe. But those evenings with her mother were so long ago. Here, things seemed different, or perhaps it was that she herself had changed. She felt stripped of her identity, rootless, as if she'd been turned into something else; a fraud.

She slept fitfully and the dreams that came to her were strange, of corn dolls, children running, shadows, shouts, flames. Several times she woke in the night thinking she had heard a cry, but there was only the sound of the wind, the spatter of rain against the windowpanes, the wash of the waves outside in the bay. She had come here to escape, and yet she felt oddly captive, for she had not the funds to leave, nor anywhere to go. And more than that, she felt that she was watched.

After dinner on the thirteenth day, Miss Buchanan summoned Audrey to the library. The candles in the chandelier had been lit, patterning the room with a tangled forest of shadows.

'Do you know what this is?' She held a small glass bottle, the colour of wet grass.

'I confess I don't. What is it?'

'A witch bottle.'

The older woman lowered herself onto the chair, her face contorting with retained pain. In the candlelight her cheekbones seemed more prominent, her eyes more hollow. 'Until recently they were still making them on the island. This one was procured for me by a woman at Loch Coruisk.'

'I've read about them – they contain . . .' Audrey hesitated. Urine, toe clippings, pins, blood.

'Not any more.' Miss Buchanan gave a slight smile. 'I'm assured this one holds rosemary and red wine.' She set the bottle down on the table before her. 'The point is that they have stopped making them. The traditions are dying. The people are leaving. It's nearly a fortnight now that you've been on Skye. Where are you with your story-collecting?'

Audrey swallowed. 'I'm not as far along as I would have wished. I've visited several of the people on your list, but the crofters have been reluctant to speak to me. They've been busy with the harvest.'

'Did you explain to them clearly what your purpose was? That you were not here to reprimand them for their practices, but to record them?'

'Yes, Miss Buchanan, I have done my best to gain their confidence.'

'And you told them you were yourself from Scotland? You told them about your mother?'

'I did. I explained that I was brought up on these stories.' She shook her head. 'Perhaps I need to try a different approach. Perhaps I am speaking to the wrong people.'

'The names on the list are people I have been reliably informed are tellers of the old tales. If they are not revealing them it is because you've yet to convince them of the value you place on these stories.' Miss Buchanan rested her hand on the table, running her fingers over the grain of the wood. 'I begin to wonder whether I made the right decision.' She spoke quietly, as if to herself.

Audrey felt the blood rush to her cheeks. 'You were right to have given me this opportunity, Miss Buchanan. It's just a matter of me finding a way to gain their trust.'

She could not fail. She could not go back. She thought of the front parlour in her father's house: the wax flowers under a glass dome, the smell of polished wood, the silence. She imagined standing there asking to be allowed to return. She knew what he would say.

Miss Buchanan picked up the green glass bottle and turned it around in her hand. 'I hope so, I truly do. I see something in you that reminds me of myself; the same independence, the same resolve.' She smiled. 'It's not easy, is it? People expect us to want something else entirely. They think we need to occupy our time simply because we cannot avail ourselves of a husband.' She set down the bottle again. 'But you must understand that if you're unable to gather the stories as I require, I will need to look for another assistant. Apply yourself as best you can, Miss Hart. Most people will take you at your own valuation. Approach the crofters with more self-belief and they will have confidence in you. You have another fortnight. See what you can do.'

Audrey left the room with her eyes on the floor. She couldn't leave Skye, for she hadn't yet carried out her purpose; she hadn't visited the places where her mother had collected stories, nor seen the place where she'd died. Even if Miss Buchanan were to give her the wages to cover her journey back to London, she had nothing to return to, nowhere to go. She could not be a governess, for she had no references. Certainly she could not ask the orphanage to recommend her now.

She caught sight of Mairi kneeling near the door, cleaning a stain from the polar bear skin rug. The girl looked up as she passed. Had she heard her conversation with Miss Buchanan? If she had, she gave no sign. She simply nodded at Audrey and then, like a good servant, looked away.

Sitting at her dressing table, Audrey unpinned her hair and let it fall loose to her shoulders. In the poor light, her face looked bloodless and queer. She picked up her wooden brush and, stroke upon stroke, brushed her hair through. There was order in it, a rhythm that allowed her to think. Why would the people not talk to her? It was like being back at school again with the smirks and whispers of the other girls, the notes passed, the skin pinched. She had not been English enough for them in London, not normal enough, not rich enough. And yet here on Skye she was too English. Too rich. For no matter how dismal her prospects, she was a long way from the stark poverty in which these people scraped an existence.

She applied the cold cream her stepmother had bought her, dense and greasy against her skin. She had to credit Dorothea: the woman had done her best to make her marriageable – washing her hair in vinegar to make it shine, applying arsenic wafers to keep her skin pale; elocution lessons, dancing lessons, drawing lessons, piano. Audrey had tried to accept these things graciously, but they had felt like an attempt to disguise her. Every correction to her complexion or diction had acted as a reminder that she was a misfit for London society, an outsider trying to get in. At all events, it was pointless because most men saw beneath the potions and the pomades. By the second or third meeting they had concluded that she was not wife material. She was pretty enough, but she had peculiar ideas; she couldn't dance, she had no conversation, and worst of all, she had little property. Her only real suitors were old or objectionable: a financier with yellowed teeth and diminishing hair; a friend of her father's with two wives dead and five children alive. She could not even pretend to be kind to these men, and for that Dorothea would not forgive her.

'Life is not a fairy tale, Audrey. Or at least not the kind that ends well. There is only what we make for ourselves.'

And now Audrey was nearly twenty-five. Nearly an old maid. *They think we need to occupy our time simply because we cannot avail ourselves of a husband.* Was that what people thought of her now? That she wished for intellectual fulfilment only because she was unmarried?

As she stared at her reflection, she remembered sitting before the looking-glass on All Hallows' Eve, eating an apple and brushing her hair, waiting for her future husband to appear – an unknown face in the glass. Perhaps there would be no husband, no lover, no children. If she could make something else of her life, maybe that did not matter. She thought briefly of Alec, his long face, his dark lashes. But that was foolish. She should have learnt her lesson by now. She thought then of that other Samhain tale, of the girl who peered into the mirror to see staring out at her the face not of her future husband, but of Satan: black-eyed, victorious. She pressed the brush harder against her head so that it pulled at the hair and made her skull smart. Silly, silly girl.

A screeching sound came then, just as it had on her first night at Lanerly. Audrey laid down her brush, moved over to the window and looked out. It was past seven o'clock and the dying sun bathed the bay below in a muted silver light. The waves washed up onto the rocks and slid away, leaving tangles of dulse and bladderwrack. A storm petrel, wings back, prodded at unseen fish beneath the water.

Then she saw it: a dark shape lying at the water's edge. For a moment she stood transfixed, then she scrabbled for the key to open the window and leant out into the evening air, salty and chill. Even now she could not be sure of what she saw. She did not believe it. Her mind, or the light, was playing tricks.

Not wanting to alert any of the household, lest they thought her delusional, she crept along the dark passage and downstairs to the hall, where all was silent save for the slow tick of the grandfather clock. She unlocked the front door, wincing at the noise of the rusty bolts as she pulled them back, and hurried down towards the sea. There was a steep descent over wet grass and stones, and Audrey, in her evening slippers, had to cling onto the rocks to prevent herself from falling.

Within a minute she reached the bay beneath her window, her teeth chattering, though with fear or cold she did not know. Lying just out of the water was a girl, her hair straggling like seaweed over the stones, her skirts twisted about her body, small waves lapping at her feet. Her face was upturned, and as Audrey bent over her, she caught her breath. The features were swollen and alien, white and blue, and the eyes, just visible beneath the hair, were empty sockets, but she knew who it was. It was Isbeil. The boat girl.

By the time Audrey reached the mansion, her hands and feet were coated in mud from where she had slipped climbing the wet path. The door had shut behind her and she banged on it with the heavy knocker. She heard the running of feet, then the door opened and Effy stood before her in an apron, her eyes wide.

'Effy, get Murdo. Something terrible has happened.'

Alec stepped out from the shadowy hallway, a glass in his hand. 'Miss Hart? What on earth is it?'

Her voice emerged strange and stiff. 'There's a girl in the bay beneath my bedroom. She's dead.'

The colour seemed to bleed from Alec's face. 'I'll need to bring her in. Effy, please prepare one of the rooms.'

Effy looked at him, startled. 'In here?'

'Of course in here. Go.'

The girl hesitated for a moment before rushing away.

Alec walked quickly past Audrey and down to the water. She stood above the bay, watching him as he bent over Isbeil's body, then lifted her. She hung awkwardly from his arms, her head lolling back like a ghastly doll. Audrey turned away and hurried back into the house. She found Effy with Mairi in one of the rooms on the ground floor, draping a sheet over the mantel-place mirror. 'What are you doing?'

'You have to cover the looking-glasses,' Effy said brusquely, 'so that they can't be sucking in the dead soul and trapping it.' She turned and stared at Audrey. 'Who is it, Miss Hart? Did Master Alec recognise her?'

Audrey looked over at Mairi and the girl brought her hands up to her face. Somehow, she knew. 'Mairi, I'm so sorry.'

'Who is it, then?' Effy asked.

'It's Isbeil, the girl who worked at the shop in Broadford.'

Effy raised her eyebrows. 'Is it indeed? Well, we must make sure all o' the windows are shut and the clocks stopped.' She left the room, her skirts rustling.

Audrey and Mairi stood in silence, Mairi still with her hands at her face. Audrey wanted to say something to comfort her, but she could think of no words that might blunt the sharp horror of it all. They heard the heavy tread of Alec's footsteps and she ran into the hallway to direct him into the room. He laid Isbeil gently on the bed. Her skin, against the sheets, looked less white now, more yellow. He pushed her wet hair back from her face and shuddered.

'Can you go and fetch another sheet, Mairi?' Audrey needed to get her away from the body.

Once she had gone, Audrey moved closer to the bed. 'Do you think she's been in the sea for long?'

'I couldn't say. Maybe, given the eyes.' Alec shook his head. 'Poor, poor girl. I'll go for Dr McGilvray, get him to look at her. I'll call for Murdo Maclean too and ask him to ride out to the minister.'

Mairi and Effy returned, Effy holding a sheet, which she began to spread over Isbeil's body. 'Help me, for goodness' sake, girl.'

It was Audrey, however, who stepped forward. As she came close to the far side of the body, she held her breath: the skin on Isbeil's forehead, just below her hairline, was deep pink, almost purple.

Effy brought the sheet up to cover the girl's bloated face, seeming not to notice the mark, then smoothed the fabric and stepped back from the bed.

'May God level the road for her soul.'

Within the half-hour, Alec returned with the doctor, a young man with a grey-tinged face and a harried manner, dark smudges beneath his eyes. He opened his leather case and removed some gloves. 'I'm afraid I must ask you all to leave while I examine the body.'

Effy and Alec walked from the room, leaving Audrey standing alone. The doctor gave her a disapproving glance. 'This isn't something for a young lady to see.'

'There's a mark,' she said, 'below her hairline.'

'Oh aye? Well, I'll inspect her.'

Accepting that he would not begin until she had left, Audrey walked into the dark, cold hall, where she found Alec standing at the window looking out onto the bay.

'Strange,' he said.

Audrey stood next to him and saw that movement in the sky above the bay: birds or bats, their shapes indistinct. There must have been more than fifty of them, circling. Birds, they were definitely birds, she could tell by their flight. Their movement, their mere presence, made her feel unaccountably sick. The bird in her bedroom, trapped. The girl in the bay, drowned. It was as though they were strange offerings, left for her to find. 'Maybe they've seen something to eat,' she said.

'Yes, fish discarded from the salt-packing station, perhaps. That might be it. But I've never seen them fly at dusk.'

As Alec and Audrey watched, the birds gradually dissipated, flying into the darkening evening, specks of black against the granite sky.

In the parlour, Effy was building up a fire. Alec picked up a bottle of whisky and poured himself a good measure before taking a seat on the sofa. Audrey sat beside him, staring into the flames.

Mairi appeared carrying a tray. Her expression was blank, her movements slow and dreamlike. It was the numbness of shock, Audrey thought. She had felt the same after her mother's death, wading for weeks as though through thick fog, not really there in the moment, but somewhere just behind or in front of it.

'Leave that, Mairi,' she said, before the girl could pick up the coffee pot.

Mairi stared at her.

'We can manage,' she said softly. 'You go to your room now.'

Mairi nodded and left the parlour, her head bowed.

Alec poured the black coffee into the delicate rose-printed cups and passed one to Audrey. She took it in both her hands and raised it to her chin so that the rising steam warmed her face; the smell was rich and bitter.

'What happened to that girl?'

Alec turned to look at her. 'She drowned herself, surely.'

'Why "surely"? Girls don't just drown themselves.'

'Ah, but they do.'

He was right, Audrey supposed. She had heard of girls in London throwing themselves into the Thames to escape starvation or degradation, but it seemed so unlikely here. 'I saw her on the boat over to Broadford when I arrived. She was unwell. Perhaps she was dying.'

'Possibly.' Alec had turned away from her and was poking at the fire with iron tongs.

'Do you know anything about her?'

'No.' A silence. 'Forgive me: I'm a little shaken is the truth of it. She was so young.'

Audrey listened to the rain that had begun to thrum on the windows and thought again of Isbeil's upturned face, of her bare feet, white as fish-flesh. She could have fallen on the rocks, she supposed, her layers of skirts soaking up seawater and dragging her down to the depths, but it was too much of a coincidence, too peculiar, that she should have washed up in the bay beneath Audrey's window, the very girl she had tried to help that first night on Skye.

The cat jumped up onto the sofa and arched his back, then settled himself beside her. As she stroked his silver-smooth fur, she wondered why Miss Buchanan remained in her room.

'Where is your aunt, Alec? She can't have slept through all this.'

'Yes, she can.' He looked at Audrey and breathed out. 'She suffers. She is often in pain. The doctor helps her. I do not judge.'

Audrey said nothing. Chloral, laudanum, the poppy's tears; the popular prescription for those in pain. They had given it to her when she was barely eighteen. She had returned from Miss Gorton's Academy to a future she did not want, and had kept to her bed for days on end.

'We all go through these interludes,' Dorothea had told her. 'You need to pull yourself through it. This should help.'

It was not a bottle she had needed, however, but a friend. A purpose.

'That coffee smells good. Any left?' The doctor had appeared, drying his hands on a cloth.

'I'm afraid not. I'll get you some fresh,' Audrey said, startled from her thoughts. 'How did she die?'

'She drowned.'

'Well, yes, but how?'

'I don't know for sure, but sadly, it's most likely that she drowned herself.'

'The mark on her head?'

'Caused no doubt while she was in the water. That's what happens when a body is buffeted about against the rocks.'

Alec turned to him. 'Then she'd been in the sea for some time?'

'Oh, I'd say only a day or two.'

'But the eyes,' Audrey said. 'Would the eyes really have gone in that time?'

The doctor frowned. 'These are not exact matters, Miss Hart. Now, that coffee.'

Audrey nodded curtly, rose and walked towards the door, knowing she'd been dismissed. Once in the hallway, however, she stopped. Alec and the doctor were talking in low voices but she could hear them clearly enough.

'A nasty business,' the doctor was saying.

'You're quite certain she drowned herself?'

'I would say so, in the circumstances.'

'The circumstances?'

There was silence for a moment. 'She was with child.'

It was raining heavily by the time the Reverend Carlisle arrived, his dark hair flattened across his forehead.

'A very sorry affair,' he said, shaking the doctor's hand. 'I was sore at heart to hear the news, though not surprised.'

'How so?' Alec asked. He stood leaning against the wall.

The minister glanced around the room, his gaze alighting on Audrey. 'I don't think now is the time to be discussing the matter.'

'It was I who found the girl's body,' Audrey said. 'I doubt that anything you say now will be more distressing than that.'

The minister stared at her for a moment. 'What is revealed to me in confession is not for me to be telling the world, Miss Hart.' He took a seat near the fireplace, stretching out his hands to warm them.

'We are hardly the world,' Alec said quietly.

No response, just the crackle of the fire, the tapping of the minister's foot on the floor. Audrey thought of Isbeil's hunched frame as she sat on the boat, her ashen face, the bloodless lips. Perhaps she had tried to rid herself of the child. Perhaps that was why she had travelled to the mainland.

At length the minister spoke. 'She disappeared a few days since. The shopkeeper told me she'd taken her wages and quit without notice. I suspected she had her own reasons for going.'

'What reasons?'

A peat on the fire burst in a shower of sparks.

'She came to me,' the minister said. 'She told me that she was bearing a child, but she wouldn't tell me who the father was. I wasn't pressing the matter.'

'What did you say to her?' Alec asked.

'I said what I would say to any young lass in her unfortunate situation: that she should pray for forgiveness and redemption.'

Audrey stared at his damp hair and his long face, which seemed suddenly ugly and cruel. You told her, she thought, that she was a sinner, that she was condemned.

'Did you offer to help her in any way?' Alec's tone was cool.

'It was for her to find her way.'

'As indeed she did,' Alec said. 'Into the sea.'

'I hardly think you can be laying the blame for the poor girl's actions on me. I did what any man of the cloth would do in my situation.'

'But should we really assume that she drowned herself?' Audrey said. 'I mentioned to the doctor that there was a mark to her forehead.' Her own head was throbbing now and she pushed her fingers to her temples.

'As I explained, Miss Hart, the bruising will be from the rocks – from the body being tossed about by the waves.' The doctor spoke with the quiet irritation of one used to explaining simple subjects to stupid women.

'It could be, but couldn't it also be something else?' Audrey thought of a young servant girl of whom her father had once spoken, beaten by her mistress until she had lost consciousness. *They told me, of course, that she'd fallen down the stairs.*

The minister was frowning at her. 'What in the Lord's name are you suggesting, Miss Hart? That someone harmed the girl?'

'Would that be so ridiculous?'

He laughed. 'Perhaps not in London, but here, aye. Skyemen are a law-abiding people. There's almost no crime here: the odd stolen sheep, but that's about the size of it.' When he spoke again, his tone was conciliatory, cloying. 'The sad truth of the matter, Miss Hart, is that Isbeil felt she had no choice.'

'Because you gave her no choice.' Alec's voice was quiet and cold. 'Your God gave her no choice.'

'*My* God? Alec, I don't care for that kind of talk. Are you forgetting our work together?'

'Oh no. I am remembering it.' Alec turned away.

'There will be a post-mortem, I assume,' Audrey said quickly.

'Post-mortem?' The minister smiled. 'Someone has been reading too many novels, I think.'

'My father is a physician,' Audrey said curtly.

'And who will be paying for this "post-mortem"?'

Audrey felt her face flush. 'In England—'

'In England,' the doctor said, 'there is a coronial system, yes. In Scotland, the matter is only reported to the procurator fiscal if the death is suspicious.'

Audrey looked about at the men. 'You can't be sure that it's not, can you? You can't know for certain that she drowned herself.' She thought of the birds. Of Isbeil's hollow eyes. Of the dead starling, its legs curled forward as though clinging to a branch.

The minister smiled again. 'We've all of us had a shock. Perhaps you could ask Effy to fetch some tea.'

'Ah yes,' Alec muttered. 'Tea, that remedy for all ills. Audrey, I'll come with you.'

They walked through the great dark hall. Audrey thought of the mark to Isbeil's head, the empty eyes. Was that really the work of the water, the rocks and the fish?

The girl had looked as though she had been drained out, emptied of life.

'There should be a post-mortem,' she said quietly.

'Yes, there probably should, but my father won't pay for one, not for a crofter girl.'

'What about your aunt?'

'You think she has money of her own? She's entirely dependent on him. That's why this place has never been properly patched up; why we dine on broth, boiled beef and potatoes almost every night. He's a mean bastard.'

Audrey flinched at the word and it occurred to her that Alec must be drunk.

'I'll go and speak to Effy about supper.'

Alec seemed not to hear her. 'Redemption,' he said, as if to himself. 'Pray for redemption,' he told her. 'In the afterlife.'

When Audrey entered the kitchen, she found Effy and Mairi already preparing food: platters of cheese, bannocks and butter, hard-boiled eggs and blackberry jam.

'If I'd have known we'd be feeding half of Broadford, I might've gone to the store this morning,' Effy grumbled.

'Well,' Audrey said, 'I don't think anyone could have predicted this, could they?'

Mairi turned suddenly to look at her, her eyes dark and liquid, and Audrey felt a pulse of fear. It was as she had thought before: somehow the girl had known. She had foreseen that her friend would die.

'I'll help you carry the food through to the gentlemen.'

She picked up one of the trays and walked ahead of Mairi down the dimly lit corridor towards the parlour. Through the doorway, she saw the doctor and the minister standing by the bureau. The doctor was leaning over a piece of paper, a pen in his hand. There was something conspiratorial in the way they conferred that made Audrey stop. She turned back to look at Mairi.

'They'll be writing the death certificate,' the girl whispered.

Audrey walked into the room softly and placed the tray on a side table. The men looked up. The minister smiled. 'Ah. Very good. Thank you, Miss Hart, for getting us in order.'

Audrey poured a cup of tea and set it down next to the doctor. Over his shoulder, she was able to see what he had been writing. Mairi was right, it was Isbeil's death certificate. Before the doctor moved the paper away, she glimpsed the final sentence:

Cause of death: self-murder by drowning. No further investigation required.

Chapter 4

For Kilmeny had been, she knew not where,
And Kilmeny had seen what she could not declare;
Kilmeny had been where the cock never crew,
Where the rain never fell, and the wind never blew.

The house seemed full of movement that night, of stirrings, rustlings, footsteps, whispers. Audrey lay awake listening to the creaking of the house and the sea sucking at the shore, thinking of Isbeil and the death certificate. She thought too of Rose, one of her pupils at the orphanage, her sharp face even thinner, skin stretched over bone. 'No one cares about girls like us, Miss Hart. They think we're bad from birth.'

'You mustn't think that,' Audrey had told her. But of course what the girl said was true.

For a long time she stared at the shadows that the candle threw on the wall, trying not to think of the events that had come after that. She focused instead on memories of her mother, of their house in Aberfeldy, the stream that ran through the garden, the pink-tongued spaniels they had left behind. But when she did finally sleep, it was to dream of Rose and the other girls floating on a calm black ocean, their arms spread wide like the wings of dead gulls, their hair swaying gently with the tide.

She awoke and dressed early. She descended the stairs and paused outside the room in which Isbeil was laid out. Through the half-open door she glimpsed the interior, still shrouded in white. She needed to look at Isbeil again. She wanted to check the injury to her head. When she stepped into the room, she drew in her breath. An old man was seated near the bed. He was slumped forward, apparently asleep. He must, she supposed, be a relative, or someone brought in to watch the body. She stepped carefully forward until she was at the bedside. A plate of salt had been placed upon Isbeil's chest: a charm against the devil.

'Wanting to touch her, are you? Before she's screwed down?'

Audrey started at the man's voice – rough and dry like sand. His face, turned to her, was withered and shrunken.

'No, no.'

'It's fair enough. It's what we all do here. Makes sure they don't come back to haunt us, eh?' He stared at her with rheumy red-veined eyes. 'You're the lass that found her, aren't you? Aye, it was as they said it would be. Here.' He pulled back the sheet so that Isbeil's arm was exposed. 'Go on, she won't be biting you.'

Audrey forced herself to look. The skin of the arm was so white it was almost transparent. Over the knuckles it was wrinkled and loose. Isbeil's hand was curved as though at the moment of death she had been gripping something; rigid, like a bird's claw.

She left the room, sickness spiralling within her, and took a seat at the dining room table, which was already spread with breakfast dishes: a porringer and an urn of tea, a plate of oatcakes and biscuits, wafers of salt butter, pots of glistening jam. She did not touch them. She felt very cold and strangely empty. Apart from the tick of the clock over the mantelpiece, everything was silent, and she sat still, thinking of the frozen body, the old man's words. *It was as they said it would be*. After a time, she became aware that someone was watching her. Mairi had appeared, dressed in a faded green gown. Her face was puffy and pale.

'Good morning, miss. Will you be wanting anything else?'

'No. No thank you.' The girl turned to go. 'Wait. Mairi, the man with Isbeil. Who is he?'

'Some old *bodach* from the village. There must be someone watching over her till she's buried. And no one came for her, you see.'

'Did she not have any relations?'

'Only an uncle.'

'Has anyone sent word to him?' Perhaps the uncle would ask questions about the death, press for the answers in a way that Audrey, an outsider, could not.

'I don't know,' Mairi said. 'He's in Suisnish. It's a fair way off.'

'But you could write to him, couldn't you? He should

know that his niece has died. He'll want to arrange the funeral, presumably.'

Mairi stood for a moment looking at Audrey with her dark, knowing eyes. 'I don't have any writing things, miss.'

'No, of course.' Audrey cursed herself. It was unlikely the girl could write.

'If you could lend me some?'

She looked up, surprised. She had assumed wrong. 'Certainly.' She removed the pocket notebook from her dress, opened it up and tore out a page. 'Here.'

Audrey knew what her father would say were he here now. 'Have you learnt nothing? Why must you interfere in matters that have nothing to do with you?' But it was precisely because she had been too afraid before, too ashamed to fight, that she needed to make sure she did all that she could to help now.

She passed Mairi her pen. 'Just to let him know.'

That evening, as she readied herself for dinner, Audrey heard the sound of wheels on the driveway, hooves on the ground. She thought for a moment that it might be Isbeil's uncle come to claim her, but surely a crofter would not travel by carriage; nor would he have arrived so soon. Through the rain-streaked window she saw two figures approaching the steps: a tall man in a black hat, Murdo's boy by his side, straining to keep an umbrella above the man's head. Despite the rain, the man walked in a measured and stately manner, as though he was aware she watched. This, perhaps, was Lord Buchanan.

At seven o'clock, the gong for dinner rang out. When
Audrey entered the great hall, she found Alec standing by
the drinks cabinet, sipping whisky from a crystal tumbler.
The tall man and Miss Buchanan were engaged in
conversation at a low table.

'I simply do not see why she cannot be taken to the
shopkeeper or to one of the crofters' houses.' His voice was
strident, with only a hint of a Highland accent.

'Do you not think that our family's reputation among
the people is low enough as it is?'

The man looked up as Audrey approached them, then
stood.

'My brother,' Miss Buchanan said by way of intro-
ducing them.

'Miss Hart, a pleasure.' Lord Buchanan dipped his head
in a bow.

Audrey took in his sleek grey hair, his finely made suit.
She gave a slight curtsey. 'How do you do, sir.'

His eyes moved quickly over her, assessing her. 'Have
we met before? In London?'

'I don't believe so.'

'No, perhaps not. We were just talking of the dead girl.
A terrible business. Most unpleasant for you.'

Audrey was not sure how to answer. She was hardly
the victim in all this. Lord Buchanan, however, did not
seem to be expecting a response. 'I gather you're helping
Charlotte with her stories.'

Charlotte. The name did not seem to belong to Miss
Buchanan; it seemed too girlish, too conventional.

'I'm doing what I can.' She looked at Miss Buchanan, but the woman did not return her gaze. Evidently she had not yet proved herself.

'And how are you finding Skye? Your first time here, I take it?'

'No. I came here many times as a child.'

'I had no idea,' Alec said. 'Why didn't you say?'

Lord Buchanan studied her curiously. 'Had you been to Broadford before?'

'I don't believe so. We usually stayed in the north-west of the island.' Audrey did not want to talk of that time now, with strangers. They were her private memories, not for sharing. 'It was a long time ago.'

She was aware of Miss Buchanan staring at her, her expression unreadable.

The moment was broken by Effy, her cotton skirt rustling. She wore a clean apron and her hair was pinned neatly back. 'Dinner is ready, my lord.'

'We should wait for Murdo,' Lord Buchanan said.

'Murdo?' Alec barely attempted to keep the scorn from his voice.

'I need to discuss some estate matters with him.'

'We will dine now, Effy,' Miss Buchanan said. 'We will not eat our broth cold because the man has not the manners to arrive on time.'

'He's out on an errand for me. Reports of a crofter's dog chasing off the sheep. He'll be here shortly.'

Miss Buchanan did not respond but walked through to the dining room. After a moment the others followed, and

Lord Buchanan took the seat at the head of the table. 'Well, Miss Hart, you must be finding it very dull here after London. Unless, of course, Charlotte, you have taken to entertaining guests?'

Miss Buchanan looked at him steadily. 'I think it a little late for that.'

'I assure you it has been very far from dull,' Audrey said. Dull, in fact, would have been a relief. 'I've been much occupied.'

'I'm sure. Nevertheless, a change from the city. Where in London do your family live?'

'In Marylebone, on Blandford Square.' She spoke quickly, hoping to close the matter. She did not like his connection to London, or his insistence on asking her about her life there.

'What does your father do?'

'He's a physician. He has his own practice.'

'Has he indeed?' Lord Buchanan was still looking at her, evaluating her, and she could guess at his conclusion: a middling address, a middling profession. She was of little consequence, but he would remain polite.

'And what did he make of your coming out here to work for my folklorist sister?'

'He understands that the stories are my passion; that this would be an opportunity for me.' As untruths went, this was surely not so bad. She noticed then that Miss Buchanan was regarding her with a slight smile upon her face. She knew Audrey was lying, or had guessed at it.

Lord Buchanan turned to his son. 'And how have you

been occupying yourself these past days, Alec?'

'In the same way as usual, Father – writing my stories.'

'Ah yes, of course. The stories. The nursery tales that no one will publish.'

'In fact, I have this very week been in correspondence with publishers in Edinburgh who are interested in my work.'

'Are they indeed? And who, then, will be running the estate while you're off peddling your stories?'

Alec took a sip of wine from his glass and did not reply.

Effy set down a soup tureen and lifted the lid, releasing the aroma of kale, herbs and mutton.

Miss Buchanan took up the ladle and spooned a small amount into her own bowl. 'This is all the doing of Jacob and Wilhelm Grimm. If they'd presented the stories verbatim, no one would have latched onto this notion of turning them into nursery tales. The original wonder tales are the creations of adults, for adults. They are tales of the dead.'

Audrey glanced at Alec, whose face remained impassive. 'Well, of course they're sometimes dark and distressing, but I grew up with such stories. They've done me no harm.'

Alec smiled. 'Exactly so, Miss Hart. They're told to children every day. I am simply putting them in a more merchantable form.'

Lord Buchanan was buttering a piece of bread. 'It's bad enough to be a writer of books for adults, but a writer of children's books? Ridiculous. It is time, my boy, to admit to your duties.' He spoke with a jocular air that fooled no one.

'We have discussed this.' Alec's tone was flat, weary.

'And yet nothing appears to have changed. Time, I think, to grow up.'

Something tightened within Audrey. Her own father had used almost the same words when she had begged not to be sent back to school after that first summer. 'They don't like me,' she had told him at last. 'They mock me.' She had not been able to bring herself to tell him the worst of it.

'There are more important things than being liked, Audrey,' her father had said. 'It's time you grew up a little. Learnt to face the world.'

But staying at school had not made Audrey grow up so much as turn in on herself.

She looked at Alec. The colour had risen in his cheeks, but he said nothing.

Lord Buchanan was sitting back in his seat, his wine glass in his hand. 'You probably think, Miss Hart, that I'm being too harsh on Alec.' He smiled. 'But the sad truth of the matter is that there's much work to do on the estate. The land is far less remunerative than it once was. The people cost me a huge amount of money in starvation funds. Of course, it's not as bad as it was in the years after the potato blights, but the crops still fail. The land is exhausted, the people too. No doubt you've heard plenty of tales of evil landowners evicting their tenants to make way for sheep and deer forest, but few of us landowning folk would pursue such actions without good cause. It is hard for all of us.'

Audrey's eyes fixed on Lord Buchanan's gold pocketwatch. She thought of the crofters' cottages; of the thin children, the scrawny hens. She looked over at Alec. He was stirring his soup with his spoon but had not eaten anything. Why did he not leave this place and make something of himself elsewhere? It was not, she thought, that he felt cowed by his father. He seemed merely irritated by him. So why put up with it? If she, a woman, could leave her home, her family, then so could he. Unless, of course, there was something else keeping him here.

'However,' Lord Buchanan continued, 'it may be that our difficulties in that regard are at an end.'

Miss Buchanan looked up. 'You're not intending to sell.'

'Merely to rent out the shooting, dear sister. There has been some interest. From an earl.'

The door opened to admit a gust of cold air and the tall figure of Murdo Maclean. He seemed more gaunt than when Audrey had last seen him, his skin drawn tight over his cheekbones. He nodded at the assembled company and took the chair next to Lord Buchanan.

'Here you are, man. Dealt with the blasted dog, have you?'

'Yes, my lord. I've done as you asked.' As he took his seat, Murdo's eyes met Audrey's. She looked away.

★

Audrey excused herself after dinner, pleading a headache.
She could not bear the strained politeness, the resentment
beneath the veneer. It was like the meals she had sat
through at her father's table in the weeks before she left
London. The icy formality, the encased anger, the words
unsaid louder than those that were spoken.

'Why can you not simply do as your father asks?'
Dorothea had murmured as they sat in the parlour after
supper. 'You make life difficult for us all.'

'Because I have done nothing wrong,' Audrey insisted.
'And because to do so would be a betrayal, it would be
giving up.'

Dorothea had sighed softly. 'There are battles that are
worth fighting, and there are those that are not, Audrey.
You will never win this one, you have no weapons.'

'Women never do.'

'We use what we have: our faces and graces. Now go
and tell your father that you concede.'

Audrey's eyes alighted now on a portrait of a girl in a
white dress staring boldly out of a gilded frame, her face
sharp but graceful, her features somehow familiar. As
she crossed the hallway towards the portrait, she saw that
Mairi was standing at the bottom of the staircase, her gaze
as dark and smooth as the waters of a loch. Audrey stopped
before her.

'What is it? Has there been word from Isbeil's uncle?'

Mairi shook her head. 'No, nothing. I was just wanting
to tell you that there's a ceilidh tomorrow.'

'A ceilidh?' Audrey knew these were local storytelling

evenings, but Alec had told her that they were rarely held these days. 'Where?'

'At Mr Mackenzie's house, in Sculamus.'

'You are going yourself?'

'I am.' A pause. Still the girl watched her. 'I can take you with me, if you like.'

Audrey hesitated. There had to be a reason why Mairi was helping her. 'Thank you, but the crofters – might they not object to my presence?'

'No, miss. They won't.'

Audrey waited for the girl to explain why the people would accept her now, the stranger they had refused to speak to in the weeks since she arrived on Skye. Mairi said only, 'We'll set off after dinner. Don't be letting anyone know I was asking you.' She nodded. 'Goodnight, then, miss.'

She turned and walked back across the hall, her slippered feet whispering on the floor, her small form swallowed by the shadows of the doorway.

Alec was not at breakfast the following morning. Audrey made her way through to his study, wanting to check if Mairi's Mr Mackenzie was on the list of storytellers he had previously shown her. The door was ajar, but the room, disordered as ever, was empty. She walked over to his desk to see if she could locate the relevant notebook, but the chaos of papers made her task impossible. Volumes of fairy tales and Celtic legends were stacked on notebooks, journals and sketchpads; drawings of winged things littered the tabletop. On the far side of the desk she saw a small framed photograph of a girl with fair hair. She peered closer, thinking it resembled the girl depicted in the portrait in the hall, but as she leant in, she heard the voices of Lord Buchanan and Murdo outside the room.

'No, not a word more,' Murdo was saying. 'Nor do I expect any. She knows it's too late now. We'd not take her back.'

Audrey had no wish to see them, or to be caught in Alec's study alone, skulking like a thief. She left by the door at the opposite end of the room and walked quickly and quietly along a darkened corridor until she reached a spiral staircase. Assuming this would lead back up to the floor on which her room was located, she climbed the steps, treading softly. When she reached the top, however, she realised that she had emerged onto a different wing, one she had never seen before.

As in the east wing, the corridor was panelled in dark wood. Here, however, there were no paintings, and the carpet had been removed, leaving the floorboards bare. Audrey's heeled boots clicked against the unvarnished wood. A door further down stood open and she peered through the gap, pushing the door ajar. Evidently it was a room that had not been used for some time, for the furniture was shrouded in white sheeting and the windows were shuttered. There was the dusty, unused smell she would expect, undercut with a hint of something more pungent. She heard a rustling, scratching sound. It stopped, then began again. Listening closely, she perceived the noise was coming from the adjoining room.

She tiptoed back out into the corridor and put her ear to the next door. There it was again, a scratching as if from an animal or an insect. She thought with a shudder of the bird in her bedroom, trapped and terrified, but after a moment she recognised the noise as that of pencil on paper. She pushed the door open a crack and glimpsed Alec, his back to her, sitting at a desk before a glass case, drawing.

He turned as the door squeaked open. 'Audrey. Are you spying on me?' He smiled. 'Come in.'

She stood before him, her face flushed, like a guilty child. 'I came the wrong way.'

'Well, you have found the storage room. It's full of delights. Come and have a look at these.'

Audrey glanced about the place. Wooden boxes were stacked against one wall, and taxidermied animals watched from a shelf above them – a forlorn-looking fox, its ears eaten away by time; a once-proud eagle with dust-coated wings. As in the first room, the furniture, save for Alec's chair and desk, was covered in sheeting. She walked closer to the desk and squinted at the creatures in the glass case before her: stout, hairy things with brown and black wings, yellow bodies, and ugly markings almost like human faces.

'What on earth are these?'

'Moths.'

'I can see they're moths, Alec, but they're enormous, hideous.'

Alec continued with his sketching. 'Oh, I don't know. I think they're rather handsome fellows. They're death's-head hawkmoths. *Acherontia atropos*. That skull-like pattern you can see on the thorax has made them the stuff of superstition, which is of course why my aunt wanted them. They arrived just before you did. Only you're rather prettier.'

Audrey gave a short laugh. 'Not much of a compliment. I was trying to find you, in fact. I wanted to take a look at that notebook you showed me, the one with the list of storytellers.'

'Of course, yes. I'll get it for you.' Alec put down his pencil and looked at her. His smile faded. 'Audrey, I'm sorry you had to witness my father in all his beastliness yesterday. He's always worse when he has an audience. He thinks I should be taking over the running of Lanerly, you see, given that my brothers have quit the place.'

'You're not tempted to do the same?' she said, and immediately thought better of it.

Alec's face tightened. 'This is my home. It's difficult to leave a place that carries your fondest memories with it.'

'Yes, I understand that.'

'You're already homesick, I think.'

'No!' She smiled and looked away. 'No. Or at least not for London.'

'For someone, then.'

She met his gaze, surprised at his bluntness. 'No. Not that either.'

For a moment she felt the flutter of wings within her. She looked away, to the frayed woven carpet that covered the floor.

'Forgive me.' Alec stood up. 'I haven't had my coffee

today and it's made me a terrible brute. Let's get you that notebook. I believe the moths will wait.'

Audrey and Mairi set off for the ceilidh at half past six that evening. Already the night was coming in, the clouds dark purple in a primrose sky, and the sheep were settling, lowering themselves into the grass for the dark hours ahead. As they left Broadford, a chorus of animal cries rose on the wind.

'What is that? Cows?'

'Aye. It's the calves crying. They're taken from their mothers in September.'

Audrey felt a pang of pain. It was a tearing, lonely sound.

'They only keep at it for a day or so,' Mairi said, looking at her. 'It's the same every year.'

They moved on, and half a mile or so past Broadford the lowing died away, leaving only the calling of the birds, the occasional bleat of a strayed sheep, the whistle of the wind over the red grass and dying heather. Mairi walked a few steps before Audrey, her dark hair streaming behind her into the breeze.

'The man who is hosting the ceilidh – this Mr Mackenzie – is he a friend of yours?' Audrey had found no mention of him in Alec's notes.

'He's one of the *seanchaidhean*, the old storytellers. He used to be known for the ceilidhs, for the songs and that, but he doesn't hold them so often now.'

'Because people disapprove of them?'

'Aye, you heard the minister at kirk, and the schoolteachers are the same: no stories, no Gaelic in the schoolroom. So he's having them only once in a while now.'

They fell into silence. Audrey thought of the children forbidden from speaking their own language, from singing their own songs. A community starved of its own culture; a land deprived of its people. Was that why her mother had loved the island? Because she understood? At the sound of their footsteps, a grouse started into the air as at a gunshot, and they watched as it flew away over the moor.

'Were you at school near here?' Audrey asked.

'No, I went to school near where I grew up, in Boreraig, but not for long. My family were needing me on the croft.'

'You learnt to read and write, though.'

'Aye, that was mainly my father. He was a big one for the books. It was his doing that I was at school at all.'

'Are your family still in Boreraig?'

Mairi paused. 'No. My family's dead.'

And then, perhaps to prevent further conversation, she began to hum a tune.

Sculamus, when they reached it, was a bleakly beautiful place, flat and treeless, the snow-laced mountains of Applecross rising behind it into the clouds. As with the other townships, the land was divided into long rectangular crofts: bronze stripes on the green. Before one of the houses, a group of children had gathered around something. As Audrey walked closer, she saw that it was a frog that gave off a horrible screaming sound as the children prodded at it with a stick.

Mairi glanced at them, then said to Audrey, 'The Mackenzies' croft is a bit further along.'

Audrey was tired now, unused as she was to walking long distances, and she felt a surge of anxiety as they neared the house. These people would never agree to admit her, the woman they had shut out from the first. She had a sudden urge to be home. But where was home? Not London, not Lanerly. When she turned back to look the way they had come, the hills beyond Broadford looked threatening, like a dark giant rising out of the earth.

'Here we are,' Mairi said as they came upon a squat-looking blackhouse, the stone walls lined with lichen. They could hear the murmur of voices, though the door was closed and Mairi had to call through it. A male voice answered. Audrey didn't understand everything that was said, but the murmur of conversation ceased. Eventually the door was opened and a man's face appeared, gnarled like the bark of an old oak tree and with deep brown eyes that moved shrewdly from Mairi to Audrey.

'Good evening to you,' he said in Gaelic. 'You'll be the English lady, then.'

Audrey winced inwardly. *The English lady*. 'My name is Miss Hart,' she said. 'I'm collecting the local lore for Miss Buchanan.' When he did not reply, she continued: 'I've been interested in folklore my whole life, so to attend your ceilidh would be a great privilege.'

The man gave her a piercing look. She knew her words sounded as stilted to him as they did to her. She felt hopelessness steal over her and waited for him to refuse her entry, but he stepped back from the doorway. 'Well then. Come in.'

A strong fire blazed in the centre of the room, bathing the occupants' faces in its amber glow. Men and women sat around the fire, some on chairs or stools, others on a rag rug on the floor where they plaited bent long grass into baskets. In a hollow to the far side of the room two children sat cross-legged, a plaid draped around them.

Audrey smiled nervously as she entered. No words of greeting were spoken, but there were nods of acknow-ledgement and two of the men stood up to offer Audrey and Mairi their stools. After that there was silence save for the crackling of the fire and the creaking of the chairs. A fishy smell pervaded the place – the oil, Audrey supposed, from the cruisie lamps. Above the fire a soot-blackened cooking pot hung from a wrought-iron chain.

She was glad of the dim light, for she felt her face flame knowing that the people's eyes were boring into her, judging her.

After a few minutes, there was another knock at the door. 'At last,' Mackenzie said, standing up. 'That'll be Mistress Campbell.'

A grey-haired woman with strange pale eyes was admitted. She nodded at Mairi, who gave a rare smile, then took a seat on the settle and began spinning on her distaff, watching Audrey while her thin fingers worked.

Mackenzie looked at Audrey. 'As I think you all know, our lady guest here is on Skye to help Mistress Buchanan, the story collector.' A pause. She wished herself anywhere but there. 'Miss Hart, we've agreed you're to stay and listen to the tales that are told. But you mayn't write anything down, mind, nor name the folk who tell the stories. There's those that think against it.'

'Thank you. I understand.'

'In return,' Mackenzie continued, 'we'll be asking something of you.'

Apprehension ran through her like a knife. 'Ask what of me, exactly?'

'We'll come to that.' His dark eyes were still on hers, reading her. 'Now,' he turned to the others, 'who will have a *strupach*?'

A rusty kettle was set to boil, and Mackenzie passed around a jar of whisky. As they drank, the people began to speak in their own language of local rumours and news, of whose crops had failed, whose children emigrated. Audrey sensed from the way they talked, the way they occasionally glanced towards her, that something was being held back. She realised that they were speaking of 'the laird's man', Murdo Maclean.

'I don't blame the lass, with that for a father.'

'It's made him crueller, though.'

'So it has. As though her very going was the fault of the people.'

'What are they talking about?' Audrey whispered to Mairi.

'Murdo's daughter. She left Skye some two or three months since.'

Audrey frowned. Had he not told her he was childless?

A fair-haired woman with a thin, anxious face nodded.

'She didn't want to be staying and watching him any longer. She had a good heart on her, didn't she, Mairi?'

'He's the very devil, that fellow,' another woman interjected. 'He was after shooting our dog in front of the children. Said it was scaring off the sheep.'

'Not worth his porridge,' said an older woman, crowlike and bent, as she looked up from her basketwork and jabbed the air with her hand. 'He turned my son out into the cold, though we told him we'd be giving him the money for the rent. What did the man say but that it was too late. He wanted him to clear out straight away. So he had to move on, to Tarskavaig. Start over again. The man said he couldn't let my boy lodge with me, or it would be the high road for all of us. I dared not open my mouth after that.'

Mackenzie nodded. 'Same as in '52, during the clearances.'

'Aye. That lass they threw out into the snow when they knew full well it was her time.'

Audrey looked from one face to another, trying to work out if she had understood correctly. The woman with the distaff caught her eye. 'That's the truth of it. The lass was put right out there in the cold to have her bairn. And he said that if any of us took the poor woman in, we'd be cleared out too. So.' She pressed her lips together.

The people were silent for a time. Audrey wondered if this was the full story. Murdo seemed a hard man, but to throw a woman in childbirth out into the snow suggested a different kind of cruelty. Surely if something so terrible had happened there would be some kind of uprising. She would have heard about it; the papers would have printed the story. The faces of these people, however, suggested real pain, and perhaps guilt. None of them, after all, had taken the girl in.

'Now,' Mackenzie said, 'as the host, it is I will be telling the first tale. Here's something I heard only a few weeks ago.'

It was years since Audrey had heard a seasoned storyteller speak to an audience, and she had forgotten how the experience was something fresh and alive, quite unlike reading words from a book. Mackenzie told of earth spirits that had led a man into insanity, filling his mind with delusions and visions, taking him on wild ramblings across the moors and the mountains until he was exhausted to the point of death. 'His family did all that they could,' he said. 'But they couldn't bring him back. He went wrong in his mind and died a hollow man, a shadow.'

'It puts me in mind of another story,' said the man to Mackenzie's right, who spoke of a boy from Barra who had been sent out into the storm at night. 'It rattled his brain, so they said. He was never right again, poor lad.'

More muttering and agreeing that it was a sad thing, a terrible thing, but nothing could have been done, such was the way of the world.

A girl stood to sing in a sweet, tremulous voice of a woman who had lured her rival down to the sea. She had tied the woman's long dark hair to the rocks and left her there at the return of the tide.

'And they will find me,
After being drowned,
My blue skirt
On the surface of the brine.'

They progressed around the circle, each person narrating a tale or a riddle, a story or a ballad they had learnt as a child. Audrey could not understand everything, and occasionally Mairi, seeing her confusion, would lean closer to explain. Mrs Campbell, the pale-eyed woman with the distaff, told of the *each-uisge*, the water horse, who took the form of a handsome young man to ensnare young girls and drag them down to the dark depths of a loch. Audrey listened carefully, trying to keep a mental note so that she might write it all up later, but at the back of her mind were Mackenzie's words: *We will be asking something of you*. And as each person around the fire told their story, she knew that it was coming closer to the time when she herself would have to speak.

The thin-faced woman seated next to her began to talk of an infant that had been found one day with blue marks about its arms, as though it had been pinched by unseen hands. 'From that day forth it dwined and dwined. It yammered and yowled for milk, and could by no means be quieted, though the parents fed it all they had.' She spoke with animation, but by this stage Audrey was barely able to concentrate. 'When quarter-day came, they dug a grave in the fields. They put the changeling child in the grave, though it screamed and clawed at them. They left it there all the night long. And in the morning, when they came back, what did they see but their own true child, as bonny and as healthy as can be.'

Audrey had heard tales of terrible things done to children believed to be changelings – beatings, burnings, brandings and drownings. But not that. Not a burial.

The room grew quiet, and she knew that it was her turn. Her test.

'Would you like me to tell you a story from Perthshire, where I come from?' Her throat was as dry as dust. 'Or perhaps one of the tales my mother collected on Skye?'

The room was silent. All eyes remained on her. Finally, Mackenzie spoke. 'Miss Hart, Mairi here told us that it was you who found the lass in the water.'

It was as though an icy hand had touched her. 'Yes. It was.'

'Tell us now what it was that you saw.'

She stared at the faces before her, lit strangely by the flickering flames. Mairi met her gaze, unflinching. This, then, was why they had brought her here: to tell them what she knew.

'I found the poor girl's body on the rocks in the little bay beneath Lanerly.' She paused. 'I'm not sure what more you want me to say.'

'What did she look like?' Mackenzie asked.

Audrey saw again the hollow eyes, the purplish bruising. 'She was changed. From being in the sea, perhaps.'

'How do you mean, changed?' the pale-eyed woman said quickly.

Audrey hesitated. 'Her eyes were gone. The fish, I suppose.'

'No,' the woman said firmly. 'That was never the fish.'

The room was still now. The children no longer whispered; the basket-weavers held off their work.

'Then what?' Audrey asked.

Mrs Campbell fixed her with her watery grey eyes. 'You saw them, didn't you? Mairi did too. Bird-like creatures circling in the sky.'

Audrey thought back to the swirling cloud of black birds, to the curled hand. 'Yes, but I thought they were just that. Birds.'

The woman shook her head. 'They were no birds.'

Audrey felt fear trickle through her. Mairi sat motionless, her face lit white by the fire's glow, her dark eyes seeming very large in her pale face.

'Forgive me,' Audrey said to the woman. 'I don't understand.'

Mrs Campbell moved her stool forward so that she was only three feet or so away. 'I'll tell you the story. But you must not be writing it down. If you speak of it at all, it must be in whispers.' She gestured to the air around her and then hissed, 'They listen.'

They. Audrey looked about her. On a shelf above the fire, small painted figures glinted, reflected in the broken mirror behind. Mrs Campbell began her story.

'Not long ago, there was a young lass called Eliza Fraser, fourteen years old. A small, bonny child. She was living up at Strollamus, biding with some other girls in a croft house near the shore, not far from the farm where they all worked. Then, one night, six weeks since, she was taken.'

'Taken?'

'Went to bed just as usual and then, during the night, gone.' The woman gave a strange sort of smile. 'Of course, you're thinking there's plenty of reasons a young lass might take off. But here's the thing.' She leant forward towards Audrey, her voice now little more than a whisper. 'When the girl's friends went out to look for her, what did they see in the night sky but a flock of black birds, whirling above the house like a dark cloud. And they heard a noise, they said, a great rushing sound full of bells and laughter, like a breeze of wind o'er the heather.'

Audrey thought all at once of the illustration in Alec's book: the scrawny bat-like creatures dragging the man into the sky.

The woman nodded, then said very quietly: 'The Sluagh.'

Sluagh. *Sloo-ah*. The Host. They were the spirits, Audrey's mother had told her, of the unforgiven dead.

'They steal the weakest,' the woman whispered. 'The poorest.'

'And they take the form of birds?'

Mackenzie was sitting with his arms folded. 'From afar,' he said, 'they can look like birds. But close up, they are not birds at all.'

Audrey thought again of the picture in Alec's book. She thought of the girls in Strollamus shouting into the night sky at the dark shapes above.

'And what happened to Eliza? Where did they take her?' She was imagining a girl dropped from the air, broken like a snail's shell.

'No one knows,' Mackenzie said. 'Maybe into a hole in the earth. Maybe into the sea. Most-times they use them and destroy them. Only sometimes do they bring them back. And when they do, they are sorely changed.' He nodded. 'So now you see why we ask you about this.'

Audrey nodded. She thought of the folk tales she had read from other places, of nightjars carrying off the souls of unbaptised children, of albatrosses circling the skies as the restless spirits of sailors. How often the dead became birds.

'Did the girls report Eliza's disappearance?'

Mackenzie raised an eyebrow. 'To whom would they be reporting it, now?'

'I don't know. The police? The procurator?'

Mrs Campbell shook her head. 'Some of the fellows from the farm were after looking for her, but found nothing. There's only one constable in Strath, and I don't see him coming all the way out here to look for a missing crofter lass.' She paused. 'After all, we've lost so many already, to sickness, to hunger, to the boats. They don't give a button about another one gone.'

Outside the wind had picked up and it had begun to rain so that drops fell down the chimney and hissed on the peats in the fireplace. The woman spoke again. 'You're thinking we're foolish ignorant people.'

'No,' Audrey said quickly. 'No, not at all.'

'You don't know this island as we do. You haven't seen

the things it can do or the ways the spirits move among us. They are here with us all the time, but only some of us can see them.' She gestured to her own pale eyes. 'I see them. Even when I'm not wanting to. I see the ghosts of the children who take the fever on the boats; I know they're gone long before the letter comes. I see winding sheets about the faces of folk I know, and dare not tell them that they've little time left. It's my gift, they say, but it's also my curse. I knew the lass would be found at Broadford Bay, and I foresaw it would be a stranger that found her.' She nodded, and Audrey felt her body tense, her face set. How many had refused to speak to her fearing she was the stranger, the woman who brought death to the island?

The woman continued, facing the circle. 'I see too that the Sluagh are not done with us yet.'

There were mutterings from the others.

'What do you see, Mistress Campbell?' Mackenzie asked.

'Last night I saw the lights again.'

The room grew silent once more, the people listening. From the corner the children's eyes shone out, glassy with fear. The fire spat red and gold.

'I saw the spirit-lights burn at Broadford Bay.' The woman looked at Audrey. 'You know what the lights mean, do you, miss?'

Audrey had read of such things. Spectral lights above the water, will-o'-the-wisps, portents of death.

'One day soon,' Mrs Campbell said, 'another girl will be taken from Broadford Bay. I don't want it to be true, but it is.'

Audrey watched the faces around her, lit orange in the glow of the fire: they were rapt, earnest, believing. In that moment she almost believed it herself.

Outside the shower had passed and a silver slice of moon threw enough light upon the ground for them to see their way back over the moors, but everything had grown unfamiliar, the grass jewelled by the strange light, the paths deep grooves of black. At first the glow of the fire and the sound of Mrs Campbell's voice stayed with Audrey as she walked, but gradually the magic drained from them and the warmth left her. She thought only of a frightened young girl taken in the night; of Isbeil's cold body lying unclaimed.

'There's still been no word from Isbeil's uncle in Suisnish?'

'No,' Mairi said. 'Nothing.'

'Then I will go and find him. Tomorrow.' For all at once she could not bear for the girl to be still laid out in that room, in the house in which she slept; for her to be alone there, unwanted and unburied. 'I can ask Murdo to take me in the gig.'

'No,' Mairi said quickly. 'It's the Sabbath tomorrow. I'm not needed in the morning so I can take you myself. It's a fair distance, but it may be that someone will be giving us a ride upon the road.'

'Very well, if you're sure you won't be missed.' Was it just that Mairi hated Murdo as the other crofters did, or was it more than that? Audrey thought of Murdo's dark brows and hard face. She had never seen him smile. Small wonder, perhaps.

'You knew Murdo's daughter, didn't you?'

'Aye, well enough.'

'What was she like?'

'Christy was a deal kinder than him. Spirited, too. I'm not surprised she went.'

They walked on in silence awhile, the wind rustling the red grass, the stars growing brighter as the darkness deepened.

'You took me to the ceilidh this evening so that they could question me about Isbeil, didn't you?'

No answer.

'You might have told me, Mairi.'

'But then you might not have come. And you got your stories, didn't you?'

She was right, of course, but Audrey felt tricked, out-manoeuvred. She said nothing.

'You don't believe us,' Mairi said suddenly. 'About the takings.'

Audrey thought of the crofters' faces. She thought of her mother – her mother who had believed the old stories, who had told her of the Sluagh herself, had written of them in her book.

'I believe that the girl, Eliza, was taken.'

'But not by them. Not by the spirits. You think you can explain it away.'

'I don't know what to think, Mairi. Truly I don't.'

An owl called softly and they both looked up, but there

was only the great bowl of the sky, shot through with stars.

Once in her room, Audrey took out her mother's journal and, in the lamplight, leafed through the pages until she found the story she sought. It was not from Skye, but from an island in the Outer Hebrides.

Tale from Benbecula: The Host

The beautiful daughter of a local laird was taken up by the 'Sluagh' – spirits of the restless dead. They carried her about with them in the air, over lands and seas and into the earth. After three years they took her to the island of Heistamal in Benbecula, where they laid her down in a greatly injured state and left her there to die. An old woman walking across the fields chanced upon her and listened as the girl told of the lands to which she had been carried, of the cave in which she had been kept, and the hardships she had endured. She believed that she had been gone only for a few weeks, having no notion that three years had in fact passed. The woman could not save the girl and she died that same day. They buried her where she was found.

Audrey woke with a jolt to the clock in the hallway striking seven. She rose from bed, her legs aching. It had been years since she had walked as far as she had the previous day. In London, she would walk only from the house to the orphanage, or to museums or parks, watching nurses with perambulators, children with dogs, and men and women arm in arm. Usually she walked alone.

She dressed, rinsed her face with cold water, then left her room, taking care not to let the door slam shut, and descended the stairs quietly.

'Ah, Miss Hart.' She froze. Lord Buchanan stood in the hall, looking up at her. 'Good morning to you.'

'Good morning.' Her voice sounded strangely loud in the silence.

'Will you be joining us at kirk?'

As she descended the stairs, Audrey looked at the closed door of the room in which Isbeil lay. 'No,' she said, 'not today.' She doubted that the minister would mention Isbeil in his sermon; presumably she was not to be spoken of within the kirk at all.

'I can't say I much blame you. Alastair's sermons are a little monotonous.' Lord Buchanan smiled at her. 'And of course you must be tired.' He struck a match to light his pipe. 'I understand the kitchen girl's been taking you on night-time jaunts.'

Audrey felt the blood rise to her face. 'Mairi offered to take me to a ceilidh, to hear some of the crofters' stories.'

'Well that was kind of her, wasn't it?' He drew heavily on the pipe and released a wave of smoke. 'She's a funny little thing. Perhaps she's taken a liking to you.'

Audrey did not respond.

'My sister tells me you taught girls at an orphanage in London.'

'Yes.'

'Which one?'

'The Asylum for Female Orphans. On Westminster Bridge Road.' Her mouth felt dry, her throat tight.

He nodded. 'A noble endeavour. You must have been sorry to leave.' A pause. 'But then I suppose that there, unlike here, you worked for free.' He smiled, but his eyes did not; he was reminding her of the indecency of a woman being paid a wage. 'A letter came for you, from London. I think Effy has taken it to the breakfast room. And now you must excuse me: I have to find my errant son. It won't do for him to be missing kirk, too.'

He walked from the hallway, leaving a trail of smoke in his wake. Audrey watched him go, but her mind was on the letter. Surely no one knew she was here.

Effy had left the envelope resting against a cup by her place at the breakfast table. It was white, with a blood-red seal. Audrey cracked the wax and unfolded the paper, her heart beating too fast, too loud.

London, 4th October, 1857

Dear Audrey,

I trust you are enjoying your adventures in Skye. It is, however, unfortunate that you ran away from London in the manner of a child, rather than letting us discuss matters as adults. As I said in my previous letter (which I have on good authority that you received, though you did not reply), I believe you misconstrued what happened and I am anxious to ensure that false information should not be passed to others. It is not clear to me why Miss Hodge took the action she did, and I dearly hope that it was not your words that misled her.

I think it is in both our interests that this business is kept between us. Naturally I am thinking of your reputation as much as of mine.

You would oblige me greatly if you were to write by return confirming that you understand my concerns and agree to honour my request. And then, of course, I shall leave you in peace to continue with your fairy stories and live happily ever after.

I remain ever, yours most sincerely,

Samuel Kingsmere

She folded the letter, feeling quite sick. She had told no one that she was coming to Skye. Not even her father. And yet Samuel had found her and sent her this poisonous little letter. *Your reputation.* It was a threat, prettily worded: retract your claims or I will destroy you. Audrey poured tea from the urn, doing her best to keep her hand steady. She had nothing to fear. She had done nothing wrong. She added milk from a little jug, watching as it spread like a storm cloud through the tea. It was mere words, false words. *Words will never break me.*

Audrey and Mairi set off for Suisnish on foot, taking the path towards Torrin across the strange, flat purpled moorland, the occasional tree twisting before them. It must have rained again overnight as the rowanberries glistened red and the wet rock faces glinted in the angled morning light, giving the landscape an otherworldly aspect. As they approached an abandoned church, tombstones protruding from the ground like broken teeth, a man in a cart stopped and offered to take them as far as he was travelling. They were already tired, and accepted gratefully, sitting amongst the hay behind him, their legs tucked under themselves as the cart bumped on over the stony road. Audrey looked back at the red hills, their pinnacles veiled in thin vapour. She wondered again how Samuel had located her. Did he know someone on Skye perhaps? Or had he employed someone to track her down? Either option was unsettling. She had come here to be free of him and of her own failure, but he had followed her, just as her conscience had.

The cart driver set them down where the road ended, at Kilbride. 'It's still a fair few miles from here,' he told them.

'Aye,' said Mairi. 'I know.'

They walked across stream-scarred moors and past black peat bogs until they reached the coast, a stretch of empty rocky beach. Here they rested for a few minutes, eating the bannocks they had brought with them, and then took the rough path leading gently uphill. The way was almost silent, save for the whispering of the wind and the occasional whistling of a curlew.

'Mairi, what did Isbeil say about her uncle?' Audrey asked after a while.

Mairi carried on walking, a little ahead of her. 'That he was her only kin still living. And that he sent her money sometimes, when he could. That's how she bought that pretty bonnet of hers.'

'Did the shopkeeper not pay her?'

'Almost nothing. Said she was lucky to have a roof over her head. They weren't kind to her, those people.'

'Then why did she stay?'

Mairi turned back. 'Isbeil was like me. She'd almost no one, and nowhere to bide. She didn't have a deal of choice.' She faced the way ahead once more and continued along the barren path, past the low leafless trees. The earth felt vulnerable and unprotected, offering no form of shelter from the wind or rain.

Audrey stared across the water at the strange black mountains, brown hills undulating beneath.

'What happened to your family, Mairi?'

Mairi continued walking. After a few moments she said: 'We were living in Boreraig, close by Suisnish, me and my ma and pa and my brothers and sisters. There were five of us. I was twelve when the men came. They made us leave.'

'What do you mean, they made you leave? Who made you leave?'

'The factor's men. They took our milk and they poured it on the fire – the milk we needed for the little ones. They took our belongings and threw them out onto the ground. They told us that they had an order that said everyone in our township must leave. We couldn't stay there anyway, because by then the thatches were alight and the doors padlocked.'

They passed a rippling burn, low bare bushes, their black branches deformed by the wind.

'We walked for miles and miles. I don't know how far. My da had to carry two of the little ones and put them down and come back for the third. And on and on like that for hours. We bided the first night under an upturned boat and then we made a shack on a boggy bit of land up by the coast. Maybe that's why they got the fever.'

Audrey walked beside Mairi now, watching the girl's face. Mairi kept her eyes on the ground as she spoke. 'The two little girls died first. Then my younger brother. Then my ma.' She wiped her nose. 'Me and Da and my big brother, Finlay, tried to nurse them, but there wasn't much we could do. We had nothing to give them: no word of medicines; hardly any milk. They went quickly, at least. Then Da got ill. Then Finlay. And then it was just me.'

In the sky above them, a storm petrel called.

Audrey wondered if she should touch Mairi's arm, make some gesture of sympathy. She had the feeling, however, that Mairi would not have wanted that.

They continued walking, the only sounds those of their boots crunching on the stones, the bleating of the sheep on the moors. Tiny birds flickered across their path: stonechat, blue tit, yellowhammer, linnet.

When they had reached the brow of the hill, Audrey paused, out of breath. 'But how did you end up in Broadford?'

Mairi shrugged. 'I couldn't stay in the shack. Not with them all dead. And I couldn't go back to Boreraig. So I walked and walked and I lived out awhile, in different places. One day I was after getting a ride with a family who were going to Broadford to look for work. I got out where they did and I slept, as I often did back then, in a stable. Master Buchanan found me there in the morning.' She looked at Audrey strangely. 'I thought he would throw me out, like they usually did, but he didn't. He asked his aunt if I might stay.'

They walked on, past shrunken trees and burbling burns, until at last Audrey saw stone shapes in the distance – some sign of previous habitation. As they drew closer, she saw that the ground was scarred by the remnants of lazy beds and peat-cuttings, the ridges and furrows a silent testimony to those who had lived here. Dry-stone dykes still marked the land, but they were covered now with moss and heather. The stone clusters she had seen from afar were the remains of houses, their centres blackened and scorched.

'They burnt them,' Mairi said as they reached the first house. 'The factor's men burnt the houses to stop folk going back to them.'

Here and there traces of human life remained: a lintel atop a doorframe, a burnt-out pot, a ladle.

'Where did they go?' Audrey asked.

Mairi shrugged. 'Some went on boats to Canada. Some were moved to different townships: Sconser, Drumfearn, Tarskavaig, Breakish. From what Isbeil told me, it was the same as I was seeing at Boreraig. People walked for miles pushing the weaker ones in carts, or carrying them. There was one woman, ninety-six years old, who returned to her house to find it boarded and barred.'

'Didn't the people fight back?'

'Aye, a few did, and they were arrested and imprisoned in Portree, then marched all the way to Inverness for their trial.'

'Were they convicted?'

'No, but they might as well have been, as their families were cleared out that Christmas while the men were away. An old woman who refused to leave was dragged out into the snow on her blanket. They were left like that, the young ones, the old ones, to survive or no.'

They walked further, past another destroyed house, overgrown with moss, bracken and nettles. It was as though they had come upon the remains of some prehistoric society. Surely no one was living in this place now. All at once, however, a man emerged from one of the houses, his face pinched and white. He narrowed his eyes at them. '*Madainn mhath.*' Good morning.

'*Madainn mhath,*' Mairi replied. 'We're looking for a man by the name of Neil McKinnon. We heard he lived here.'

The man nodded. 'I knew McKinnon, but he's long gone. Left on the boat to Canada many months since with all the others.'

'He can't have,' Mairi said sharply.

Audrey stepped forward to explain. 'McKinnon's niece, Isbeil, has died. We wanted to tell her uncle. We understood that he'd been sending her money until recently.'

'No, no. I'm telling you, McKinnon left this place back in May last year to get the boat to Canada, together with a few other fellows who were living here. And I don't see as how he'd be having any money to send her. You see how we live.' He gestured to the destroyed houses around him; the parched earth. How *did* they live? Audrey wondered.

'Did she no' have any other kin hereabouts?' Mairi asked. 'Perhaps it was not him she was talking of.'

The man shook his head. 'It's only a few of us now that's left here. We're allowed to stay to keep the sheep, do you see? McKinnon, he had no one else. His wife died after the clearance, and the lass too. That's why he went: nothing to stay for.'

Audrey glanced at Mairi, who looked pale as paper.

'Maybe he was sending money back from Canada?'

The man shrugged. 'Aye, maybe he was. That could be it. I never heard from him, though. Some of the others were writing to say how they were faring, but not him. No, from what I've heard, things haven't gone so well for McKinnon. There are a few who've done not too bad for theirselves, but not him.'

'I see,' Audrey said. 'Well, thank you anyway.'

The man nodded. 'I'd offer you lasses some tea after your journey, but I've no milk. No cows any more, you see.'

Audrey knew then that she should have brought something with her: some oatcakes, some biscuits. Anything. For he had nothing.

'That's very kind of you, but we'd best be going.'

She turned away.

★

They walked back towards Kilbride in silence, the wind blowing hard against them.

Mairi stopped suddenly. 'She told me it was her uncle. She told me he was writing to her every month from Suisnish and sending a little money.'

Audrey faced Mairi. There were spots of deep pink on the girl's cheeks.

'She told me that was how she bought the bonnet. She lied to me.'

'Yes, it seems she did.' No one living in that place could have anything to send back.

Mairi began to walk more quickly, striding first, then running into the wind. Audrey tried to keep up, but she was exhausted now, her feet blistered, and the gap between them grew wider, Mairi's form receding until she was un-identifiable, just a small grey figure against the vast blue sky.

The following morning began bright and fine. In the mansion gardens, the last of the year's bees buzzed about the Shirley poppies and the tall pink foxgloves that sprang out along the borders of the lawn. The ground was soft beneath Audrey's feet where apples had been allowed to fall and ferment, and the scent of roses and jasmine mingled with the smell of decay.

She found Miss Buchanan in a sheltered corner, at a little table set up amongst the unpruned roses. She sat bent over a manuscript, pen in hand. For a moment Audrey saw her as she might have been when she was young. With her fine features and large blue eyes, she would have been handsome, beautiful even. Had her injury deterred suitors, or had she spurned them? Perhaps she had feared being diminished by marriage – being turned into a wife, not a person, not a folklorist. But if she had desired independence, she did not have it here. Her brother monitored her spending and her activities, and it seemed she was too debilitated or too loath to meet with others, to even walk to the village. She was confined here, in this strange house. No, Audrey thought as she watched her, Miss Buchanan was the same as her: she had not chosen solitude but had had it forced upon her. And now she had abandoned the outside world altogether, save for its stories.

She did not look up until Audrey was a few paces away, when she pushed her spectacles down her nose and peered over the frames. 'You have found me in my garden retreat.'

'Effy told me you were here. I wondered if you had a moment to speak with me?'

Miss Buchanan removed her glasses and pushed back her chair, leaning heavily on her cane as she rose, the red garnet eye of the handle glinting in the morning light. She moved over to a wooden bench and gestured to Audrey to join her. 'Well?'

'Two days ago, Mairi took me to a ceilidh in Sculamus. The people there were willing to tell me their stories in part, I think, because she was there.' She would not mention the real reason they had admitted her. 'And she was able to translate when I didn't fully understand.'

Miss Buchanan said nothing, but her lips tightened.

'My suggestion is that I engage Mairi as an assistant in my work. She can accompany me to these people's houses, seek out those who may be able to tell us old stories, and interpret where my own Gaelic is not sufficient.'

Miss Buchanan did not answer immediately. She turned her spectacles in her hand. 'Do you know how Mairi came to us?'

'She said Alec had found her.'

'Yes,' Miss Buchanan said. 'She had been sleeping in the straw next to the horses. She was a tiny, dirty thing. He brought her into the kitchen for some food and drink, though Lord knows, many would have simply turned her out. She stayed on the hearth in the kitchen for a few days and began to help with the most basic tasks. She was almost feral, but quick. Sharp.' She looked at Audrey. 'So I decided to keep her.'

Audrey watched a red admiral butterfly settle on one of the roses. The woman made it sound as though Mairi were an animal of some kind – another cat.

'But I'm not sure that she has ever really taken to our world,' Miss Buchanan said. 'She is still a creature of the moors. And she does not always do as she is bid.'

Audrey thought of Mairi's young, smooth face; her slight figure. 'I think she can do what is asked of her in this instance, and I believe her assistance will make all the difference. People will be more willing to offer their stories with her present at the meetings. Is it not worth trying what I suggest, at least for a short time?'

Miss Buchanan gave a slight smile. 'You may try, as you

are so insistent, but you must keep a close watch on her, and she must still be able to complete her duties about the house.'

'Of course. And in terms of payment?' She herself had not yet received any monies, and she thought uncomfortably of Lord Buchanan's comment the previous day: *Unlike here, you worked for free.*

'I will speak to her.' Miss Buchanan regarded Audrey closely. 'Would you say, Miss Hart, that you were a good judge of character?'

Audrey blanched. 'Usually, yes.'

'Mairi is not predictable.'

'I see.'

Predictable. Was anyone truly predictable? Audrey could not have predicted how Samuel had acted, or her father. She could not even have predicted how she herself had behaved over the summer.

'What were the stories?' Miss Buchanan said.

'I beg your pardon?'

'The stories you heard at the ceilidh – what were they?'

'There were several: a water horse, a changeling child.' Audrey hesitated. She did not want to tell Miss Buchanan about Eliza – it seemed a betrayal – but after all, this was what she was here to do. 'They also spoke about a young girl who recently vanished.'

'Vanished?'

In a low voice, Audrey related the story of Eliza as it had been told to her. Under Miss Buchanan's blue gaze, however, the tale that had unnerved her became risible.

As she described the birds that had been seen whirling overhead, Miss Buchanan actually smiled. 'The Sluagh,' she said.

'Yes, that's what they think.'

Miss Buchanan's eyes gleamed. 'Of course they do. They believe that the Sluagh are incapable of reproducing and therefore steal young children, or young mothers.'

'This girl, though. Eliza Fraser. She hadn't had a child. At least not as far as I know.' Audrey thought of Isbeil and her hidden pregnancy. She would not tell Miss Buchanan of the crofters' belief that Isbeil too was a victim. Not yet. 'That's not the reason they gave for her being taken.'

Miss Buchanan glanced up, her hand tightening on her stick. 'Mr Maclean. Something is amusing?'

Audrey turned to see Murdo looking down at them, a smirk upon his face. He had clearly overheard their conversation as he approached. 'Only, Miss Buchanan, that Eliza Fraser wasn't taken.'

'No?'

'No.'

'Then where is she?' Audrey asked.

'She has, like many young folk before her, gone to the Lowlands seeking work. That's what I heard, from a far surer source than the *cailleach* who told you that tale, I'd wager.'

His smirk fell away and his mouth was now a cruel line. Had he always been this hard, this dismissive, she wondered, or was there once some kindness in him?

'Mr Maclean,' Miss Buchanan said coldly, 'you are here

for a reason, I assume. What was it you wanted?'

'One of your brother's creditors is here, making a fair nuisance of himself, and Lord Buchanan is nowhere to be found.'

'Very well. Miss Hart, we can continue this conversation later.'

Audrey rose, nodded to Murdo and walked back through the garden, past ageing plum trees with their decaying fruits melting into the ground. She stopped by a small fountain where moss had crept into the scalloped edges of the bowl. In the centre stood a sculpture of a small child holding a large shell atop his head, his face and body streaked brown and green with mud and lichen.

'I would thank you,' she heard Miss Buchanan say to Murdo, 'not to mention these matters in the presence of others. My brother's affairs are not for public discussion.'

Audrey spent the rest of the morning sitting in the library window seat, continuing to write up the stories the crofters had told at the ceilidh. Her mind returned to the birds whirling, to the girls calling for Eliza, to Isbeil, whose body still lay in the white-shrouded room, unclaimed. She stared out of the window at the sky, now blurred by clouds, and at the great hill that looked down upon the mansion – the hill of the old woman, they called it. Beinn na Caillich. A giantess presiding over Skye.

'So here you are.'

She turned. Alec stood before her, a small velvet box in his hand. He held it out.

'Take it.'

She put down her book. 'What is it?'

'Open and see.'

She took the box and removed the lid. Inside was a silver apple, exquisitely crafted, a delicate leaf folded into its side. Holding it in her palm and looking at it carefully, she saw that it was itself a small box, lined with red velvet.

'It's beautiful,' she said. 'Where on earth did you get it?'

'A gift from the fairies.' Alec settled himself into a chair and winked. 'My aunt gave it to me some years ago. Bought it from a travelling silversmith and thought I'd appreciate the fairy-tale significance. But I thought you might like it.'

She turned the apple in her hand. The forbidden fruit. 'Are you sure?'

'Yes, yes. I've no real use for it myself.'

She looked up at him, his eyes a cold blue but the lines about them kind. He seemed so very different from Samuel, but then Samuel had been so different from how he had at first appeared.

'What are you doing in here anyway?' Alec asked. 'I haven't seen you all morning.' He took the seat beside her.

Audrey touched the notebook in which she had been writing. 'Recording the stories I was told the night before last.' She told him about the ceilidh. About Eliza. About the birds.

'It's just like in your book, Alec. They truly believe she was taken by spirits.'

'Well, I suppose it gives more purpose to their lives to believe that mystical forces are at work.'

Surely that is what we all do, Audrey thought. We believe in things that make this life seem better, that give it meaning. But perhaps Alec believed in nothing – not even in God.

'They are genuinely afraid,' she said.

'Better to be terrified than miserable. If the reality is that people die of starvation and illness, drown themselves out of shame, or leave their impoverished homes in search of a better life, then maybe it's preferable to think that the fairies are taking people away to serve some greater purpose. Anyway,' he said, standing up, 'if you've been in here all morning, you need some fresh air.'

Drown themselves out of shame. Audrey looked out of the window again to the sullen sky. 'Not a very lovely day for a walk.'

'If you let the weather on this island deter you, you'll never leave the house.' He got up and reached out a hand to her. 'Come on. I want to show you something.'

Grey clouds, black-edged, were scudding in from the west, and already there was a faint smirr of rain on the air. Audrey drew her travelling cloak closer around her and hurried after Alec, who was already halfway across the garden. 'Up this way!'

The wind grew stronger and buffeted Audrey's hair. Leaves gusted across the path. She felt exhilarated, even happy. 'Where are we going?'

Alec turned back and smiled, but did not answer. A moment later he pointed. 'Look!'

A flock of dark birds flew low overhead. Audrey put back her hood and gazed up at them.

'They must know that a storm is coming,' she said, remembering the words of the man on the boat.

'Or maybe,' Alec shouted back at her through the wind, 'they're spirits of the dead come to carry off another crofter girl.'

Audrey ran to catch up with him. 'You're heartless,' she laughed.

'So they say.'

They walked close together now, so that they could hear one other against the wind, and their shoulders occasionally touched. Audrey thought that he might link his arm with hers, but he did not.

'Did you come across any similar stories? Of the Sluagh? Of spirits taking the form of birds?'

'No, not in the stories I myself collected. The motif occurs in fairy tales, of course. The milk-white doo who flies out from the little boy's bones after his mother kills him; Cinderella's mother as the birds that peck the rice from the soot.'

'But those tales are both about the souls of the dead taking the shape of birds, aren't they? This is different. Here, the Sluagh are carrying the *living*, spiriting them into holes in the earth.'

They had reached what seemed to be the remains of an ancient wall, a carved door with an ornate shell-work surround built into the middle. Taking a key from his waistcoat pocket, Alec unlocked and unbolted it, then led the way inside.

At first, Audrey could see only gloom, but when Alec lit an oil lamp, the place was illuminated with a flickering multicoloured light. It was a grotto, the walls covered with glass fragments and iridescent shells of all kinds: blush-pink cowries, pearly fan shells, great scallops and angel wings. Here and there glimmered the green of jade, the red of garnet, the pink of quartz.

'Some of the stones were hacked out before we thought to lock it up properly,' he said, moving the lamp to the wall to show her where rocks had been removed.

Audrey looked up at the ceiling, which shone with hundreds of tiny white shells. 'It's magical. How long has it been here?'

'My mother had it built before I was born; this and the tea house, which is now little more than a wreck. She was very fond of entertaining, apparently.'

'You don't remember her?'

'Not really. She died when I was young. My sister told me they collected most of the shells together.' He took a seat on a rock shelf and gestured for Audrey to join him.

Looking at the glinting glass, the black marble floor, Audrey had a sudden memory of being on a beach with her own mother the last time they had come to Skye, their bare feet testing the waves, the sea breeze billowing their skirts. Where had that been? How soon after that had her mother died? Then, like a rush of night air, came an understanding. 'Alec, that first evening I was here, Effy gave me some clothes that belonged to Miss Buchanan's niece. They were your sister's?'

Alec gave a strange smile. 'Yes. It was a peculiar thing for her to do.'

Audrey saw again the framed portrait on his desk. 'What was her name?'

'Flora. She died when she was fourteen. Here.'

'Here?'

'In the bay. In the sea.'

She watched him in the glow of the lamp. She could not bring herself to ask how. 'What was she like?'

His gaze remained on the lamp's flame. 'She was only three years older than me, but she looked after me when our mother died.' He smiled. 'Flora was terribly stern with all of us. I suppose she felt she had to be, with our mother gone and Father often away. And she was beautiful – not at all like me, in fact. Fine-boned and fair.' The smile vanished and his eyes dulled. 'Not that she was beautiful by the time they found her.'

The candle flame quivered. For a long moment there was silence.

When he spoke again, his tone was bright, false. 'It's not so surprising that the crofters believe the Sluagh carry the living into the earth. The fairies are always hiding people underground. Do you know the poem "Kilmeny", by James Hogg?'

'Oh yes, I know it well,' Audrey said, relieved to be on more familiar ground. '"For Kilmeny was pure as pure could be." But that was about a child taken into heaven, wasn't it?'

Alec frowned. 'I don't think so.'

Audrey closed her eyes, remembering the words: '"Kilmeny had been where the cock never crew, Where the rain never fell, and the wind never blew. But it seem'd as the harp of the sky had rung, And the airs of heaven play'd round her tongue." That's heaven, surely.'

'"A land where sin had never been; A land of love and a land of light, Withouten sun, or moon, or night; Where the river swa'd a living stream." That's fairyland.'

'Not the fairyland around here,' Audrey laughed. 'You yourself have told me that the fairies are hardly things of love and light.'

'Maybe not. But these are good fairies. They return Kilmeny after seven years.'

'How generous of them.'

'If you read the poem carefully, you'll see that they were protecting her.'

There was a hint of irritation in Alec's voice, and Audrey sensed that her tone had been too light, too mocking. 'I'm sure you're right: I suppose I always felt sorry for her.' For she had known what it was to be alone; what it was to be trapped.

Alec ran his hand over a pattern of shells in the shape of a heart. 'Read it again. I think you'll see it differently now. In any case,' he stood up, 'we should get back before the storm sets in.'

★

Miss Buchanan was in the hall when they reached Lanerly, speaking to a thin-boned man dressed entirely in black.

'If they have made the arrangements, then that is all well and good, though it is unfortunate that they left it to you to communicate this to us.'

'My apologies, Miss Buchanan, I thought you had been informed. They were concerned that she shouldn't be left too long unburied.' The man bowed his head a little. 'Matters of the soul.'

Miss Buchanan turned to Alec. 'Mr Gillies here has been sent by the shopkeeper to make the coffin. Did anyone mention this to you?'

Alec shook his head. 'No, I can't say they did. When is the burial?'

'Tomorrow,' the man said, and then in a lower voice: 'But in the circumstances it will not be in the kirkyard.'

'No,' Miss Buchanan said coldly. 'The minister is very particular about that, isn't he?'

Audrey found Mairi in the kitchen, scrubbing a heap of copper pans. 'It shouldn't have been them to arrange it,' the girl said to her. 'Not them.'

Audrey watched Mairi's face. 'What exactly did they do to Isbeil?'

Mairi stopped her scrubbing. 'They didn't care a straw for her and they'll make sure her burial is as mean as can be. It'll just be me and a few others.'

Audrey hesitated. 'Are women allowed to attend funerals here, then?'

'Oh, it won't be a proper burial. Not with them saying what they're saying. Not with that man and his little pimple of a wife organising it. It'll be outside the kirkyard wall at dusk. That's all she'll be getting.' She returned to the pans but Audrey could see she was near tears.

'Then I will come with you.'

Mairi stared at her. 'You will?'

'Yes. I would like to be there.' After all, she was the one who had found Isbeil, the one who had tried to help her. It was right that she should pay her respects in some way.

And besides, she wanted to see who else would attend.

Back in her room, Audrey re-read Samuel's letter, the smooth sentences and the embroidered threats. It was his skill, she now knew, to persuade and coerce, a trick so well practised he had managed to permeate the shell of a girl who had tried to close herself off to the world. A girl who had told herself she had given up on obtaining the approval or companionship of others, but who still held out a small, secret hope of friendship or love. When Samuel told Audrey he thought her intelligent and interesting, she was surprised and disbelieving, but he did not give up. 'You are not like other women, Audrey. You should not pretend to be. You are worth a thousand lace-clad debutantes.'

He had attended Audrey's lessons as she assisted the orphanage girls with their reading and writing. At first they had talked only briefly after the classes, Audrey sitting straight-backed as he praised her teaching abilities and her knowledge, gave gentle advice on how to improve still further, and offered to speak to the girls himself. After a few weeks, he suggested that they walk together in Regent's Park, taking her arm as they strolled about the water-lily house and the botanic gardens. He even hired a little boat and rowed them up and down the lake, talking to her about her favourite books, asking her about folk stories, drawing out details about her childhood as though it was the most natural thing in the world.

There was nothing improper in it, she assured herself. He was married and was a friend of her father's. She didn't think it possible that he could have any interest in her of that sort; she assumed that his attention was benign. By this stage in her life Audrey had concluded that most people thought her unlikeable and awkward. She had walled herself in, polite enough but never attempting intimacy with anyone. Samuel, however, had not seemed to notice her gaucheness, her plain dress, her hair that continually struggled free of its pins. When he looked into her eyes, he seemed to like what was there.

She knew now that he had been looking only at himself, reflected.

All night it rained, and all throughout the following morning; heavy, fat drops driving at the roof and windows, drenching the remaining flowers, and seaming the mountains with white, as the burns became torrents that rushed down to the sea. By dusk, the rain had reduced to a dull drizzle, and Audrey put on her cloak, boots and hat to walk together with Mairi to the burial ceremony. The air smelt of moss, earth and the bark of the birch trees; the mud sucked at her boots and spattered on her legs. The graveyard was beyond the manse, near the sea, where stone slabs and crosses ran down to the shore.

It was a small gathering – Mrs Campbell, Mairi's pale-eyed friend from the ceilidh; a girl of about fifteen whom Audrey had never before seen; the sexton, and an old man wearing a flat woollen hat. The last to arrive were a stout, greasy-looking man and a small, bland-faced woman who scurried behind him.

'Now there's a sight to sicken a sow from its supper,' Mrs Campbell muttered when she saw them. 'Beat her into the ground and come to see it covered over.'

Audrey glanced at Mairi. 'The shopkeeper and his wife,' the girl confirmed.

For a few minutes they stood listening to the doleful murmur of the sea. It was the old man who began singing. The girl joined him, then Mairi. Audrey understood only fragments of the song, which were carried into the wind: *She is gone on the mountain . . . She is lost to the forest . . .*

She watched the faces of the shopkeeper and his wife, he with the jaundiced tinge of a drinker, she with the furtive eyes of a mouse. They did not sing. Their expressions seemed hard. Why had they arranged the burial if they cared nothing for Isbeil? Audrey thought again of the girl's bruised head, her hollow eyes. She thought of her father's case of the beaten servant. As the song ended, the shopkeeper's wife put her hands to her face and seemed to breathe in. When she dropped her hands, her eyes met Audrey's for a moment.

The old man walked to the freshly dug grave, bowed his head and crossed himself. The shopkeeper and his wife followed, then the young girl. Mrs Campbell took Mairi's hand and they walked together over the muddy ground. Audrey followed behind and saw that the coffin was still visible beneath a scattering of earth. For a moment she thought of her mother and the funeral she had not been allowed to attend. She had seen only the closed coffin, white lilies laid across it. Her father had left her alone in the undertaker's room, to 'say goodbye', but she had not quite believed that her mother was there. She did not wish to think of her body shattered into pieces; she preferred to think of her floating somewhere in the ether, like a protecting spirit or a good fairy.

Muttering in Gaelic, Mairi knelt down and placed a sprig of rowan on the coffin. At first Audrey thought she was praying, but after a moment she understood that Mairi was speaking to Isbeil.

'Why didn't you talk to me? Why didn't you tell me?'

Part Two

Chapter 5

The little man led Bainne through the forest, and before long they came upon a huge tree, as wide as a castle. The man approached the tree and whispered some words that Bainne could not hear. All at once a door appeared in the trunk and sprang open to admit them. This, of course, was the door to fairyland, and as soon as they entered Bainne could hear the sound of laughter, music and tinkling bells. They followed a path down beneath the earth, the sound of merriment growing ever louder, until they reached a wide hall bedecked with flowers and lights. In the centre of the hall was a long table piled high with dishes of delicious food: shining fruits, glimmering jellies, delicate pastries, sugared cakes. Around them danced boys and girls all clothed in green and gold, their faces as beautiful as angels'.

'Dance with us!' said one of the girls, running to Bainne and seizing her hands.

'But I have never danced,' Bainne said. 'I do not know how.'

'Then we will show you,' the girl said, leading her towards the other children. 'It's never too late to learn.'

All night she danced with her new friends, stopping only to drink sweet wine and feast upon the foods the fairies offered her: jugs of frothing milk, butter fresh from the churn, treacle scones and bramble jelly.

Outside, however, Bainne's parents were searching for her. They might not have loved their daughter, but she was theirs – their blood and bone – and they had no intention of letting her go.

❧❦❧

The grocer's shop consisted of one plain room lined with wooden boxes of goods: meal, oats, potatoes, turnips, bunches of withered greens and, on a shelf, brown rolls of tobacco and a few dusty pots. Behind a counter stood the shopkeeper, his wide face the colour of raw meat left out too long.

'Can I help you?'

Though it had been Audrey's idea to come, it was Mairi who spoke. Her voice was quiet and cold. 'I came to collect Isbeil's things. Whatever she left.'

The man shrugged. 'You can take them if you want.'

At the back of the shop a door led onto a narrow dark room, a bed in the corner, a rush-backed chair beside it and a small wooden *kist* against the wall.

'I'll be leaving you to it then.'

He stood with his hand on the door handle, his thick fingers curled around it.

'When did you realise Isbeil had gone?' Audrey asked.

He frowned. 'Two days before she was found. It was just after I paid her wages, so we were thinking she'd left without notice.'

'You didn't see her go?'

'No. She ate her supper and went to bed in her room here. Next thing, it's the morning and she's away.'

'Did you alert anyone?'

The man narrowed his eyes. 'As I was saying, we thought she'd upped and left. I told the minister when we saw him at kirk. Now if you'll excuse me, miss, I've a shop to be minding.'

Audrey looked about the room. It was little more than a cell: a small window, whitewashed walls, no pictures, no books. Nothing to make it cheerful or homely.

'The *kist*,' she said.

Mairi nodded and moved over to the chest to open it. There were only a few items inside, which Mairi transferred into a box she had brought with her: a pair of worn-down shoes, a little prayer book, the pretty blue bonnet and a pair of gloves. Audrey took the gloves and ran her hand over them. They were good quality and pale blue, almost grey.

Mairi stood up. 'That's all.'

'Did she have other things?'

'She had two dresses, but I suppose she was found in one, buried in the other. I don't know if there was anything else.'

As Audrey folded the gloves, she felt something move within one of them. She shook it and a small object fell to the ground.

Mairi gave a sharp intake of breath. 'Whatever's that?'

Audrey stooped to collect it and held it in her palm. It was a small silver bird, no bigger than an acorn. Peering closely, she discerned a loop for a chain. 'It's a pendant.' She turned it over.

Etched into the silver was a tiny tree.

As they neared the drive, they heard the sound of hooves and wheels and a shining black carriage shot past them, neither acknowledging them in any way nor reducing its speed. Miss Buchanan was standing in the hallway when they reached the house. She looked briefly bewildered and lost, an old woman alone, but when she saw Audrey and Mairi, her face reverted to its usual unreadable mask.

'Was that Lord Buchanan?' Audrey asked. 'Is everything all right?'

'Yes, yes. He's off to London again. He never stays long.' She nodded towards the box that Mairi carried. 'What have you got there?'

Mairi hesitated. 'Isbeil's things. There was no one else to take them.'

'I see. Poor girl. Well, along with you now, Mairi.'

The girl gave a quick bob of her head and darted across the hallway, the box in her arms.

When Audrey turned back, she realised that Miss Buchanan was regarding her closely. 'I understand you attended the girl's funeral.'

Audrey felt her throat constrict. 'Yes, I did. I wanted to

see whether there were any particular burial customs.' Even to her own ears, this sounded ridiculous. Why was she defending herself?

'And were there?'

'Well, there was no speech or rite, just a lament – I'm afraid I didn't catch all the words. And they laid rowan wreaths.'

'Nothing more?'

'Nothing more. But then I suppose it wasn't a typical burial. There was very little ceremony, in fact.'

'There never is for a suicide.' Miss Buchanan looked away. 'Has there been any more talk of abductions?'

'No,' Audrey said. 'Not that I've heard.'

Miss Buchanan's eyes were on the painting of the girl in white.

'She is very striking,' Audrey ventured.

'Yes. She was. My niece.' Miss Buchanan's face was rigid and pale.

'Alec told me a little about her.'

Miss Buchanan nodded. 'He was very fond of Flora. As was I.' She looked back at Audrey. 'What will be your next steps in terms of collecting the tales?'

'Well, I thought that tomorrow we would go to Strollamus, to speak to the girls who saw the birds in the sky the night Eliza vanished, find out exactly what they saw, what they believe.' Audrey considered telling Miss Buchanan about Isbeil's silver bird, but she was not yet sure what to make of it herself.

'Good, Miss Hart. A sensible idea. Ascertain why they

linked the birds they saw with the Sluagh, and whether
there are any legends specific to the area. In fact, there's a
man living near Strollamus Farm who's said to know many
of the old tales. It was Murdo who told me of him; he
should be able to take you.'

'Really, that won't be necessary. I'm quite happy to
walk.'

'Miss Hart, I don't want you wasting time tramping
about the countryside. Strollamus is at least three miles
away. I'll speak to Murdo. You need hardly worry about
putting him out. And while I think of it, I want you to
arrange to visit another folklorist with whom I've been
corresponding.

'Oh yes? Who?'

'A Mr Shawfield, in Trotternish.'

'Trotternish.'

'It's in the north-west section of Skye. You'll have
to arrange for a wagonette. Take the girl with you. They
have some distinct superstitions there that I want you
to investigate, and apparently several willing storytellers.'
She turned. 'Come with me to the library now and I'll
give you the necessary details. You should go in the next
week.'

Audrey walked behind Miss Buchanan, her eyes on the
polished wooden floor. Finally she would be returning to
Trotternish. The place where her mother had died.

Tale from Staffin, Trotternish: The Little Bird

A man at Woodend, whose first wife had died, married a second time. The only child of the first marriage was a delicate little girl. The stepmother was far from kind to this child, giving her tasks to do that were beyond her strength, and allowing her no rest or peace. One day the poor child was set to winnow corn, a task much too hard for her. The stepmother was watching her, but it was impossible for the child to get on with her work, for a little bird persisted in following and interrupting her. The child at length had to abandon the task, and for that time, at least, she got some rest. That night the stepmother had a terrifying vision. A spirit appeared to her, saying she was the child's dead mother. This spirit warned her that if she did not behave better to the little girl, dreadful consequences would follow. She said that she was the little bird that had so annoyed the stepmother that day. The woman took the lesson to heart, but too late to save the child's life, for she died soon after.

This belief in souls turning to birds is quite common. L says that people report having seen flocks of souls rising in the air in the form of birds.

'It's not a long drive,' Murdo told Audrey as he handed her up into the gig the following morning, then took the seat beside her and flicked the reins to prompt the horse. He was clean-shaven, she noticed, and smelt of soap. Mairi sat behind them, curled up on her seat, and seemed to go back to sleep, but Audrey remained awake and alert, as they passed through sparse woods where the birch and hazel trees had left a path of yellow and gold and where rabbits raced before them, their tails flashes of white. The morning air was cold and sharp, with a smell of late clover and wild thyme. Murdo seemed less stilted and resentful, occasionally pointing out landmarks: the bay at Camas na Sgianadin, the corn mill, the schoolhouse.

Audrey thought of the orphanage schoolroom with its bare wooden tables and its smell of limewash and chalk. Two months after she had started teaching the girls, they had come to her with a present. 'For your birthday, miss. It's just a little book we made you.' It was a collection of poems that they had copied out by hand, with pictures in the borders, carefully drawn. It was the first time since her mother had died that anyone had made her a present. It was the first time in a long time that anyone had shown her any real kindness. And how she had repaid them.

'Murdo, is there a silversmith on Skye?' she asked on impulse.

He glanced at her. 'I doubt it. Maybe in Portree. Is this to do with that box Master Buchanan gave you?'

Audrey tensed. What did he know of that? 'No,' she said shortly. 'It's nothing to do with that.'

Murdo nodded. 'He's a strange one, Alec Buchanan. Has some funny ideas. I'd keep my distance if I were you.'

Audrey turned away from him, pale with anger. What right had this man to cast aspersions, or to assume that he understood anything about Alec, or her? For the remainder of the journey she did not speak, but watched the clouds as they scudded by.

'Well, this is Strollamus,' Murdo said, as they came upon a group of crofter houses straggling down to the sea. 'I'll take you as far as the farm.'

They smelt the farm before they saw it – the stink of pigs, the stench of manure – and they heard the farm hands, already up and at work, feeding the animals, shouting to one another, whistling.

A boy carrying a curved spade looked up as Audrey and Mairi climbed down from the gig. 'Will you be wanting Mr Hewitt?'

Audrey smiled at him. 'No, we're looking for some girls. I don't know their names, but I know that they lived with Eliza Fraser.'

'Eliza.'

'Yes,' Audrey said, walking closer to him. 'I wanted to speak to the girls who were with her the night she disappeared.'

The boy stared at her. 'It's only Marjory that's still here. The others are gone. She'll be at the milking.'

'Can you take us to her?'

He looked about, then set down his spade and took them through the farm to the cattle shed, where several young women sat on low stools pulling rhythmically at the udders of the cows. The air was pungent with the smell of the animals and of the warm milk, and rang with the sound of the milk hitting the pails, the lowing of the cows, the chatter of the girls. The boy approached a large girl with fair hair, who continued her work.

'What do you want, Evander?'

He nodded over to Audrey and Mairi.

The girl turned from the cow and squinted at them, before standing up. She was not more than sixteen, Audrey thought, but buxom and full-faced, as though she'd been drinking the cream off the milk each morning. Her cheeks were pink with the exertion of her work.

'We wondered if we could talk to you, Marjory.'

The girl wiped her hands on her apron. 'Oh aye. What about?'

'About Eliza.'

The place quietened as the other girls held off their milking to watch them. Marjory picked up her bucket and walked away from them, looking back at Audrey to indicate that she was to follow. She poured the pail of foaming milk into a large wooden trough. 'I can't be long,' she muttered, 'or I'll catch it.'

'We won't keep you.' Walking alongside the girl, Audrey explained quietly that they were assisting Miss Buchanan.

'Oh aye. Down at Lanerly Hall. She's a queer one, I heard. Never goes out. Just takes our stories and keeps them in books. The young ones say she's a witch.'

'She's a folklorist,' Audrey said, suppressing her irritation. 'She's recording the stories to ensure they're not lost.'

'Well, what happened to Eliza was no story. It was the truth. I saw it with my own eyes.'

'And what did you see?'

Marjory looked from Audrey to Mairi, her face hard. 'Why should I tell you? So you can write it down in some book?'

Mairi met her stare. 'Because another girl has died. And folk are saying it's the same thing.'

The hostility in the girl's face mingled with something else – curiosity, surprise. 'What happened to her then, this other lass?'

'She was found drowned at Broadford Bay,' Mairi said. 'And the rich folk are saying she drowned herself. Others, though, think it was *them*. The spirits.'

'What did you see?' Audrey asked again.

Marjory hesitated, seeming to consider. 'Blackish birds I thought they were at first, but now I know they weren't.'

'What kind of birds did you think they were?'

'Rooks, maybe. It was rightly dark so it's hard to say.'

'And what makes you think they weren't just birds?'

The girl looked at Audrey as though she were stupid. 'Because they took her, didn't they?'

'Why do you think they took Eliza?'

'She was there when we went to bed. Said nothing about leaving, just undressed down to her shift and got herself ready as she always did. The next thing we knew, she was gone.'

'You were asleep when she left?'

'Aye. But I woke up in the chill and saw the door was open.'

'And you went outside.'

'Sure I did. I ran out to call for Eliza, and that's when I saw them, circling in the sky above. And there was a noise too, a great rushing sound.'

'The wind?'

Marjory shook her head. 'That was never the wind. There was something else in it – music, maybe. Bells. Whispers.'

'And when did you decide it might have been the Host?'

The girl gave her a long, appraising look as though she were judging the quality of a horse at market. 'I knew there and then that there was something strange in it.'

'Strange, yes, but did you think then that it was the Host, or was it afterwards?'

'We talked of it later.'

'Later that night?'

'What the devil does it matter when it was?'

Audrey pressed her lips together. 'I'm just trying to understand exactly what happened. And why you came to the conclusion that it was the Sluagh.'

'Because you think it nonsense, is that it?' The girl's face was hard again, closed.

'No, no.' Why must she always say the wrong thing? 'I don't think that at all. But you must see that in those circumstances, it would be possible to assume that something else had happened to Eliza.'

'That what had happened to her?'

'Well, couldn't she have left the house for some reason?'

Marjory narrowed her eyes. 'Left the croft in the middle of the night to go and meet some fellow, is that what you mean? Is that what they've been saying?'

'Is that what who's been saying?'

'Folk talk. They always talk.' She was angry now. 'Folk will always be down on a lass just because she might once have been seen talking to a fellow.'

'Which fellow?' Audrey said cautiously. 'What man did they say they'd seen her with?'

'All talk, I tell you. And even if there'd been an ounce of truth in it, she'd never have gone walking in the night to meet him. She wasn't a fool.'

'What was she like, then?' Mairi said.

Marjory paused, assessing this other girl, taking in the thinness of her, the dark hair, the clever eyes. 'She was a quiet one, always thinking.'

'Did she have family on Skye?' Audrey asked.

Marjory shook her head. 'No, not a soul. Came over on a boat from Lewis with her brothers a few years back, and then they went off to seek their silver in America and left her on her own. That's family for you.' She looked at Mairi. 'This other lass – your friend. Why do they say it was spirits?'

'The birds. The night Isbeil was found there were birds flying out in the sky above the sea. Or something that looked like birds. So.' Mairi nodded.

'That's all of it?'

Mairi looked at Audrey, who reached into her pocket and held out her hand towards Marjory so that she could see the silver bird there, nestling in her palm.

'Did Eliza have something like this?' she said.

Marjory looked closely, shook her head. 'No, nothing like that.'

'Did she have anything unusual? Expensive, perhaps?'

'You think girls like us have money?' she said, the hardness returning to her voice. 'You think lasses like me and Eliza have bonny bits of jewellery for wearing when we're about milking the cows?'

'No,' Audrey said. 'And I don't think Isbeil had money either. That's precisely why—'

'I have to be going back now,' Marjory said, cutting her off. 'Or I'll be for it. I've been long enough as it is.' She turned on them and walked back towards the cattle shed, her black boots stirring up the straw.

From the farm, Audrey and Mairi walked up a narrow track to the home of the crofter Miss Buchanan had wanted them to visit. He was a bowed little man with wet blue eyes in a small brown face like a shrivelled apple. His house was even more bare and dark than those Audrey had already seen: a narrow opening in the ceiling allowed smoke to escape, but there were no windows, and only a stool and a chair, the plaited straw of the seat coming away after years of use. The man was wary at first, just as the other people had been, but it did not take long for Mairi to put him at his ease. She told him of their visit to Mackenzie's ceilidh and of how his guests had told Audrey their stories. 'There's no harm in it,' she assured him, sitting by his side. 'Miss

Hart only wants to be writing down the tales to make sure they're safe, not lost forever.'

Some herrings were baking in the embers of the peats, and in the smoke-filled room the smell was overwhelming. Audrey took out her mother's journal, and held it out to him. 'It's a book of stories my own mother collected on the island many years ago. She speaks here of stories about souls taking the form of birds. That's what I'm most interested in at the moment. Can you tell us anything connected with birds?'

The man's apple face wrinkled further in a smile. 'Oh, I know a few tales, I should say.'

He told them then of the Boobrie, a gigantic black bird that lived in lochs and fed on cattle; of the Cailleach, a hag who appeared in the form of a raven and feasted on corpses. When they asked him about Eliza, he nodded his head and spoke in a hushed voice of the circling birds, but he told them nothing that they did not already know. Indeed, the phrases he used were the same as Marjory's: the bells and whispers, the rushing of the wind. It was already a legend, passed between people.

'Have there been other stories about the Sluagh in this region?' Audrey asked. 'Anything similar?'

'From some years ago, aye. Before my time. A child was taken up and returned after one night and one day. He was found, poor lad, back in his house with the palms of his hands in the holes in the wall, and with no life left in his body.'

Audrey felt quite sick. This sounded nothing like the Eliza story.

'Why was it believed to be the Sluagh?'

'His uncle had seen them taking him, so he said.'

Audrey nodded slowly, wondering how many crimes had been concealed by claims of the mystical. Maybe this was what the minister had meant by dangerous beliefs: delusions so deep that they obscured abuse. 'And there's been nothing since then? Nothing until Eliza?'

'Not that I know of. But, well now, we wouldn't always know. Folk were scattered with the clearances. There are so many now without families, without anything at all. They often take the ones that aren't cared for, do you see? They take the friendless ones. The ones they think none will miss.'

Audrey thought of being sent away to school, unwanted. She thought of the house in London and her empty rose-papered room.

'That's why they're coming now,' the old man said. 'Because they see things have got so bad that folk no longer care properly for one another. It was not so in my time, but this is what they've done to us. This is what we are.'

As they made their way back towards the road where Murdo had left them, a terrible groaning sound carried across on the wind. At first Audrey thought it must be someone in great pain, but as they came closer, she saw that it was a cow, surrounded by a group of men. They seemed to be trying to push the animal to the ground.

'What are they doing?'

Mairi would not meet her eye. 'It may be that it's

diseased, miss. If one cow gets the sickness, they have to be curing it or it'll be after infecting the whole of the herd.'

They watched the men push the animal into a hole. 'But what are they doing to it?'

'Burying it to rid it of the sickness.'

Audrey felt her heart slow. 'But Mairi, the animal is alive.'

'Aye, it's a cruel thing. But it's the only way.' Mairi turned away. 'Time we were making for home now, miss.'

After dinner that evening, Audrey retired to her room and retrieved Samuel's letter from the bureau. She supposed she would have to respond, but in what way she did not know. As she lifted the bureau lid, an icy feeling crept over her. Was it her imagination, or had things been moved? She thought she had left her mother's journal at the back of the bureau. Now it was further towards the front, resting on a pile of papers.

A wild roaring sound came from outside – she knew now that it was the red deer stags, calling to each other across the hills, but tonight they sounded more disturbing, more monstrous. Her own heart seemed to beat strangely – too fast, too light.

As she removed Samuel's letter, she knocked over a pot of ink, sending the black liquid spilling over the desk. Cursing at her clumsiness, she used her pocket handkerchief to mop up the ink, smeared thickly over her mother's journal and the papers beneath it. She picked up the precious journal and took it over to the lamp to clean it.

She saw then that the fabric had rubbed the ink into a strange shape. In her distressed state, she fancied that it looked almost like wings.

Chapter 6

When seven lang years had come and fled,
When grief was calm, and hope was dead;
When scarce was remember'd Kilmeny's name,
Late, late in a gloamin' Kilmeny came hame!

Audrey awoke, disturbed, to a cold, sullen morning. A
dank mist had settled over the island and the sea was
steel-grey, angry. Her dreams had been vivid and terrible:
black-feathered creatures with the faces of children, their
wings clipped so they could not fly.

At breakfast, Miss Buchanan wanted to talk more of
what they had learnt in Strollamus. 'Why the Sluagh?
That's the interesting thing. Why not assume that the girl's
spirit had taken the form of a bird, as happens in so many
stories?'

Audrey wondered how Miss Buchanan could retain her
academic distance. She appeared to have no sense that
things were converging, intensifying. Flatly she told her of
the other legends of which the old man had spoken, the

Boobrie, the Cailleach, the child found dead, his hands in the wall.

'Fascinating.' Miss Buchanan sat back in her chair. 'Perhaps you are finally getting somewhere, Miss Hart. I knew you could do it. I only wish I could have travelled with you. There's a man in Heaste whom you must visit too. I was assured he knows many stories passed down to him by his father.' She was animated today and full of energy. How much was the opium, Audrey wondered, and how much was her?

'I will go this afternoon.'

'Very good. And you've arranged your trip to Trotternish?'

Audrey swallowed. 'I have. We leave tomorrow morning.'

'Excellent. I will be interested to hear what you make of our Mr Shawfield. When you return, I'd like you to show me where you are with your work.'

'Yes, of course.' Audrey could take no comfort in Miss Buchanan's enthusiasm. There was something morbid about it. She could not eat. She felt a sickness in her stomach as though of terrible foreknowledge. Despite the rain, she had to leave the house.

Outside, the damp sea-mist shrouded the bay and clung to her skin like cobwebs. Amidst the bracken she saw dots of colour: wild raspberries, blackberries, tiny purple elderberries. From above her came the mournful call of the curlew. Halfway down the path to Broadford the mist grew thicker, swallowing the trees, reducing the pier to an outline, and she could barely make out the way. All at once she came upon a young deer, its ears back, listening. She took a careful step forward and the deer turned its head towards her, its eyes shining darkly. For a moment they looked at one another, and then the deer bolted, its delicate legs a whir of brown and white. Audrey stood still. Although she had left the house simply in order to escape, she knew now where she was going.

The door squeaked as she entered, and she was greeted by the smell of apples and wood shavings. It was not the shopkeeper behind the counter, but his wife, with her flat, small-featured face.

'Good morning,' the woman said dully.

Audrey picked up a dusty pot of honey and brought it to the table. The woman nodded and began to wrap the pot in a piece of brown paper.

'How are you managing without Isbeil to help you?'

'We are managing just fine, thank you.' She continued her wrapping.

'Did you know she was with child?' Audrey knew her question was abrupt, rude, but she felt slightly delirious today, as though something within her had been released.

The woman stared at her for a moment, her mouth a thin line. 'No, we didn't know. We wouldn't have been employing her if we had.'

'But you knew she was ill, didn't you? You must have done.'

No response.

'I met Isbeil when I first came to Broadford and she was obviously sick. Did you not think of getting a doctor for her?'

The woman's face took on a bitter aspect. 'What happened to Isbeil was a sad thing, but it was not our doing.'

'Did she ever go out at night, to meet someone?'

'I don't know.'

'Well, she must have met someone, somewhere.'

The woman's face flushed and her voice was tight with anger. 'I didn't keep a guard on the girl. I was her employer, not her gaoler. As far as I knew, she wasn't wandering out at night like a tink and never met any fellow. As far as I knew, she was a good kirk-going girl. Now,' she set the wrapped pot down on the counter with a small thud, 'that'll be sixpence.'

Slowly Audrey counted out the money onto the counter.

'She wasn't happy working for you, was she?'

'I'd be careful, miss, of assuming that you, a stranger to this place, know anything about it. She may have been unhappy, aye. She may have been ill. But that's not what killed her.'

Behind her Audrey heard the shop door open. The woman's face contorted into a smile.

'Effy. What'll you be wanting?'

The maid walked up to the counter to stand beside Audrey. 'Morning, Miss Hart. You're out early.'

Audrey picked up her pot of honey and turned to face the girl. Effy's expression was carefully bland, but her mud-brown eyes slid away from Audrey's, uneasy.

★

Audrey walked back alone, along the coast. The mist was clearing now, and above the water she saw the whiskered head of a seal, watching her with its gleaming black eyes. The souls of the drowned – that was what her mother used to say; or selkies who shed their skin to walk on land as humans. In the stories, men stole the selkies' skins so that they would have to stay on dry land as their wives. Sometimes, when her mother seemed sad, when her father spoke to her sharply, Audrey had wondered whether her mother was like the selkie women, trapped in a marriage, yearning to escape.

Instead of following the usual route to Lanerly, she took the path leading up from the sea, beneath hazel and birch trees, their crinkled, rust-coloured leaves forming a carpet over the ground. After a few minutes she came upon a small clearing, and her heart contracted. In the centre stood a large tree, a piece of fence fixed across it. Hanging from the fence were the withered and shrunken corpses of birds, their necks pierced through with nails. Buzzards, ravens, eagles, hawks, all in rows like shrunken coats on pegs. She stared at a line of crows and rooks – there must have been fifty of them. And then, behind, another row of smaller birds: blackbirds, blackcaps, buntings, starlings.

For a moment she stood transfixed. Then she shuddered, turned and walked quickly down the path, back towards Lanerly.

★

She found Alec in the library, writing.

'Why are there dead birds hanging from a tree? On the walk from Loveress?'

He turned to look at her. 'Pretty ghastly, isn't it? It's Murdo's gibbet – his little project for scaring the predators away. There have been a few sheep taken.'

Audrey had heard talk of eagles taking the eyes of lambs, but surely crows didn't harm sheep. Nor starlings. She felt for the silver bird in her pocket and placed it next to Alec's notebook.

He put down his pen. 'Where did you get this?'

'It was with Isbeil's possessions. It seems strange that she should have had any jewellery at all, and I wondered if you knew where it came from, or whether it signified anything.'

Alec leant to look more closely at the bird. 'Well, it might mean Skye itself: *An t-Eilean Sgitheanach*.' He sat back. 'Some think that means the Winged Isle, because of the island's shape. It might just be a bird. But I agree it's odd that she should have had such a thing.' He seemed deep in thought for a moment. 'Travelling tinkers sometimes hammer silver objects into charms or brooches for the crofter women – I've seen them wearing them on their shawls. But not anything as prettily done as this.'

Audrey held the bird on her open palm. 'That looks like it might be a hallmark, a tree.'

'I suppose it could be, yes, though it's unlikely to be a hallmark from Skye. We're not exactly known for our trees.' A shadow flitted across his face. He picked up his pen again.

Audrey hesitated. 'Isbeil was receiving money from someone. She told Mairi her uncle had been sending her money, but he emigrated some time ago. And the girl we spoke to in Strollamus yesterday suggested that Eliza, the missing girl, had been seen talking to a man.'

Alec narrowed his eyes.

'You know who it might have been?'

'No. But I know *what* it might have been.' He paused. 'People say that there's no crime on this island, no vice. That we are a moral and law-abiding people. By and large that's true, but remember that in my work with the minister I see the way the poor live, I see what they do in order to survive, and in some ways Skye is just like everywhere else. Maybe Eliza was making money in a way that people don't talk about. Maybe Isbeil too. You understand me?'

Audrey saw Isbeil, alive. She thought of the girls at the orphanage, the girls she had failed. *They are juvenile prostitutes, Miss Hart. That's the way of it. They might tell you otherwise, but I see them for what they are.*

'Yes,' she said to Alec. 'Yes, I understand.'

Audrey left Alec and walked slowly from the library, past the grimacing cat and the case of moths, now housed alongside the beetles. She thought of Rose, at the orphanage, of how she had grown thinner, shrunken somehow. But no, she had assured Audrey, she was not ill, she was not unhappy; she was quite all right. She would not look Audrey in the eye, however. She no longer spoke in class. A week or so later, Cora followed, growing quieter and more withdrawn. She no longer asked questions, and she no longer laughed. Her skin had lost its bloom.

Perhaps the cause should have been obvious to Audrey, but she refused to see it. Because it could not be possible, could it, that the man she had learnt to trust, perhaps even love, had been using that trust, that love, as a blindfold?

She could not believe it until she saw it.

It had been late July, the corridors a cool relief from the stench and heat of London. She had returned to the classroom after her lesson ended, realising she had left her workbook there. Unusually, the door was closed, and before she turned the handle it occurred to her to check if there was someone inside. She put her ear to the door and heard a sharp drawing-in of breath, a rustling, then a whimpering. Lowering her eye to the keyhole, she saw through it what she should have seen weeks before – the hand on the thigh, the skirts pushed back – and she heard a voice plead, 'No!'

She had had no time to think. She simply rattled on the door handle, wanting it to stop. Murmuring, footsteps, and then Samuel was at the door, smiling. Even within a few seconds, he had regained his composure. 'Audrey. I was just helping Rose with her reading.'

Audrey stared at Samuel, having no words to question or accuse him. She looked over his shoulder to Rose, who sat expressionless, her skirts rearranged, on one of the wooden benches. Audrey had walked over to the table, picked up her workbook and left the room in silence. Once in the corridor, she had pressed the book to her

chest, quickened her pace, and then run until she was out
of the orphanage and in the dust-filled street, where for
once she was glad of the noise and chaos and anonymity
of London.

It was a clever move on his part, to prey on girls who
were under his protection; who were eating food bought at
least partly with his money, and who slept under a roof
that he had helped to provide. He had saved them from
the streets, so they owed him a little repayment. And who
would speak out against someone so powerful and so
popular? Who would believe that a man so charming would
need to thrust his hand up the skirts of a thirteen-year-old
girl?

As Audrey walked back home, she had cursed herself
for a fool. Of course he didn't find her interesting. Of
course he didn't want to listen to her dull stories about her
mother or her past. He had been laughing at her, enduring
her, in order to make use of her students. Worst of all was
that she had credited any of it. She had allowed herself to
be duped and her charges to be degraded.

She never challenged him. She never spoke to him of it
at all. What would she say? What words would she use?
Ruin? Corruption? Dishonour? Shame? In any event, he
would deny whatever she charged him with. She had no
proof, save for her own eyes.

Instead, she had gone to Rose and taken her into her
arms, her thin shoulders, her scent of neglect. 'I will tell
Miss Hodge,' she had said. 'He cannot be allowed to
continue.'

Rose had drawn back with a shake of her head. 'No one cares about girls like us. They assume we're bad from birth.'

'You mustn't think like that. Miss Hodge won't, I'm sure of it. People will recognise this for what it is – a wanton abuse of power.'

Rose had stared at her, her eyes swimming. 'I know you mean well, Miss Hart, but saying anything will only make it worse. That is how it is.'

For two days, Audrey had thought it over. Should she go to the board of guardians, even to the police? But she could imagine the response. Accusing a man of Samuel's status and wealth was pointless. Men like him were never prosecuted, she knew that. Certainly not for the abuse of orphans, unwanted children over the age of consent. No, she would go to Miss Hodge. The woman would have to find a way of dealing with Samuel, of stopping him once and for all.

She dreaded having to speak of it. She knew that the conversation would be excruciating. She steeled herself for the meeting, envisaging the other woman's disbelief and distress. What she had not prepared herself for was the hatred – for Miss Hodge's face, ashen with anger, and for the words she vomited out.

'Virulent minxes, all of them. I should have known what they were about.'

'This is not their fault, Miss Hodge,' Audrey protested. 'This is not something they brought upon themselves; they were not willing participants.'

The matron had laughed. 'Women like you, Miss Hart, coming here with your worthy intentions and your ignorance. A girl of thirteen years is perfectly competent to judge of her own fitness in these matters. This lot have made their beds, and they will lie in them. You want me to speak against Mr Kingsmere? Do you think me a fool? I would be finished here.'

'But he will continue to interfere with them.'

'And so he might, but what evidence have you got? The word of three damaged and corrupted girls – girls this society has tried to help.'

Audrey had been stunned, unable to find the right words with which to fight. Thinking back to that meeting now, she burnt at the injustice of it, at the hypocrisy and cruelty of this woman who, faced with evidence that girls in her care had been abused, had rushed not to protect them, but to punish them.

'Dirty little wretches. We will not keep them here, or the whole barrel will rot.'

Rose and Susan had been sent to a home for fallen girls, Cora to a reformatory school. They were deemed to be a polluting presence, a curse. No industrial school would take them.

What could Audrey do then? Perhaps she should have steeled herself and gone to the board of guardians, but after Miss Hodge's reaction, she had lost all faith in human kindness, and in herself.

She had reached her room now. The window was open and she could smell the sea. She lay on her bed and watched the lace curtains drift in and out like ghosts.

Audrey and Mairi left for Trotternish early in the morning when the land was still shrouded in dark mists. The grass was pearly with night-frost and everything was silent, even the birds, as though for a moment the world had stopped spinning.

Audrey part-opened the window of the wagonette so that she might breathe in the briny morning air. They travelled northwards, theirs the only coach on the road, up and down hills, over little stone bridges and bronzed moorland, past black peat bogs and lonely lochans glinting like sheets of silver. Every now and again they saw crofter hamlets clinging to hillsides or clustered in valleys, the familiar stripes of the lazy beds before them, the whirls of blue smoke above. Occasionally they passed women who spun wool on their distaffs as they walked, bending beneath the weight of a creel of goods or a sleeping child strapped to their back.

Audrey, already uncomfortable, looked at Mairi, who sat with her knees folded under her. 'I've been thinking, Mairi, about the silver bird. About who might have given it to Isbeil.'

The girl cocked her head to one side. 'It was them, Miss Hart.'

Them. 'But Mairi, how can a spirit leave a silver charm?'

'They can leave whatever they like. Mrs Campbell says that one time they left an egg, a tiny blue egg. This time they chose a silver bird.'

'What about the other things? How do you explain the money that Isbeil had? The bonnet, the gloves? Did the spirits give her those too?'

Mairi shook her head. 'I don't know. I don't know that. I only know that she didn't lie, not the whole time I was knowing her. That wasn't her way. If she did so at the end, it was because she had a great fear on her.'

Audrey sank back into the seat. Fear, yes. But fear of what? 'Miss Buchanan said that they prey on those who are carrying babies, or those with newborns.'

'Aye, I heard that too. They want the bairns for theirselves. That's why I'm thinking that maybe Isbeil and the baby are not dead at all. Maybe they still have them, beneath the earth.'

'Mairi, I saw her body. You did too.' The fish-white flesh, the hollow sockets.

'We saw something,' Mairi said. 'Sometimes they're after leaving a stock, a trick, to stop people trying to get the real person back.'

Audrey pressed her lips together. That was not a stock. 'When my mother died, I believed something similar. That she must have been taken for some purpose, that she was not really dead.'

Mairi stared at her. 'When was she taken?'

'Oh, many years ago, when I was ten years old. It happened here, on Skye. In Trotternish.'

Mairi sat up straight, attentive. 'What happened?'

'She fell. From a ridge.'

'I'm sorry, miss.'

Audrey smiled weakly. 'I lost my mother. You lost your entire family.'

'Aye. But they're never truly gone. They're still with me, all of them. I carry them with me.'

'Yes, I understand.' For Audrey's mother was still there, still near her, just beyond her reach. She was there in the hours before dawn and in the ruby ring. She was there in the stories, every time she read them. But she was not alive in the way that Audrey had imagined as a child, nor in the way that Mairi thought of Isbeil. Isbeil and her baby were cold and dead and they had taken the answers with them.

They stopped only once on their journey, to stretch their cramped limbs, rest the horses and take some food at an inn. By late afternoon, they were progressing up the drive to Elishader, John Shawfield's home.

'You must have a hunger on you,' he said as soon as they had been admitted. He was a broad man with large meaty hands and a florid face partly covered in grey beard. 'Come through to the parlour and let me get you a good tea. I'll have your cases taken up to your room.'

Mairi and Audrey warmed themselves before a bright fire in the drawing room while Shawfield went to the kitchen. The room was smaller than the parlours at Lanerly and more cheerful, crammed with rosewood furniture, paintings of flowers, pottery ornaments, and a large mounted fish above the mantelpiece.

He returned within a few minutes with two glasses of

milk, the cream thick upon the top, a pot of tea, and a pile of bannocks silky with butter and heather honey. 'It's glad I am to be seeing some fellow story-collectors in my domain. I've been writing to your Miss Buchanan for a year or so, but of course she couldn't visit herself. It must be a trial to her not being able to meet the people, nor to receive visitors.'

Audrey smiled, and took a cup of tea from him. Surely Miss Buchanan could have visitors, but chose not to. She could have taken a gig into Broadford or further if she wanted, but she never did. She had made a decision to seal herself off, though whether because of her injury or for another reason, Audrey still could not decide. 'She told me you'd done much to collect the stories from this area.'

'Oh, I've a passion for the old ways and old tales, and the folk seem willing to talk to me. But these are bad times on Skye. So many are leaving, and so many are being told their stories and their language are worth but a straw.' He smiled. 'Now, what have you young people discovered? Tell me this story of the Sluagh that Miss Buchanan was writing to me about.'

Audrey felt travel-worn and weary and had no desire to talk now of it all, but she could hardly refuse. The very purpose of their visit was to exchange stories and ideas. 'It's a strange affair, Mr Shawfield. One girl disappeared some weeks ago. Another has died. Local people attribute it to the Host.' She spoke quietly, but John Shawfield did not seem to notice her reticence.

'Ah yes. The Sluagh Sidhe. A vengeful, angry lot, forever rolling and dragging folk off, trouncing them in mud and mire and pools. It wasn't that long since that a local woman was telling me the boils on her skin were burns from the Sluagh.' He smiled, exposing crooked front teeth.

'Are there stories here of them taking people?'

'Oh yes. Children, mothers, old men heavy with the drink – all taken off into their own fairy world.' He put down his cup. 'Aye, I've heard plenty of tales of folk vanishing, but I've not heard of many deaths blamed on them – not around here. What is it that they're saying then about this lass?'

Audrey saw again Isbeil's white face, the wet hair twisted about it. She thought of the birds hanging from the tree like rotten fruit. For a moment she could not speak, and it was Mairi who told him of Eliza and Isbeil and the black birds in the sky; of Mrs Campbell's premonition that they would take another girl.

'Well,' Shawfield said when she had finished, 'that is indeed a terrible and strange thing.' He tugged at his beard. 'I've never before heard any tale of a lass drowned by the Sluagh.'

'On Skye, you mean,' Audrey said.

'Not Skye, not anywhere. And I've heard a deal of stories of them in my time. Returned exhausted, yes. Replaced with a doll or a log, aye. But drowned? No, no, I was never hearing of that.' He drummed his fingers on the table. 'Well now, it'll be something to ask the crofting folk tomorrow. They will know stories I don't. They always do.'

★

Breakfast at Elishader was not for the faint-hearted: great bowls of porridge with fresh cream, newly baked girdle scones with butter, eggs and bacon, strong tea with sugar. 'You need feeding up, the pair o' you,' Shawfield told Mairi and Audrey, pouring more tea. 'And you'll be needing your strength for today.'

'Mr Shawfield, I wanted to ask you. Is there another folklorist in this area?'

'Sadly not, no. It is just myself.'

'And elsewhere on Skye?'

'Well, there are those that tinker, but it's only myself and your Miss Buchanan who are well known for it, I'd say.' He sipped his tea. 'Why? Are we not enough for you, Miss Hart?'

Audrey smiled. 'My mother collected folklore here many years ago. I still have her journal. Where she records stories from Skye, she refers here and there to information given to her by an "L". It could be that she was quoting from a book, but I get the impression it was someone she knew, who helped her.' She shrugged. 'I suppose it could be anyone.'

'I wonder that I never met your mother myself. What was her name?'

'Matilda Hart. Her maiden name was McColl.'

'Matilda Hart. Where was it that she stayed?'

'We usually stayed at a guest house in Valtos. I wondered if we might go there. To see if there's anyone who remembers her.'

'Oh, indeed we must. It's not so far, we can pass by there later. See if anyone knows your mysterious L.'

They spent the morning amongst the crofters in the Staffin district, John Shawfield taking them from house to house to meet his most trusted storytellers: a bent old man with eyes narrowed from a life squinting against the sun and rain; a woman with flax-white hair who offered them cups of buttermilk and asked Shawfield to read her letters she had received from children and grandchildren left for Glasgow, Canada and America. They liked him, these people; they accepted him, and Audrey could not help but feel a small twist of envy.

The crofters here were different, she decided. They were poor, yes, but perhaps not quite as deprived as the people of Strath, and those she spoke to seemed less cowed and more openly inquisitive. They asked questions of Audrey: where were her family from? How had she come here? What was it like in England, in London? Groups of barefoot children followed them as they went between the smoke-choked houses, watching Mairi and Audrey with eyes as round as pennies, listening to the fireside tales of witches and water horses, curses and blessings.

At a river, they came upon a group of women, their skirts hitched up above their knees, their white forearms covered in soap suds, washing their laundry in the icy water, pounding the clothing against the rocks. John Shawfield approached them, and within a few minutes they were laughing, teasing him, and agreeing to tell Audrey and Mairi their stories. He had a way of dealing with these people – joking with them, sharing his tobacco, drinking their tea – that put them at their ease. Watching him, Audrey felt herself more awkward than ever. If only she could emulate his warmth, his bumbling confidence. It was how her mother had been: at home in her own skin.

As they travelled between townships, Audrey gazed at the solemn mountains and the still, dark lochs and tried to remember if they had come this way before, when she was with her parents. Perhaps her mother had travelled this same road; seen these same villages. But there was only one story from Trotternish in her journal – 'The Little Bird', from Staffin – and that now seemed curious to Audrey, for they had come here many times. Could there have been another journal? She might have spoken to Mairi about it, but the girl seemed distracted and distant. Audrey had given Mairi a notebook of her own in which to record stories, but today she seemed only to draw little pictures in the margins.

'What is it?' Audrey asked eventually. 'You've been quiet all day.'

Mairi shrugged. 'Nothing. Only it's odd, isn't it, that Miss Buchanan wanted us to come here now?'

Audrey stared at the girl, at her sullen sharp face in profile. 'It was important to her that we met Mr Shawfield. She's been corresponding with him for some months.'

'Aye, maybe, but why was she not asking you right at the beginning, then? When you first came to Skye?'

Perhaps Mairi had a point. Miss Buchanan had not

mentioned Trotternish or Shawfield until a few days ago, but that did not necessarily mean anything significant. The woman was not exactly forthcoming on most subjects.

'You think she wanted us out of the way?'

Mairi's face was still petulant, like a child. 'Och, I don't know, but I want to be back.' She shook her head. 'I've a bad feeling on me is all.'

As the dusk came in and the sky grew pink, John Shawfield directed the gig towards Valtos. It was easy enough to find the guest house, for it was the only one in the village – a whitewashed building with a slate roof and neat front lawn. Audrey had not thought she would remember the place, but as soon as she saw it, she knew it. She approached the house alone, a strange feeling of excitement and nervousness uncoiling in her chest. She recalled the black front door now, the iron knocker in the shape of a hand. But she had little memory of the woman who opened it, a fierce-looking character with raven-dark hair.

'Oh, fine I remember her,' the woman said to her questions. 'She was a pretty one, wasn't she? Big grey eyes like yourself. Aye. Very gracious. Not like many that come here from the mainland, with their airs and fancies, not slow at complaining. No, she was a decent type. Insisted on helping me with the breakfast. I remember you too. A wee thing you were.' She did not smile.

'You were here when she died?'

'I was, aye. A bad business.'

'What were you told of what happened?'

The woman regarded her suspiciously. 'Not much. Your father said that it was an accident. I was here looking after you that day. You were sick. You don't remember, maybe.'

'I remember, but not clearly.' Audrey hesitated, thinking the woman might invite her inside for a *strupach* – tea and scones – as was traditional. Perhaps there was something she was supposed to do or say, some social convention she had missed.

'I wondered: did my mother have a friend here that you know of? Another folklorist, perhaps?'

The woman's black eyes darted towards hers. 'A friend?'

'I think someone may have helped her with her story-collecting, but I don't know their name. Only that it began with the letter L.'

The woman stared, shaking her head slowly. 'I can't help you, I'm afraid.'

'Was there anyone else here? Anyone else who might remember?'

'I can't say there was.'

'That's a shame. I very much wanted to find out about my mother's last days here, about anyone she may have known.'

'Your father was here through all of it, wasn't he? If anyone can tell you, it'll be him, like as not.'

Audrey's throat tightened. She had of course asked him about L many years before and had received the same dismissive, annoyed response she always had. *I've no idea, Audrey. What your mother wrote in that book was her affair. And*

I do not wish to speak of it, as you well know.

Audrey hesitated, trying to find the courage to ask for more information, for a proper account of the day her mother died.

The woman, however, already had her hand on the door. 'I'd best be getting in, I'm afraid. I've guests arriving soon.'

'Yes, of course. I'm sorry to have troubled you.'

'No bother,' the woman said. 'Good evening to you.'

Audrey turned and walked back down the gravel path, feeling dark eyes burning into her back.

They continued their work the following morning, gathering tales of fairies who wove tweed or cut corn overnight, of a little boy stolen away by an old woman dressed in red, of a man turned mad by witches. Audrey thought again of the landlady, her grudging words, her doubtful eyes. *If anyone can tell you, it'll be him.* She was implying her father had lied.

At midday, when Shawfield helped her into the gig that would take them back to Elishader, Audrey said, 'I wondered, Mr Shawfield, if we might look at the Quiraing.'

'Indeed. You must see it. It's not far from here.'

'Well, I don't want to inconvenience you. Only it's our last day in Trotternish.'

'Then we must go,' Shawfield said firmly. 'We can take dinner at the Staffin Inn.' He helped Mairi into the gig and took the seat next to the driver.

They continued along a rugged road, the countryside

around growing stranger, rising into rocky ridges and sinking into dark hollows, until they came to the inn at Loch Staffin, where they took a brief luncheon of bread and cold mutton. The road beyond the inn ascended for two miles, bringing them to the brow of the hill, and there Audrey saw the Quiraing: a great dark mass studded with rocky spires and needles.

Shawfield ordered the driver to stop on a path where several other vehicles waited. 'Quite something, isn't it?' he said, smiling. 'You have to do the walk to get the full effect, of course.'

Mairi was watching Audrey closely. She knew, then. Of course she did.

'You've heard the story about it, I suppose?' Shawfield said.

'The story?'

'I was thinking you wanted to come here because one of the crofters had been talking to you.'

'No. No, the reason I've asked you to bring me here is rather personal. This is where my mother died.'

The smile fell from Shawfield's face. 'My dear, I am very sorry.'

'It was a long time ago. She fell from a ridge, when I was a girl. I thought I should visit the place, see it for myself.'

'Well. I can take you further up, if you'd like to see some of the rock formations.'

They climbed a steep grassy slope until they reached a path that led through a gate and then to the edge of the cliffs. They stopped, out of breath, to look down upon a flat table of grass surrounded by dark, jagged rocks. Beyond that they could see the curve of Staffin Bay and the sea glinting silver. Others might have thought it beautiful, but for Audrey there was a malignity about the place – the warped black rocks veined with white, the thin mist atop the hills – that chilled her to the bone.

'We can go back now if you like.' Shawfield looked at her with concern. 'We don't have to be doing the entire walk.'

'We've come this far. We might as well continue.'

They walked on in silence, close to the edge of the cliffs and around several steep gullies. Perhaps it was here, Audrey thought. It was steep enough to kill.

Similar thoughts must have occurred to Mairi. 'Do you know where it was that she went over?'

Audrey shook her head. 'No, my father never told me.'

He had explained her mother's death only once. It had taken Audrey a long time to summon the courage to ask him what had happened. She had seen him only at mealtimes, a distant and oddly formal figure at the other end of the long dining table.

'Please can you tell me what happened to Mother? I still don't understand.' She remembered the words she had overheard that day. 'Did she fall?'

When her father replied his voice was flat, like a dead thing. 'Yes. We had gone out walking. You were too ill to join us. It was a mistake. We should never have gone. There'd been a rockfall only a few days before. I should have put my foot down, but your mother wanted to go.

She wandered apart from me a little, too close to the edge, which was very like her. Part of the cliff collapsed, and then she was gone.' A pause. 'It was only later that we found her, and then we brought her home. Please let us not speak of it again, Audrey. It pains me, and it does not help you. It does not help her.' He had returned to his dinner, and that was the last time they had discussed it. Only much later did it occur to her how unfair that was. And how strange.

Now she looked out across the wind-blown landscape, the sharp ridges and peaks like the skeleton of some huge animal. They took a steep path that twisted down into the dark heart of the Quiraing. Audrey tried to pay attention as Shawfield pointed to the triple summit of the rock formation known as the Prison, to the sharp stone Needle, but she wanted now to be away from the place. She wished, just as her father had, that they had never come. She did not want to think of her mother dying here. There was a sense of evil about it, of cruelty.

'You mentioned there was a story about the Quiraing?' she said as they made their way back.

'Ach, well. There's a story to every place, isn't there? But yes, it's said that a woman disappeared from here some years ago.'

Audrey felt a sliver of ice enter her stomach. Maybe this was what the landlady had been keeping from her; the piece of information her father had held back. 'I see. When was this? What happened?'

'I only know the bare bones of the story, which is that a

woman came up here and was never seen again. I suppose she must have fallen down a crevasse, or been hidden by a fall of rocks. She may have simply run away, but you know how the folk here turn things. It's their way of making sense of the world.'

It was nothing, Audrey told herself. It was mere superstition.

The sky was darkening and they walked the last mile or so quickly, their heads down against the rising wind. Despite the exertion of the walk, Audrey felt very cold.

'You're shaking, miss,' Mairi said softly when they reached the gig.

'Yes, I'm frozen through. I should have brought my gloves.'

Mairi took Audrey's marble-cold hands in her own, and for a moment she held them there tight. Then she released them, turned and climbed into the open carriage.

Throughout the journey back to Lanerly the following day, the vision of the Quiraing was there before her, dark and hostile. Audrey had thought that visiting the place where her mother died would make her feel closer to her, but what she was left with was confusion and doubt.

It began to rain – a light grey mizzle turning quickly to a lashing, pitiless downpour that pummelled at the wagonette windows and seeped through a crack in the roof. Audrey was watching the raindrops on the glass when Mairi leant forward and said: 'If they did take her, then maybe she's still out there somewhere. Maybe she's not dead at all.'

Audrey stared at her for a moment. 'I can't think like that, Mairi. It will drive me mad. I saw her coffin. She is dead.'

Mairi held her gaze. 'My mother came back. Only for a short time, but she came.'

'When?'

'Years ago, when I was after sleeping out by myself by the shore. I thought it was over for me, for I had no food save for the whelks and limpets that I was scraping from the rocks, and I was bitter cold, cold in my bones. She came to me then. I felt her hand here, on my shoulder. I couldn't see her, but I heard her voice, soft in my ear. And you know what she said? She said that she'd seen that one day I'd have bairns of my own. She'd seen the little faces of her grandchildren, a boy and a lass. She said I'd be loved. That's what she said. And I still believe it.'

Audrey stared at Mairi's solemn elfin face. A little girl, starving, grief-broken and afraid, had wished her mother back into existence. That was all, wasn't it? Mairi had seen what she had to in order to keep going. And yet a strange feeling was creeping over Audrey's skin: part fear, part hope.

The weather slowed their journey and it was almost dark by the time they approached Broadford. The rain had abated, but gusts of wind still shook the wagonette on its high wheels as they passed over the exposed earth, the horses driven forward by the driver's whip. The coach-lamp shone out over the road, throwing strange shadows before them. Audrey was still awake, but exhausted, and in that limbo when dreams begin to intrude on consciousness. It seemed to her she could see the saw-edged rocks of the Quiraing rising before her in the pale morning light, feel the wind on her face and the ground hard beneath her boots as she walked away from the other people, towards the cliff edge.

All at once she saw a white shape ahead of them. When she wiped the condensation from the glass and strained her eyes into the gloom, she saw a ghostly figure moving through the darkness. Surely she was seeing things. She was tired and overwrought. Imagining her mother's last day had confused her. As the wagonette drew closer to the figure, the lamplight catching her white form, Audrey saw that it was a girl.

They slowed and stopped. The girl turned her emaciated face towards the light, her eyes sunken within it. Her long hair was dark and wet, dripping from her shoulders like molasses.

Mairi was awake now and gripped at Audrey's arm. 'She's sick. Look at her. Sick. Don't get out. Don't touch her.'

Audrey shook Mairi off, opened the wagonette door and stepped down. The girl stared at her dully. She was shaking. Her white dress was soaked through, filthy and torn. Her feet were bare.

'Where are you going?' Audrey asked. 'Can we help you?'

The girl merely stared.

Audrey moved closer. She put her hand on the girl's

wrist, finding it icy cold. 'Can we get you to a doctor? Or to your home?'

No answer.

'What is your name?'

Silence, and then the girl said, 'Eliza. My name is Eliza.'

Chapter 7

❦

Bainne stayed with the fairies in their home beneath the earth, playing with them, feasting with them, singing their songs. Sometimes, on moonlit evenings, they would run out into the forest and gather berries and nuts. On one such evening, a crow alighted on a branch above Bainne, its feathers the glossy black of wet ink.

'Come home,' the bird cawed softly. 'Your parents miss you. Your little sister awaits you.'

'That cannot be,' Bainne said. 'For my parents do not love me, and I have no sister.'

'You are wrong,' cawed the crow. 'Seven years have passed since you last saw home, and your mother and father have a new child, three years old. Every day they weep at the loss of their firstborn and every day they wish that you would return.'

'I cannot believe you. I have been here only days. Bring me some sign that what you say is true.'

'Very well,' said the crow. 'I will do as you ask.' And he lifted from the branch and flew into the night.

Bainne watched him go and she thought of his words. What if she did have a sister, three years old? What if her parents had changed, as the crow had said? But her fairy friends begged her to come back beneath the earth.

'Mortals never change,
That much is true.
No matter what they say,
They don't love you.'

All the same, Bainne wondered at what the crow had cawed. For if her parents were still as cruel as ever, would they not mistreat another child, as they had done her? Would they not lock her too below the stairs, leaving her afraid and alone in the dark?

The driver cracked the whip above the horses' heads to urge the exhausted beasts onwards, and they raced the remainder of the way to Broadford and to Dr McGilvray. Eliza had collapsed insensible. She was as cold as death, her hair and clothing drenched, and the smell that rose from her was strange and sour, but Audrey clutched the girl to her to stop her from falling as the coach jerked and jolted over the darkened road.

When they arrived at the doctor's house, the footman and the driver lifted Eliza up the steps, her thin body seeming little more than a rag.

'What's wrong with her?' Audrey asked the doctor as

she passed him the money she had in her purse. 'Will you be able to save her?'

Dr McGilvray looked at the clutch of coins. 'I won't know until I've examined her. You were right to bring her to me at once.'

'And the police? A constable must be called.'

'We don't yet know where she's been. No doubt she'll tell us once she recovers a wee bit. Come back tomorrow afternoon, Miss Hart. I'll do what I can.'

As the horse and coach reached the front of Lanerly, Alec descended the steps to meet them, a dark figure silhouetted against the porch light. He ran his eyes over Audrey's face, seeing at once the strain and distress. 'Something has happened. Come, tell me.'

They sat together in the parlour, and as Alec built up the fire, she told him of finding Eliza on the road, of visiting the place where her mother had apparently fallen, of the story of the woman who had vanished from the Quiraing. Alec filled a tumbler with Talisker and put it into her hand. 'You've had a shock.'

The smell of the whisky rose up to her, smoky and sharp. 'Yes, but it's not just the fact of finding the girl. I'm convinced now that the two are linked – Isbeil and Eliza.'

Alec sat quietly sipping his own drink, his eyes fixed on the flames. 'We can't be sure of that.'

'No. But Eliza will be able to tell us soon.'

'You didn't get anything out of her this evening?'

She shook her head. 'She was barely conscious when I left her. She will talk in time, though. I'll go back to her tomorrow.'

'I will come with you, I think. You have been through enough alone.'

Audrey met his eyes. 'Where is Miss Buchanan?'

'Asleep. We were instructed not to disturb her.'

Audrey nodded, remembering the little glass vials she had once drunk from herself, the warm oblivion that followed. 'Tell me, why does she never leave here? I know she's in pain and walks with her silver stick, but that isn't the reason she never leaves Lanerly, or why she never has visitors.'

'No, it is not the reason. Or at least it is not the only reason.' Alec smiled. 'We all find it hard to fit into this world sometimes, do we not? You, me. Everyone, perhaps. But we force ourselves to go out there. We make fools of ourselves every day, we risk rejection and humiliation, because we haven't accepted that we must shut ourselves off entirely. We still want to be part of human society.' He put down his glass. 'My aunt has gone beyond that stage. Because of her accident, of what it turned her into, because of what others said of her, and what they did. She no longer wishes to face the prejudices and prying eyes of others. And she doesn't have to. She can stay here. At least she can until my father disposes of Lanerly.'

'Will he do that?'

'Oh yes, I believe so. It's only a matter of time. He's running out of money. Aunt Buchanan knows that. That's why she must work fast – why she must collect her stories and get them published – before he attempts to cart her off to the mainland, to Glasgow or Inverness or wherever he deems she should live. If by then she's a published folklorist, she would have money of her own, and status, too. A reason to stay on Skye.'

Audrey considered this, thinking of Miss Buchanan's waxen face, the moments when her mask had slipped. 'Why do we keep on doing it? Why do we keep on going out there, hoping for acceptance? Shouldn't we be content within ourselves? Shouldn't that be enough?'

'Well, we want to be loved, don't we? We want to find people who understand us, who make us feel that we are not entirely alone. Of course, some people are content by themselves. Some have that gift. But my aunt is not one of those people. Neither, in fact, am I.'

Audrey swallowed another gulp of whisky. Alec's eyes, she noticed, were flecked orange in the centre. The colour of the flames that burnt in the grate.

As had been the case after Isbeil's death, Dr McGilvray addressed Alec rather than Audrey when they visited. 'She has typhus. I believe she's developed internal bleeding.'

'Then she's been left untreated for some time?' Audrey said.

The doctor frowned at her. 'Aye, I would say so.'

'Will she recover?' Alec asked. 'Can she speak?'

'She will probably improve in time, but she's in a poor way. And aye, she can speak, but not one word of sense.

Has some idea that she's only been away for a few days, but of course it's weeks, isn't it?'

Audrey and Alec exchanged a look.

'And it *is* Eliza Fraser?'

The doctor turned to Audrey. 'That's what she says.'

'May we see her?'

'Briefly, if you must, but as I say, she's in a poor state. There's a nurse looking after her as best she can.'

Audrey looked at Alec. 'Perhaps I should go in alone. She has at least seen me before.'

He nodded. 'Of course.'

Audrey climbed the narrow staircase to the room and knocked. After a moment the door was opened a crack and a woman's face appeared: small button eyes and a flattened nose.

'I wanted to see how Eliza was. We came upon her on the road last night.'

Unsmiling, the woman opened the door a little further and stood back.

Inside, the light was dim and the air rank with the smell of sickness. Only a feeble glow from the fire enabled Audrey to distinguish the shape of the furniture, of the narrow bed on which Eliza lay, so still and grey that she could barely believe for a moment that she was alive.

'Eliza,' she said gently.

The girl's eyes flickered, then closed. Her breath came suddenly, quick and feverish. Audrey took a chair next to the bed and watched for a time as her chest rose and fell. Eliza's hands rested on the cover, clenched below her ragged sleeves. With a jolt, Audrey realised that the girl had opened her eyes and was staring at her directly.

'Eliza, my name is Audrey. It was I who helped you last night on the road. Do you remember?'

No answer.

'I work for Miss Buchanan. I came to see how you were.'

The girl's eyes opened wider. She began to mumble something in Gaelic.

'Eliza, you don't need to be frightened. I just wanted to find out how you were faring.'

The girl was trying to sit up in bed now. She was pointing at something beyond Audrey, but when Audrey turned, there was nothing, save for the nurse, who stood with her arms folded, watching.

'Please, don't try to get up. You are very unwell. Where have you been, Eliza? Were you hurt?'

The girl began to cry, her breath coming in gasps. 'I don't know,' she sobbed. 'I don't know where I've been. I thought I'd only been gone a short while. I don't know.'

Audrey touched her arm to try to calm her, but she shrank away.

'*Chan eil fhios agam*,' Eliza kept saying. I don't know.

The nurse moved forward to the bed and spoke to Audrey sharply. 'There's no point you asking her. She doesn't remember anything. You're only upsetting her.' She bent close to Eliza and whispered to her. When she spoke again to Audrey, her voice was hard and cold. 'You need to go now, miss. The girl needs her peace.'

Audrey stood up. 'Of course. I'm so sorry. I didn't mean to distress her. I only wanted to find out what had happened to her.'

The nurse turned back, her small eyes on Audrey. 'Please tell Dr McGilvray no more visitors today.'

Audrey found Alec in the hall below. 'Bad?' he asked, seeing her expression.

'Yes. Very bad.'

They walked back to Lanerly side by side.

'What happened to her?' Alec said.

'I don't know. I hardly know what to think.'

'You asked her where she'd been?'

'Of course, but she simply kept saying that she didn't know. She was terrified, though whether of me or something she thought she'd seen, it was difficult to tell. Perhaps, in her feverish state, she truly believes she was abducted.'

'Well, it wouldn't be the first time that someone had been abducted from this island.'

'What do you mean?'

'Oh, it was a long time ago, in the last century. People don't talk about it now, but it happened.'

She walked quickly to keep pace with him, to see his face. 'What happened?'

'People were taken. Poor people, people nobody much noticed, so no one understood what was happening.'

'And what *was* happening?'

He turned to her. 'They were sold. A ship was wrecked

off the coast of Antrim. The survivors who reached the shore said they'd been kidnapped. It turned out Norman Macleod of Unish was carrying people off to America and selling them there as slaves.'

'When was this?'

'Over a hundred years ago. Unfortunately, there is a long history on this island of the rich mistreating the poor. A long line of guilt.'

That was why Alec assisted the minister with his work, Audrey thought. It was nothing to do with God; it was about finding a way to help those whom his own family had helped to render landless.

'Do you ever think, Alec, about doing something more than you already do? You could go into Parliament, couldn't you?'

He laughed. 'I'm flattered that you think me capable of a career in politics, but I don't think they would have me. No, there are other things I can do here, though. Other things I should and must do.'

You could stand up to your father, Audrey thought. Your aunt does. But then what had defying her own father achieved other than driving him further away? Certainly it had not changed his views.

'I have plans, Audrey. If I can make enough to support myself, things will change. At the moment I can't risk being disinherited, and I have little doubt that my father would cut me off in an instant. I don't want to leave Lanerly or Skye, not yet. It's all I have left of her now, you see – my sister. So I play along, and I do what I can.'

Audrey nodded, thinking of the girl in white, captured in a frame. She wanted to ask Alec about the estate, about how much money was actually left, about how much would go to him, how much to his brothers. For was it worth staying silent for a mound of debts? But it was too impertinent, too crass a question.

'And what of Murdo? How much of what is done to the tenants is his doing? He is much hated by the crofters.'

'Oh yes, they detest him. Did you know that even his own daughter abandoned him?'

'I had heard that. But he told me, when I first asked him, that he had no children.'

'Evidently that is how he sees it. All contact is broken off, I believe. There was a letter – she told him she couldn't remain on the island any longer, not to stand by and watch what he did to the people she loved. Some thought it might soften him, but I think it's only made him harsher against the crofters, for he blames them for her leaving. And his wife blames him.'

Audrey thought of Murdo's hard, unsmiling face. 'His life must be a torment,' she said quietly.

Alec shrugged. 'Quite possibly, but he brought it upon himself.' He looked at her. 'You think me cruel, but even before that I never much liked the man. I don't trust him. My father sees him as a convenient underling, but I think Murdo resents my father as much as I do – more – for what he's asked to do, for what happened to his daughter. I think he hates my father, all of us Buchanans, and given the opportunity, he'll do us all down.' Alec smiled. 'But this is morbid talk. Let's go and look at the seals – they're pupping now on the rocks. Come on, I'll show you.'

They walked together back towards Lanerly. This time he took Audrey's arm.

When Audrey returned to her room later that afternoon, the letter was resting against the looking-glass – the blood-red seal, the handwriting that she knew – and dread washed icily over her.

> London, 14th October, 1857
>
> Dear Miss Hart,
>
> I am surprised not to have received any response from you to my last letter. I thought I had made myself sufficiently clear. Increasingly I believe that you have made fraudulent claims about me, at least to one person, possibly more, and it is vital that you stop.
>
> If you wish to avoid my explaining the true circumstances – the real reason why you may have made false allegations – please send an immediate reply confirming that you will keep silent, and if you have made any mistaken comment, retract it. I do not wish to damage your name, nor your father's, but you leave me with little choice.
>
> I await your response.
>
> Yours very truly,
>
> Samuel Kingsmere

So there in was, in black on white. Withdraw your claims or I will ruin you, your father too. Audrey's hands were shaking with fear and rage. *The true circumstances.* What would he say those circumstances were? Perhaps he would claim she was not merely peculiar, but delusional, a danger to men; creating depraved fantasies out of thin air. No one would believe an account of assault coming from a woman judged mad. Perhaps he would say they had had an illicit encounter, or that she had thrown herself at him like a lovelorn character in a book, then resorted to slander when her advances were rebuffed. A woman was her reputation – Audrey had been told that enough times to know how easy it would be for him to destroy her. And yet he had never even kissed her, no matter how much she had wished he would. Because of course it had not been her he wanted.

She folded the letter in half, then into quarters, feeling the bile rise from her stomach. She had underestimated the lengths to which Samuel would go to protect himself, the extent to which, beyond the gloss, the interior was entirely rotten.

She could not retract her comments. To do so would be to fail the girls more than she already had. For Samuel to write again he must himself be afraid that she had reported him further, to the board of guardians, or to the police. If only she had had the nerve.

She took the letter over to her bureau and placed it between two notebooks at the back of the shelf. She felt off-balance, physically sick, her heart beating faster than it should.

She pulled open the casement, then the window itself, to admit the air: cold, damp and carrying the smell of rotting seaweed and leaf-mould. The sound of the waves seemed hollow and baleful. She leant out, trying to breathe in slowly to stop the rapid beating of her heart. She heard a noise then, quiet at first but growing louder, a terrible rushing sound like the thrashing of a thousand wings or the rustling of a million insects. There were voices within it, human voices, whispering and rasping. It seemed so close that she could almost feel the feathers brushing at her ear, the wings beating, breathing, becoming things with mouths and pincers. She put up her hands to cover her ears and looked up into the sky, but could see nothing: only the darkness of the night shot through with stars.

All at once the rushing was gone and the silence echoed around her, empty.

Five days passed and the weather grew colder, shrivelling the berries on the brambles and sprinkling a hard glitter upon the dying docken and foxgloves. Most of the birds had flown and the sky was strangely empty, save for the occasional chevron of pale-bellied geese moving ghostlike over the isle. Audrey, too, felt colder and weaker, as though something had lodged inside her, poisoning her. It was as if the stories – of travellers pricked with pins by witches, of witches left to bleed to death – had seeped into her soul.

Though they continued with their story-collecting, Audrey and Mairi travelled only to places where they might learn more about the girls: to Sligachan, where Isbeil had once worked; to Heaste, where Eliza had lived before. They learnt little of use, however, only that the girls had lived quietly, working hard and attending kirk.

The doctor had sent Eliza back to her croft house, claiming she had recovered sufficiently to be treated at home. But the reports they received were troubling: that she still did not speak, that she was vacant, changed. 'Some are saying she is not the same girl,' Mrs Campbell told them darkly. 'And some are saying that she is not a girl at all.'

That was why they walked now towards Strollamus, the wind ice-cold against their faces, the frost-bound earth hard beneath their boots, and as she walked, Audrey's thoughts flitted from Eliza to the story John Shawfield had told them of the woman who had disappeared from the Quiraing.

'I'm going to return to Trotternish,' she said to Mairi as they rested by a low stone wall, 'as soon as I can get away. Someone there must know more about the tale of the stolen woman. And someone else must have seen my mother before she died. My parents can't have gone up there alone.'

Mairi did not look at her directly. 'Could you write to your father maybe? Ask him what he says of it?'

'No. No, I can't do that.' She paused. 'In fact, Mairi, he doesn't know where I am.'

Mairi stared at her then. 'Will he not be worrying for you?'

'Perhaps. I don't know. He knows that I left to take up employment, only that. He wouldn't approve.'

'Why not?'

'Because he doesn't understand why this is important to me. And because women like me are not supposed to work at all.'

'Will you go back there?'

'I don't think so. I don't think I can.'

Mairi was watching her curiously. 'You had a falling-out.'

'Yes. He didn't support me when he should have. He put his reputation before my happiness, as he always has, and I decided I didn't have to endure it any more. That's all.'

'Was it to do with a fellow?'

'Yes, but not in the way you think. It was a man who abused his position, and who hurt some girls I was trying to help.'

She had not explained the situation to her father until he questioned why she did not visit the orphanage. At first she said only that she no longer wished to go, but that annoyed him. He, after all, had organised the whole endeavour.

'What will Samuel think of you simply not bothering to attend?'

'He can draw his own conclusions.'

'And what conclusions might those be? That my daughter is lazy and unreliable?'

'He will know that it is because of his own actions that I do not go.'

'Meaning what, exactly?'

It was the arrogance with which her father spoke that had driven Audrey to tell him. That his influential friend, this man he so much admired, had been interfering with young girls, girls in his own care.

Her father had looked away from her. 'You did not accuse him of this, I trust.'

'No. I went to Miss Hodge, the matron. I had to tell somebody, to prevent him from continuing. But she refused to do anything about it.'

When he turned towards her, she saw that he had gone quite white with anger. 'You have badly misjudged the situation, Audrey.'

'I know what I saw.'

'You have made a mistake.'

'I did not make a mistake.'

'Oh yes you did. A very serious mistake. You should have come to me first.'

'And what would you have done?'

'I would have dealt with this privately.'

'You would have done nothing.'

His voice when he spoke was quiet and cold. 'You are wrong. You are exactly like your mother. As wilful and selfish and stupid as she was. You will retract whatever you have said to this matron woman. You will do so at once.'

It had been confirmation of what she had suspected for many years: her father avoided her not because he had loved her mother, but because he had hated her.

★

As Audrey and Mairi neared Strollamus farm they heard a scream, shouts, a dog howling. They quickened their pace and when they reached the gate they saw a cluster of people, some with their hands to their faces, others trying to hold back a woman at the centre of the group. Moving closer, Audrey realised that it was Marjory, the milkmaid, but there was no surliness about her now. She was red-faced, crying, trying to wrench free of the hands that held her.

Audrey ran then, over the tufted grass and dead heather, towards the knot of people, for she had a sudden and sickening notion as to what was wrong.

'What is it?' she asked a woman standing on the outskirts of the group. 'What's happened?'

'It's a terrible thing. An awful thing. They had no right, no right to do it.'

'To do what?'

The woman looked at Audrey, shook her head. 'I shouldn't be telling you, it'll be the law on them.'

'On who? Has someone hurt Marjory?'

'No, not her. The other one.'

The other one. 'You mean Eliza.'

The woman did not answer, and Audrey, desperate to know, pushed her way towards Marjory. She saw then what they were all clustered around. It was a pit, a shallow grave. It was empty.

'Marjory? Where's Eliza?' Audrey came right up close to her. 'What's happened here? Can I help?'

The girl seemed dazed. 'I doubt but anyone can help now. They've done for her.'

'Who?'

'Angus Steele and his men.'

Audrey thought back to the Steeles' miserable little house, their tales of punishments for stories told, and her heart went cold. 'What did they do?'

'They burnt her.' Marjory's breathing was ragged. 'They said she wasn't Eliza at all, but a changeling brought back to trick us all. They burnt her to make her admit what she was and where she'd been and then they left her here overnight.'

Something settled in Audrey's stomach like a stone. 'Where is she?'

'They've carried her by horseback to the doctor, just now. But it may well be too late.'

Audrey walked back to Lanerly in a numb silence, Mairi by her side. Though she tried to shut her mind, images pushed their way through to her consciousness – a shackled girl, a fire, a mouth open in a scream. She had heard tales of people using fire to make a changeling speak with its true voice, but for it to be real, for it to have happened here, seemed inconceivable.

Once in the hall, they heard voices from the parlour, the minister's the loudest amongst them. When Audrey entered the room she saw that he stood, his face mottled pink and white, gesturing towards Alec and Miss Buchanan as though preaching at them from the pulpit.

'The whole thing is madness. Pure havers. This is exactly why I've been warning folk against the old beliefs:

they're not just wrong, they're dangerous. They've near killed the poor lass and for what? For their wretched fairies? I hope that you see and hear this and learn from it.' He was pointing at Miss Buchanan now. 'These aren't mere folk stories, for goodness' sake. This is evil. Your collecting of tales is only encouraging these practices and superstitions. They must be stamped out.'

Miss Buchanan's face had set hard. 'It is their super-stitions that drove them to this, is it? And tell me, Reverend, when the English slaughtered the Irish in the name of Christ, was it their God that drove them to it? When American Christians hunted Indians with packs of dogs, did that mean that Christianity should be stamped out? Much worse things have been done in the name of your religion.'

'It is not *my* religion, Miss Buchanan, it is our religion. You may refuse to come to the kirk or take part in our community, but it is religion that is driving this dangerous superstition from our doors.'

'It is religion that is driving the people from this country!'

'Religion?' The minister was angry now, his face flooded with red. 'No, it is the likes of your brother and his henchmen, and you may be prepared to stand idly by while innocent folk are harmed, but I am not.'

'What do you mean by that?'

'You know what was done in your brother's name during the clearances. You know what is done now. I have not heard you speak against it.'

Miss Buchanan banged her stick on the ground. 'What is done in my brother's name is done in his alone. I have no control over his men, as you very well know. Let me remind you that it was my brother who secured your appointment. It is not the first time you appear to have forgotten.'

Alec was sitting forward, his hands to his face. 'Has she said anything? Has the girl admitted to where she's been?'

The minister turned to him. 'You think that matters now?'

'We need to know who took her,' Audrey said, coming into the room. 'It may be that others are in danger.'

The minister shook his head. 'No one "took" her, Miss Hart. Your theories are as deluded as those of the crofters.'

'Then where has she been, Minister?' Miss Buchanan spoke coldly.

'That I do not know. What I do know is that she's an innocent child who's been dreadfully harmed as a result of ignorance and superstition. And I am asking you to cease with your folklore-collecting, lest it provoke more of the same.'

Alec looked up. 'You seem terribly concerned about a mere crofter girl, Alastair.'

'As you know, that is my pastoral duty.'

'Is it?' Alec said.

The minister looked at him and frowned. 'You have been with me to visit these people. You have seen what I do.'

'Yes,' Alec said. 'I have.' His tone was flat. Audrey could not interpret his expression.

'I do my job to the best of my ability,' the minister said, his tone patronising. 'I care for these people. I guide them.'

'As you guided Isbeil,' Audrey said softly.

The minister turned to her. 'What do you mean by that?'

Audrey shook her head. 'I mean nothing.'

Miss Buchanan stood up, leaning on her stick. 'We are all shaken, Reverend Carlisle. You must forgive us. Terrible things have happened and we are all reacting unwisely. What we need is to ensure that the child is safe. Perhaps we should bring her here.'

'Yes,' Alec said. 'Clearly she's at risk among the community.'

'No, no.' The minister shook his head. 'Better that she remains with the doctor and with her friends. She's confused enough as it is. The constable has arrested those responsible; no doubt he'll make an example of them. I will play my part too, and make clear to the folk what this means in terms of their lives beyond this world.' He moved towards the door. 'In fact I will speak to young Mairi and Effy now. They must understand that it is not the spirits and the fairies that they answer to. It is God.'

A light knock came at Audrey's bedroom door. She set her mother's ring in the little silver apple box, put it in the dressing table drawer and turned from the table to see Mairi already standing in the doorway watching her. She looked small and forlorn.

'Mairi. What is it?'

'The minister came to see me.'

'Yes. I'm sorry. He believes we should stop the story-collecting. He thinks it's to blame for what happened.'

She turned back to face the mirror. For an instant she saw not her own face, but Eliza's, burnt and black. She shut her eyes.

'What I keep asking myself,' Mairi said quietly, 'is why Eliza wouldn't say where she'd been. Even then. What was it she was so afeared of?'

'I don't know, Mairi. I don't know.' Audrey could imagine, though: shadowy shapes, the brush of wings, a prison beneath the ground.

She caught Mairi's reflection in the mirror. The girl was looking at the dressing table. After a moment she said, very softly, 'It could be them, of course. The spirits. It could be that she's so afraid of what they might do that she can't be saying a word.'

Audrey watched her, thinking of the baby born with no mouth. She said nothing.

'Miss Hart, do you mind that day at the kirk when I was talking to Isbeil?'

'Yes, I remember.'

'Well, like I told you, she wouldn't say what was worrying her. But I'm wondering now if it wasn't the minister that was upsetting her.'

Audrey turned to her. 'Why do you think that?'

'There was the prayer book, wasn't there, in her things?'

Audrey stared at her. 'That's not unusual, is it, to have a prayer book?'

'No.' Mairi fiddled with a loose strand of hair. 'But I'm thinking now maybe she was afeared of him that day.'

'The minister told us that Isbeil had asked for his guidance. She would have been frightened of what he would think and say.'

'Maybe, aye. Maybe that's it,' Mairi said.

Audrey thought of Alec's words in the dining room, and of the reverend's flushed face, his trembling hands. Why be so concerned about a 'mere crofter girl'?

'It's just that, if you're right, if someone was after giving Isbeil those things – the bonnet, the silver bird – well, then it would have to be someone who could have met with her on her own without anyone thinking bad of it. Someone, you know, respectable.'

Respectable. Audrey knew all about that. She saw again Samuel's smile, bright, confident, false.

She met Mairi's gaze. The girl's pupils were so large that her eyes seemed black. 'We must be very careful, Mairi. He is a man of the church and we have nothing to go on; no proof.'

'No,' Mairi said. 'No, we don't yet.'

Chapter 8

And a land where sin had never been;
A land of love and a land of light,
Withouten sun, or moon, or night;
Where the river swa'd a living stream,
And the light a pure celestial beam;
The land of vision, it would seem,
A still, an everlasting dream.

The winds came, gusting through the bracken and the blackberry bushes, howling down the chimneys and making the windows of the mansion shudder in their frames. In the undergrowth, mushrooms emerged, their gills spreading over tree roots and bursting from trunks. On her walks Audrey saw little brown penny buns, yellow-frilled chanterelles, deadly white angels and red-capped toadstools. She could not escape the feeling that something else grew too.

She had passed her trial period with Miss Buchanan, it seemed. 'Well, Miss Hart, it appears I was right to give you the benefit of the doubt. You've achieved far more in one month than Alec did in six. But perhaps that's not surprising. I should never have asked him to help.'

Audrey should have been pleased. She should have felt a sense of accomplishment. But the people had only begun to talk to her because she had found Isbeil, just as Mrs Campbell had foretold. She could not entirely dismiss the notion that her return to the island had played a part in it all: Isbeil's death, Eliza's torture. Was she in some strange way the cause? Her dreams grew muddled and bloodied. More than once she woke to a cry that must have been her own.

She and Mairi continued with their folklore-collecting, using it as an excuse to ask further questions of the crofters. Had anyone seen a silver bird or the tree watermark? Did anyone know which man Eliza Fraser had met with? No one knew the answers, or no one would say, and Audrey's unease grew by the day. No further letters arrived from London, and their very absence made her sick, for she guessed that Samuel must have given up on his attempts to silence her and was now speaking to others – the orphanage, her father. A storm was gathering. She felt it, just as the birds had.

Mairi must have sensed it too, for she stayed ever closer to Audrey. She always walked beside her now, rather than ahead. She taught her the words for the things they saw: *iolair* – the lone eagle that soared above; *siris* – the wild cherries that blazed amongst the birches. On occasion, she took Audrey's arm. Audrey was never sure whether

Mairi was protecting her, or whether she herself was afraid.

In the last week of October, Lord Buchanan returned from London and declared that they were to hold a dinner for the Earl of Ross, the prospective shooting tenant. A cook was hired for the occasion, together with a head waiter, and special provisions were ordered in from the mainland: fish, a huge turkey, wines, whiskies and port.

On the day of the dinner itself, Effy hurried about the mansion in a state of nervous excitement, commanding Mairi to carry out various cleaning and preparatory duties, such that the girl had no time to assist Audrey and they saw little of one another until an hour or so before the dinner was due to commence, when Mairi appeared in the library where Audrey sat writing. She had been made to wear a frilled bonnet and her shoes were freshly blackened.

'Yes?' Audrey looked at her expectantly.

'Himself will be here.'

'Who?'

Mairi looked at her darkly. 'The minister.'

'He will, yes.' Lord Buchanan had insisted that he be invited, and to Audrey's surprise, the reverend had accepted.

'I'm only needed for the making of the dinner and the carrying of it. Effy says I'm to stay out of the way after that. She and the waiter fellow will do the serving.'

'And?'

'And he will be here, away from the manse, and I will not be needed.' Mairi gave a slight smile.

Audrey frowned at her. 'You're not serious? How on earth would you get in?'

'He keeps his keys in his coat pocket.'

'How do you know this?'

Mairi ignored the question. 'I can take the key and run over there while everyone's here eating. See if I can find anything.'

'Mairi, quite apart from anything else, someone might well notice you leaving Lanerly.'

'I am not daft altogether. I'll leave by the servants' tunnel.'

'I didn't know there was one.'

'Aye, in the basement, but no one's been using it since the place has been shut off. No one will see.'

'Mairi, please think about this. There's nothing to say that Reverend Carlisle is involved. It's just a notion that's taken you recently. And if you were to be discovered . . .'

'I won't be.'

Audrey frowned, but could not help admiring the girl's nerve.

'The charm,' Mairi said. 'The silver bird. If there was something similar in the manse. Well, then. I'd know.'

'I thought you told me that was left by the Host.'

'Maybe. I don't know. I don't trust him, is all.'

They heard voices in the corridor outside.

'I'd best go now. You'll make sure he doesn't leave early?'

'Yes, but Mairi,' Audrey said as the girl walked from the room, 'listen . . .'

It was too late: she was hurrying into the corridor, her skirts whispering, her shoes a light patter upon the wooden floor.

The long dining table had been laid out with the finest linen, china and silverware. Crystal glasses glinted in the light of the many candles that had been placed about the room, their flames reflected in the large mirror. Lord Buchanan sat at the head of the table, next to the earl, a squat man with the jowly face of an overfed dog, who was offering his views on a new Act of Parliament. 'It's a worrying development, in my view, this divorce business. It'll encourage women to make baseless claims against their husbands, the whole thing in full public view.'

Miss Buchanan, who sat to the man's left, said coolly, 'Oh, I wouldn't worry. The odds are still stacked against the wife. As I understand it, while a husband only needs to show adultery, a wife must also prove cruelty, bigamy or something of the sort. I'd say you were fairly safe.'

'Charlotte likes to be controversial,' Lord Buchanan said, laughing too hard. 'That's why we rarely let her out.'

Audrey had been seated midway down the table, next to the minister, who omitted an odour of damp wool and eau de cologne. She had thought he might be hostile towards her, but he had reverted to his former condescending self, leaning close so that he might talk to her in soft tones of his guidance to the poor, his concern for her own welfare. 'You look tired, my dear. Are you not sleeping well?'

Audrey smiled by way of response as she cast her eyes

around the room. The chair next to her was empty. Where was Alec? Murdo, she learnt, had not been invited. Evidently he was not gentleman enough for the Earl of Ross.

Effy, flustered and pink-cheeked, appeared carrying a large soup tureen. The hired waiter, a gaunt man dressed in green, held a second silver dish, which he placed close to Audrey and lifted the lid, releasing a wave of scented steam. Eventually Alec arrived, with the heightened colour of a man who had been drinking for some time. Audrey glanced at him as he took his seat next to her, wondering what he might say this time to the minister or to the guest of honour. Lord Buchanan, perhaps fearing the same, was speaking at increased volume about the Highlands and Islands Emigration Society.

'It is said now that they have assisted nearly five thousand to reach Australia, a land far more suited to these people.'

'But this is their home,' Alec said, not quietly enough.

'It is not their land,' his father replied crisply.

'Not legally, no,' Miss Buchanan said.

The earl turned to her. 'You are a collector of folklore, I understand,' he said, directing the conversation away from the land he was considering emptying of its inhabitants.

'I'm collecting the local lore, yes.' She fixed him with her blue gaze and added, 'Before it vanishes.'

'Charlotte's interests have always been a little peculiar.' Lord Buchanan smiled at his sister.

'Oh, it's a very interesting hobby, the collection of

local lore, I'm sure. I merely think that these tales need
to be shaped a little, to impart a moral lesson.'

'There is no directing them,' the minister said shortly.
'They're dangerous. They need to be squashed.'

'Oh come, man. I know some of them are a little
peculiar, but stories in which a mother's blessing leads to
success, in which hard work is rewarded? Surely these are
less harmful than the whisky bottle.'

'The whisky bottle is not the only alternative available
to them.' The minister continued eating his bread. Audrey
could hear the click of his jaw.

'What else is there?' Miss Buchanan said. 'It's stories or
silence.'

'There is prayer,' the minister said. 'There are books.'

'English books, for the Gaelic ones have been taken
away. And in any event, most can't read. You know that.
We all need our amusements, Minister.'

Silence, save for the scrape of cutlery on plates. Alec
poured himself more wine, then filled Audrey's glass and
gave her a wry smile. Two large plates of fish were brought
to the table, then four silver entrée dishes. Audrey forced
down some of the food, barely tasting it. In her mind, she
was following Mairi out of the servants' tunnel and along
the path to the manse, turning the stolen key in the door
and walking into the darkened hallway. She should have
stopped her.

'The truth of the matter,' the earl continued, 'is that
these people have limited intelligence. How else do you
account for the continuing belief in the mystical and for

their failure to improve their living standards? They are culturally, and in every other sense, backward.'

'Indeed,' replied Lord Buchanan. 'They have no urge to self-improvement, none of what we might call enterprise. They would live in their squalid little huts raking over their famished earth until there was no life left in the land whatsoever. Better to leave the land to the animals.'

Alec sighed audibly. The minister looked at him and raised his eyebrows. They were friends again, it seemed.

The entrée dishes were cleared and a huge side of roast beef was placed before Lord Buchanan to carve. At the opposite end of the table a roast turkey was set down. Further small dishes and wines were brought in, tiny bowls in which to dip their fingers, silver goblets and another basket of bread, until the table was heaped with dish upon dish of rich foods, reminding Audrey of the banquets in fairy tales that the hero was forbidden to touch. How could they afford this, she wondered, and how could they justify such excess while others starved?

The conversation moved on to matters of Parliament and the Indian Mutiny. 'They are talking, you know, of granting an amnesty to some of the rebels.'

'After Cawnpore?' Lord Buchanan shook his head. 'If they think they will win power over these natives using compromise, they are cruelly mistaken. Such people only understand brute force.'

The minister put down his fork. 'This is hardly conversation for mixed company.'

Lord Buchanan turned to Audrey. 'My apologies, Miss

Hart. You must think us terrible boors. We will reserve such talk for after dinner.'

Audrey imitated a smile. Of course women should not be exposed to such things. Their delicate constitutions could not withstand it. Except that she had already read of the Cawnpore massacre. Women and children butchered; bloody handprints on walls; the dying thrown into a well. The darkest fairy tale of all.

More wine was poured and drunk. The minister drummed his fingers on the cloth, looked at the clock on the mantelpiece and expressed his concern that Audrey must be exhausted and wanting to retire.

'I'm fine, I assure you.' She thought of Mairi in the gloom of the manse, using a candle to light her way.

The dinner dragged on, and she abandoned any attempt to eat, pushing her plate to one side.

'No wonder you stay so slender,' the minister said, nodding at the untouched food. 'You have the figure almost of a child.'

Audrey gave a chill, flat smile. It never ceased to amaze her how many people thought it acceptable to comment on a woman's size or shape, or how much she ate.

Then came the pudding course. The waiter set a dish of macaroni and cheese at the head of the table, while at the other end Effy placed a magnificent tower of spun sugar and pastry filled with preserves. Cut-crystal dishes were laid out alongside them: white vanilla and a pink raspberry cream, a pale wine jelly, another tinted crimson.

'All this,' Alec said, 'to sell off the shooting.'

The minister wiped his mouth with a napkin. 'Aye. All this would feed the whole of Strath several times over.'

At long last the meal reached its conclusion. Effy brought in a tray of cheese, a bowl of apples, and a bottle of port, which she proceeded to decant into silver cups and hand to the men.

'You'll have to excuse me,' the minister said, standing. 'I've been up since the early hours.'

Audrey looked at the clock. How much time had passed since Mairi left – an hour and a half? Not enough for her to be sure she had returned safely.

'Reverend Carlisle, you're not leaving us already, surely?'

'I'm afraid so, Miss Hart. I've another early start tomorrow and I am not a young thing like you.' His tone was honeyed, his smile false and stretched.

'No, no, my man.' Lord Buchanan's speech was slurred. 'You must taste the brandy that I've brought up from London. Where is that waiter?'

'Don't worry, Father. I'll go.' Alec stood up.

'And there are things you and I need to talk about, Minister,' Buchanan said. 'Gentlemen, we should let the ladies withdraw rather than bore them with politics.'

Miss Buchanan pushed herself up on her stick and nodded at Audrey.

Alec followed them into the hall. 'Lucky you,' he whispered into her ear. 'An escape.'

★

As soon as Miss Buchanan had left her, Audrey ran to the kitchen, where she found Effy surrounded by dirty pots and plates. 'Where's Mairi?'

'Blessed if I know,' Effy muttered, scrubbing at one of the tureens. 'I'll skelp the stuffing out o' her when I find her.' She stopped and looked up. 'Did you come down here for something, miss?'

'Yes,' Audrey said, after a second. 'Some cocoa, if you don't mind.'

Effy frowned at her. 'Did you not eat your dinner? All that food,' she grumbled as she went about heating a pan of milk.

Audrey left the kitchen with the warm cup, feeling a tightness in her chest.

Pausing by the dining room, she could hear the rumble of conversation and could make out the deeper tones of the minister. The pain in her chest eased a little. She tiptoed up the back stairs to Mairi's attic room and tapped gently on the door. When no answer came, she pushed the door ajar and peered inside. The narrow room was cold and dark. A dress was folded over the chair. Mairi's old shoes rested beneath the bed. No one had been here for some time.

Not knowing what else to do, Audrey returned to her own room, where she pushed her chair to the window and sat with her cocoa watching the shifting sea. She would sit up until Mairi came to her, for she *would* come to her when she returned, surely. She took up Scott's *Letters on Demonology and Witchcraft* and read until the candle burnt down to a puddle. Downstairs, doors closed, footsteps crunched on the path; the great house creaked, the walls whispered. Audrey turned the pages of her book, trying to keep her eyes trained on the words of the story.

'Miss?'

The voice was both close and distant, as though from behind a wall. Audrey tried to struggle out of the darkness and open her eyes, but it felt as though they had been glued shut.

'Miss Hart.'

Was it Mairi's voice? Audrey wrenched herself from what seemed like a deep pit and struggled to the surface of consciousness.

'Shall I leave your tea here?'

It was not Mairi, but Effy. Audrey realised with a jolt that she had fallen asleep in her chair, her cloak pulled across her. 'Please leave the tray on the table. I seem to have fallen asleep while reading – how silly of me.' Her voice sounded thick, perhaps not intelligible. 'Have you seen Mairi this morning?'

'You're to come downstairs, miss,' Effy said, without turning back to face her. 'When you're up and dressed.'

Audrey coughed, trying to clear her head. Her mouth felt furred and dry. She should not have drunk any wine: what an utter fool she was. She forced herself to drink some of the scalding-hot tea, then splashed water on her face, tidied her hair and dressed as quickly as she could, though her movements felt sluggish and strange. When she glanced at herself in the looking-glass her face seemed different: older, her eyes darker. Something had changed.

'Ah. The sleeping beauty.' Lord Buchanan looked up at Audrey as she descended the staircase, gripping the balustrade. 'Join us, would you?' He signalled towards the parlour.

As she entered the room, Audrey started, for they were all there, assembled: Alec, Miss Buchanan and the Reverend Carlisle.

'We've had a wee bit of a shock this morning, Audrey,' the minister said, standing up.

'A shock?'

'When I returned to the manse last night I found that my key had gone from my pocket. Fortunately I keep a second key hidden and was able to enter the house. But I found, Miss Hart, that someone had been there.'

Audrey remained silent, her heart working too hard, her blood too thick in her veins.

'Things had been moved,' the minister said. 'Some items had been taken.'

'What had been taken?' she asked dully.

He ignored her question and continued with his story. 'I came here first thing to warn Miss Buchanan that there was a thief in our midst, but it seems my warning came too late.'

'Thief?' Audrey's thoughts were still slow and jumbled. Her tongue stuck to the roof of her mouth.

'Mairi has stolen various things, including my jewellery,' Miss Buchanan said. 'And some of the silver.'

Audrey stared at Miss Buchanan, then at the minister. 'Where is she now?'

'A very good question,' Miss Buchanan said. 'We wondered whether you might know.'

Audrey tried to read the woman's expression, unsure whether this was an accusation or a ruse to ferret out what she knew.

'I have no idea. But I can't believe . . .' She faltered. Surely it was not possible that Mairi had stolen from Miss Buchanan and the minister. 'I don't believe Mairi is a thief.'

'Well,' Miss Buchanan said drily, 'I did tell you that she wasn't necessarily to be trusted, although I can't say that I imagined she would run off with the silver. How very pedestrian.'

Audrey's heart was racing. 'Why would she do this now? If she'd wanted to steal from you, she could have done so a long time ago.'

'People act in curious ways,' the minister said, 'and have secrets within their hearts that only God can guess at.'

Alec was watching the minister. 'Perhaps she had a very specific secret,' he said. 'A reason she needed money.' He turned to Audrey. 'She didn't say anything to you?'

Audrey shook her head. 'As far as I know, Mairi had no reason to run away.' A thought pierced through her lethargy, sharp as a needle. 'She's been taken.'

Alec met her eye.

'Taken?' the minister said, smiling. 'Miss Hart, really . . .'

'We must contact the police.'

'I already have,' Miss Buchanan said. 'I sent Murdo out first thing this morning to Sligachan to speak with the constable there. That jewellery was not of inconsiderable value. I want it back. You might want to check that nothing of yours has been taken.'

Audrey felt a twist of sickness. She ran from the parlour, through the hallway, up the stairs to her room and pulled open the dressing table drawer. The little silver apple box was gone, her mother's ruby ring with it.

Audrey walked slowly down the stairs, her eyes on the faded carpet, not quite believing that she could have misjudged Mairi.

'Don't blame yourself.' Alec was standing by the window in the hallway.

Audrey stopped and looked at him.

'None of us thought she was a thief,' Alec said quietly. 'As you said, if she'd wanted to rob us, she could have done so a long time ago, when we had a lot more to steal.'

'It wasn't her,' Audrey said uncertainly.

'No? Well whoever it was knew where my aunt kept her jewellery.'

'Where was it?'

'In one of the cabinets beneath the selkie skins.' He smiled. 'Not many thieves would guess to look there.' He turned towards the window.

'And it's gone?'

'Yes, all of it. Look at that.'

Audrey joined him at the window. In the distance, a dark mass was surging through the sky. It seemed at first to be a cloud, moving towards them like a storm. As it grew closer, she saw that it was made up of tiny pinpricks of darkness. It was not a cloud at all, she realised, but birds, hundreds upon hundreds of birds, all swirling together in the sky as one.

'It's a murmuration of starlings,' Alec said. 'They fly at this time of year.'

'Why?' Her hands were at her throat. 'Why are they all flying together like that?'

They stood watching as the lines of birds merged and separated, undulating like streams of dark water.

'I'm not sure. I think perhaps they group together when they're afraid of something,' he said. 'Safety in numbers.'

Chapter 9

Seven days passed and Bainne heard nothing further, but on the eighth night the crow returned. Again he alighted on the branch above Bainne and again he cawed, 'Come home, come home. Your parents miss you. Your sister awaits you.'

This time, however, he had brought with him a little leather shoe the size of an egg, which he dropped into Bainne's lap.

Seeing the little shoe, Bainne began to fear that what the crow said was true: that she did indeed have a sister, a sister whom her parents might at that very moment have locked in the cupboard in the dark, as they had once done to her.

'No, no,' the fairies told her, 'you cannot go back. It is a trick, a wicked trick to lure you back home. You must stay with us where you are safe and happy.'

But Bainne was no longer happy. She was afraid.

Audrey watched the Reverend Carlisle as he walked towards the nave, nodding to members of the congregation. Although the terror and uncertainty were still with her, her mind was clearer today, sharper.

The minister took his place in the pulpit. A wintry sun shone through the window, lighting him from behind, throwing his shadow across the nave, long and severe.

He had been at Lanerly throughout the dinner; he had still been in the dining room when Audrey went to bed. Perhaps Mairi had somehow become trapped in the manse before he returned, or perhaps this had nothing to do with him at all.

The chanting began as before – the minister giving the line of the psalm, the congregation singing back.

'He that worketh deceit shall not dwell within my house: he that telleth lies shall not tarry in my sight.'

The psalm was a message and everyone there knew it. The voices were quieter than before, more hesitant. There was no jubilation, nothing mystical. Just misery, and fear.

Audrey glanced at Alec, seated close beside her. He too seemed dejected today, his face drawn. Audrey wondered if he shared her sense that something terrible was happening, or if he suspected anything of the minister. She could not ask. The two men worked together. They were, in a strange way, friends. Alec would consider her questions preposterous, even mad. She did not want to push him away from her.

The minister began his sermon. 'Let us not grieve when we see fraud successful. Let no man's heart fail him. It was not the intention of the Almighty that the race should always be swift, or the battle strong, lest we should fix our affections on earthly things. Sooner or later we will all receive our reward. Mercy and peace will be upon us.'

Audrey looked down at her hands. Without her mother's ring, they felt naked and vulnerable. A tiny part of her wondered if Mairi had tricked her, if she really was a thief, but she could not truly believe that. Something far stranger was happening. She folded her hands together.

'Let us pray.'

The constable must have been seated at the back of the kirk, as Audrey saw him approach the minister as he left the church. They shook hands and the minister took the man by the shoulder and steered him in the direction of the gate. Audrey walked quickly towards them.

'Oh aye, I always lock it,' she heard the minister say. 'I'm a Glasgow man at heart – I never got out of the habit.'

The constable spoke more quietly in response and she could not hear what he was asking, but the minister nodded and said, 'Yes, a peculiar child.'

They moved closer together, lowering their voices. She could not risk approaching nearer, so she waited until the police officer had left the minister and was making towards the path, then hurried to catch up with him.

'Excuse me.'

The policeman turned towards her. At this proximity,

she could see that he had the swollen nose of a drunkard, the close-set eyes of a weasel.

'I wished to speak with you, Mr . . .'

'Norris. Constable Norris. And who might you be, miss?'

'My name is Audrey Hart. I'm assisting Miss Buchanan and living in the mansion. Mairi was working with me.'

'Oh yes?' The man's small eyes ran over her, as though measuring her up for the noose.

'Yes, I got to know her well.' This wasn't strictly true: she still felt that she had only scratched the surface of what Mairi was. 'I don't believe, Constable Norris, that she stole those things and ran away. It simply isn't like her. I'm concerned that something else has happened to her.'

'And what exactly do you think has happened, Miss Hart?'

'I'm not sure.' She glanced back in the direction of the minister. 'But I'm worried that perhaps she has been taken.'

'Taken?'

She held her nerve. 'You may have heard, Constable, that two other girls have gone missing recently.'

The man frowned. 'You're not talking about the crofter girls?'

'I am, yes: Eliza Fraser, who returned. And Isbeil McLennan, who was found dead.'

'Tell me now, Miss Hart, what exactly is it that you're doing for Miss Buchanan?'

She could tell from his expression that he already knew the answer to this.

'I'm helping her with the collection of local lore.'

'By listening to the stories of the crofters.'

'Yes.'

The man pulled his face into a smile. 'I think perhaps you've been taking their stories a little too seriously, Miss Hart. I know what they say about those lasses. I also know that there's not a grain of truth in it.' He dropped the smile. 'You know what the crofters did to Eliza Fraser?'

'I do. And I'm not suggesting, Constable, that the girls were taken by spirits.'

'Then what is it that you *are* suggesting?'

'I don't know. Is it not possible that something else could be at work?'

'Such as?'

The minister was standing near the gate, watching them. Audrey felt the blood rush to her cheeks. 'I just think,' she said quickly, 'that it should be properly investigated. In London—'

The officer gave a mirthless laugh. 'Oh in *London* I daresay they'd do things very different, but this isn't London, is it, miss?' His voice was cold now.

She tried, too late, to rescue the situation. 'But surely you have some system for investigating disappearances here?'

He cocked his head. 'Miss Hart, this is Skye. Folk don't just disappear, or get their heads beaten in as happens on the streets of London. We're not having a "system". We look into things as they happen. I'll be investigating what's become of your friend, and I've little doubt but that we'll catch up with her soon enough. Now good day to you.' He touched his hat and turned from her.

Audrey watched as he made his way down the path with the unmistakable gait of a man who believes he has authority and power. A man whose mind is already made up.

She found Alec down by the water, bringing in his boat, a small skiff, peaked at both ends. The boat's iron-shod stem grated on the stones as he dragged it to shore. She wondered for a moment how he could bear to sail in the very bay where his sister had drowned.

'Ah yes,' he said, when she told him of her encounter with the constable. 'Officer Pointless.'

'You know him, then?'

'Norris comes here occasionally when there's been a ruckus or something stolen.' He was feeding a rope through a mooring ring. His shirtsleeves were rolled up and Audrey noticed the muscles taut beneath his skin. 'The man is a simpleton.'

'He thinks this is a mere case of a runaway servant. He wouldn't listen.'

'Yes, well, men like him are incapable of believing that something truly bad could happen here. They just don't have the imagination. A stolen teapot, yes; a girl killed, no.'

She watched him. 'So you believe Isbeil was killed?'

Alec kept his eyes on his work. 'I have no idea, Audrey.'

'Mairi had no reason to run away.'

'No reason that you know of.'

'But you do?'

No answer.

'Alec?'

He shook his head. 'I know nothing.'

'You *think* something, though.'

He looked at her. 'You're a determined one, aren't you?' He smiled. 'I believe you know that it was me who first found Mairi; me who persuaded my aunt to take her in.'

'Yes.'

'Well, I had a rather strange ally in that.'

'The minister.'

She had spoken too quickly. Alec frowned. 'No. Why do you suggest him?'

Audrey swallowed. 'Well, he sees it as his role to help the poor, doesn't he?'

'Oh, I see. No. No, it was Murdo. He was the one who suggested that we might find a use for her. And I've always wondered . . .' He paused. 'A few days ago, when you returned from Strollamus, I saw Murdo talking to Mairi outside.'

'What about?'

'I don't know. I couldn't hear them. But there was something about the way he was speaking; about the way she was standing. It wasn't right.'

'In what way?'

'I'm not sure. I got the idea that they might have been arguing, or that he might have been reprimanding her.' He returned to knotting the rope. 'I suppose it's possible they were talking about his daughter. I think Murdo has always believed Mairi knows where she is.'

'Were they friends then?'

'Of sorts, I think. They're about the same age. Oh, it's all speculation, nonsense. I've just been thinking about why Mairi would leave now. After all, she had nowhere else to go, had she?'

Audrey opened the door to Mairi's room and stood for a moment in the doorway. The air was chill and smelt of guttered candles and damp wallpaper. She had come here the morning Mairi had vanished, to see whether she had taken her belongings. She had not. They were still here now: a hairbrush and a small piece of soap on the little table; a dress folded on the chair; a pair of worn shoes beneath the bed. It all seemed so mundane, so empty.

Audrey sat on the narrow bed. The blanket was folded neatly at the bottom, Mairi's nightgown atop it. On the pillow rested the leather notebook that Audrey had given the girl so that she could make her own notes of their meetings with the crofters. She picked up the little book and opened it. Inside, Mairi's crude scrawl ran across the pages. There were notes about the stories they had heard together: the old woman who washed in a stream the linen rags of those who were to die; the long-haired Gruagach who lay on the roof of the byre and drank the milk of the cows. Tales of sprites and brownies, changelings and kelpies, all arranged by location, as Audrey had directed. Some had little drawings alongside them – a horse for a kelpie story, a cow for the Gruagach. As she turned the pages, Audrey was reminded painfully of the little book of poems and pictures the orphanage girls had made for her, and she thought again of Samuel and what he might now be doing to rescue his reputation, and ruin hers. Her eye was drawn to a sketch of a black bird on one of the final pages. The handwriting here was neater, she noticed.

No, not just neater: different. This was not Mairi's hand.

The writing was in Gaelic, and it took some time for Audrey to fathom its meaning, but as she read on, she felt the blood drain from her face and her heart began to pulse strangely. This was the story Shawfield had told them of the woman who had disappeared from the Quiraing. Only it was a far fuller version than he had given. Mairi must have obtained a more complete story from someone else, or perhaps Shawfield himself had written this at her request. Why, though, had Mairi not told her? Had she feared causing her distress?

She read on, feeling the nausea return, the shakiness begin again. *A man told of how, just after the woman had vanished, a flock of black birds appeared in the sky above the rocks. Hundreds upon hundreds of them, swirling in the sky like a great dark cloud. It is believed that they were the Sluagh – the spirits of the restless dead.*

Audrey was seized with sickness that evening, though whether it was due to distress or illness she could not say. For a time she lay shivering on the floor, curled in on herself, the room spinning about her. She was afraid, yes, but more than anything else she felt unbearably alone. She remembered her mother holding her head when she was poorly as a child, laying compresses on her forehead when she had a fever. She thought of Mairi taking her cold hand between hers. She lay drifting in and out of sleep. Occasionally she would hear a knocking sound, as though from below the floorboards. She dreamt of Mairi, her hand gripping hers; then of Eliza lying across her in the coach, her hand curled like Isbeil's. She woke, confused and clammy, to the sound of Alec's voice.

'Audrey?'

She hauled herself to her feet.

'Audrey, are you all right?'

She splashed water on her hands and face, came to the door and opened it.

Alec looked her up and down. 'You didn't come for dinner. I was worried about you.'

'You're very kind. I'm feeling a little under the weather this evening, but I'm sure it will pass.'

He put his hand to her forehead and let it rest there a moment. 'You are feverish, I think.'

'It's nothing serious.' She was conscious of how dishevelled she must look, her hair unpinned, her buttons undone.

'Would you like me to ask Effy to bring something for you? Some Epsom salts, perhaps?'

'Thank you, but no. I think I simply need to go to bed.'

Alec's eyes did not leave hers. She thought momentarily

of telling him about the story in Mairi's notebook, but could not bear even to think of it.

'It's this business with Mairi, isn't it?'

'Not just Mairi. All of them. Isbeil. Then Eliza. I can't help but feel . . .' She shook her head. She had not the strength to talk of it now.

Alec rested against the doorframe. 'You mustn't take this all upon yourself. It's nothing to do with you.'

'It was I who found Isbeil. I who first saw Eliza when she returned. And now Mairi, whom I'd persuaded to help me. It's too much.' She heard her voice crack.

'It's a terrible collection of circumstances, yes, but none of it is your fault. And none of it is your responsibility.'

Audrey met his eyes. There was such kindness in them that she felt she might cry.

The knocking sound came then again, though this time it was as though it was within the walls. 'What is that?'

Alec searched her face. 'What is what, Audrey?'

'That noise. The knocking sound.'

He shook his head. 'I didn't hear it, but the old water pipes, perhaps.' He touched her lightly on the shoulder. 'You're exhausted, I think. I will let you sleep.'

By the following day, the sickness and the sounds had gone, but Audrey still felt weak and strange. She kept to the house, reading and taking notes in the library. Late in the afternoon, Constable Norris called in to announce his findings. Having spoken to 'the relevant parties' and inspected both Lanerly and the manse, he had little doubt that Mairi had taken the jewellery and silver while they were at dinner, then removed the key from the minister's pocket and used it to enter his house.

'Like as not she's on the road to Inverness,' he said, putting on his hat, 'but we'll get your jewellery back, Miss Buchanan, never the fear o' it. I'll send word to our men there to look out for her. When she tries to sell the stuff, she'll be caught like a rabbit in a trap.'

'She'll be arrested, will she?' Effy asked, opening the door for him.

'Oh aye,' said the constable. 'She might be young, but she's old enough to face the law.'

'It's a hanging offence, isn't it?' Audrey said. 'That amount of money?'

The constable looked at her. 'It is, aye.'

Audrey shook her head. 'She just wouldn't have done it. Quite apart from anything else, she wouldn't have taken the risk.'

'People surprise us, Miss Hart.' He buttoned his coat. 'I've been in this game long enough to know that.'

'What if you're wrong? What if something's happened to her?'

The constable regarded her steadily. 'Miss Buchanan tells me you had a ring stolen. You didn't mention that when we spoke the other day.'

Audrey looked at her hands. 'Mairi wouldn't have taken my ring,' she said quietly. 'She wouldn't have done that to me.'

When she looked up, she saw that Miss Buchanan was watching her, interested.

'Thank you for your time, Officer.' The older woman smiled at him unconvincingly. 'Don't let us keep you any further.'

The constable gave an odd sort of a bow, wiped his bulbous nose and left.

Once the door was closed, Miss Buchanan turned back to Audrey. 'Well, we have been duped, Miss Hart, pure and simple. I, of all people, should have seen it coming.' She gave an odd, thin smile and Audrey wondered what she meant. She could not imagine anyone getting anything past Miss Buchanan, but perhaps she had been deceived before, just as Audrey had. Maybe that accounted for her distance, for why she was a closed book.

'Nevertheless, our purpose remains.'

'Yes, Miss Buchanan. I will continue collecting the stories tomorrow.'

'Good. I know you've been unwell, but we both understand, I think, the importance of pressing on, even when everything seems against us.'

Audrey nodded, trying to read Miss Buchanan's blue gaze. For a moment she had a horrible sense that the woman knew, somehow, about what had happened at the orphanage – that she knew everything about her. But perhaps Miss Buchanan was referring only to herself, to having continued her studies despite injury, despite a brother who undermined and underfunded her. Or perhaps she was remembering something else, something worse.

Audrey left the lobby and made her way to the library, trying to give the appearance of someone walking with ease. But she knew that Miss Buchanan's eyes were still on her, watching.

Audrey did not sleep that night, and by dawn she could not bear to stay any longer in the green-tinged room, the shadows from the candle flickering on the ceiling, the night breathing, the ivy tapping on the glass. She rose and left the mansion early in the morning, despite the icy rain that spat down from the granite sky. The fields were colourless and empty; the wild flowers had disappeared, leaving only faded bracken, brambles, and the occasional pink flash of rosebay willowherb. Most of the birds had flown now, but the ravens remained, calling to one another across the moors with their sepulchral croak. At a stile, Audrey came across the carcass of a deer that the ravens had already stripped bare. They looked up at her as she passed, unperturbed, glossy as wet ink, their eyes black pearls.

The ground had turned to muddy water, which oozed into her shoes and spattered her skirts as she followed the route she had walked before with Mairi. By the time she reached Lower Breakish, she was shivering, her clothes damp, and her fingers so numb she could barely feel the wooden door beneath her knuckles as she knocked.

Mrs Campbell's face expressed no surprise. She took Audrey's cold hand and pressed it between her warm palms, as Mairi herself had done. 'We'll get her back,' she said.

Water was already bubbling in the pot hanging above the fire, and for once Audrey did not care about the peat smoke. The croft was brighter than others she had seen thanks to a crude window cut into the side of the house, and the walls were covered with old sacks on which newspapers had been pasted. Spindles hung from hooks, and a spinning wheel stood in the corner, yarn stretched across it. On the back of a chair some finished blue cloth was drying, and Audrey remembered her mother telling her of the dyes they used to make colours: meadowsweet for yellow, nettle for green, blaeberry for purple. The reek of dung and damp was there but it was partly masked by the smell of toasting oats. On the hearth, the morning bannocks had been propped against a flat stone to brown.

Audrey watched Mrs Campbell as she stirred the tea in a pan with a wooden spoon. She poured it into two cups, then took down a can from the dresser. 'We've only a little milk, I'm afraid. Our Blàrach isn't getting much feeding.' Blàrach stared at them from the adjoining byre, her eyes shining pools in the gloom.

The woman handed Audrey a cup and a bannock, still hot and crisp.

'Thank you.' Audrey raised the cup so that the steam enveloped her face. 'You don't believe, then, that she's run away?'

'I don't believe she'd ha' gone without a word to anyone. Not unless she were truly frightened.'

'You think she might have run, though?'

'Mairi's had to look after herself her whole life, and she could run if she had to. But I don't think it's that. You saw the evil flying over Broadford Bay. We all did.'

Audrey licked her lips. 'Yes.' She tried not to think of the swirling mass of darkness, or of the black bird in Mairi's book, but they were there before her and she felt her resolve collapse. 'Mrs Campbell, can you tell? Is she alive?'

The woman raked the embers of the fire to set them aglow. 'Aye. I reckon so.'

'Where is she?'

Mrs Campbell shook her head. 'I've been looking and looking, but I see nothing. I can't will these things.'

Audrey closed her eyes for a second. She reached into her cloak and pulled out Mairi's notebook. Without speaking, she directed Mrs Campbell to the story and to the picture of the bird. Mrs Campbell stared at the passage for a long time, and for a moment it occurred to Audrey that she might not be able to read. But it was not that, for she turned the page, then the next. She rested the book on her lap.

'The Quiraing. It's where my mother died,' Audrey explained. 'She fell. I knew there was a story about it, but not this. I don't understand where it came from, where Mairi found the story, or who wrote this.'

The woman did not respond. She looked again at the writing, then back at Audrey. Curiously, she smiled. 'Maybe that's why you're here, Miss Hart. Maybe your mother sent you.'

Audrey swallowed. There was something awful in the idea, but it was also oddly comforting. Her mother had sent her to help the girls. To ensure they did not suffer her fate. She thought again of her mother's coffin spread with lilies, and she was convinced now that it had been empty. They had never found her. Her father had lied to make it easier for her to accept that her mother was gone. Maybe he knew about the story of the Sluagh, and knew that she would believe it. He had been protecting her, in his own fashion.

But she could not think like this; this was not how a rational person thought, nor was it the way to find Mairi. 'Mrs Campbell, is there anything or anyone you knew Mairi to be frightened of?'

'Mairi kept her thoughts to herself.'

'But you think there was someone.'

Mrs Campbell frowned. 'She doesn't trust many. Certainly not the rich folk. But frightened? I don't know.'

'Did she ever say anything about Murdo Maclean?'

The woman shook her head. 'Not really. She doesn't much like the man, but then none of us do. Why?'

'It was something that Alec Buchanan said to me, about him having seen them talking; arguing, maybe.'

'I don't know about that, but I wouldn't bide by anything that fellow says, Miss Hart. Isn't it him that's Lord Buchanan's son?'

'Yes, but he is a kind man. He has been very good to me.' She was ashamed to realise she was near tears.

'Maybe so,' Mrs Campbell said gently. 'Maybe so. But so far as I know there was no one in particular she was afeared of. No, they've taken her, sure as death. We must find a way to get her back.'

★

By the time Audrey reached Lanerly, the day had a cold brightness about it, the sun a white orb high above the sea. Rather than return at once to the house, where she knew she would face questions as to where she had been, she walked down to the cove where she had found Isbeil all those weeks ago. The waves broke softly upon the shore, dragging themselves back again, exposing black rocks heaped with tangles of tawny dulse. Redshanks and eider ducks paddled about the bay and bobbed on the shifting tides. Audrey sat on a large rock by the water, and for a moment her mind was empty and clear.

A pair of oystercatchers waded in the shallows, poking at something with their long orange bills. At first Audrey thought it was seaweed, but it was too dense, too grey. She stood up and walked closer so that the waves almost reached her feet. The birds eyed her warily but did not move away until she was only a few paces from them; then they lifted off, wings flapping in a blur of black and white. Audrey stared at what they had left behind. She knew now what it was.

Chapter 10

They bore her away, she wist not how,
For she felt not arm nor rest below;
But so swift they wain'd her through the light,
'Twas like the motion of sound or sight;
They seem'd to split the gales of air,
And yet nor gale nor breeze was there.

Audrey held out the dress, the pale grey turned almost black by the seawater.

Miss Buchanan stared at the bundle. 'What is this?'

'It's Mairi's dress, Miss Buchanan. The dress she was wearing the night she disappeared.'

Miss Buchanan took a step closer, peering at the wet fabric. 'Yes, it is, isn't it? It was the previous kitchen girl's before her, but she took it in, here and here.' She pointed to the seams where the dress had been mended. 'I wondered where she'd got rid of it.'

'What do you mean?'

'Some of Flora's clothes were taken. Mairi must have

been wearing them when she left, in order to disguise herself as a lady. Well, she was a clever one, I'll give her that.'

'I don't think so, Miss Buchanan. I don't think she would have taken your niece's clothing. And why would she have disposed of her own dress in the sea?'

'To hide it, I suppose. But I am not a detective, Miss Hart, and nor, might I remind you, are you.' Miss Buchanan's tone was almost kind. 'I know you wish to find Mairi, that you had grown to like her, but I would give her up as a lost cause. I've employed a new girl to start tomorrow. Perhaps she will be able to assist you too.' She looked down. 'Mairi deceived all of us. She is best forgotten.'

Audrey left the library hugging the dress in her arms, not caring that the seawater would ruin her own clothing.

They are best forgotten, her father had said to her. *Those girls are no longer your concern.*

The letter came the following day, but there was no blood-red seal this time.

25th October, 1857

Dear Audrey,

We learnt of your address via Samuel Kingsmere. To have wished to leave London was perhaps understandable; to have failed to tell us even of your location was unforgivable.

You are to return home immediately. I am afraid for you there.

    Your father,

        Dr Edwin Hart

Audrey read the letter twice before setting it down. She had guessed that Samuel would go to see her father, but the thought of it nevertheless sickened her. She could imagine her father shrinking before him, apologising for his silly, thoughtless daughter. Of course he would bring her under control, of course he would. He had simply had the difficulty of not knowing where she was.

This claim that he was afraid for her must be a trick to lure her home. Or was it that he feared Samuel would reach her first? But for him to travel all the way to Skye would mean that he was desperate, and she could not quite believe that of a man so self-assured and cool.

Perhaps the danger her father spoke of was entirely unconnected with Samuel; perhaps it related instead to what was happening on the island. But what did he know of that?

Eliza Fraser was still under the care of Dr McGilvray.

'There's little point in speaking to her,' he told Audrey. 'She won't be making any sense. And I don't want her upset again.'

Audrey regarded him carefully – his dark eyes, the smattering of stubble on his jaw. Who was paying his fees?

'I would like to see her. Remember it was I who found her.'

The doctor watched Audrey, understanding her meaning: it was I who paid you last time. 'Very well,' he said after a moment. 'You may speak to her for a short while.' He walked before her to the door and spoke without turning back. 'It's right to warn you that she is much changed.'

Nothing, however, could have prepared Audrey for Eliza Fraser's appearance. The flesh on the right side of her face had been eaten away by fire, leaving a battle site of red and black. Her singed hair had been cut into a rough crop. Her blue eyes stared out from the wreckage. She gave no sign of recognising Audrey.

Audrey stepped towards the bed and held out the basket of apples she had purchased at the store. 'I brought these for you.'

The girl's eyes slid over the basket, but she made no comment.

Audrey took the chair by the bedside. 'I'm so sorry that this has happened to you, Eliza. I wanted to see if there was anything I could do.'

She reached out and rested her hand on the bed sheets, rough and chill.

'Marjory told me what they did.'

Eliza did not respond.

'There's another girl. Mairi Finlayson. Perhaps you know her.'

Still silence.

'She has gone missing from here in Broadford. She's a friend of mine. They say she's run away, but I don't believe that. I'm worried that someone has hurt her; that someone has taken her.'

The girl stared, her eyes blank.

'Eliza, I know you're afraid, but you can tell me what happened. I won't tell the doctor or the minister; I won't tell the constable. I promise you. I simply want to find Mairi.' Audrey became aware that she was crying, the tears salty in her mouth. She wiped them away. 'Do you understand?'

'They'll look after her.' Her voice came in a whisper.

'Who will look after her?'

'The fairy king and queen.'

'The fairy king and queen?'

Eliza looked into Audrey's eyes. 'Aye. If she behaves herself, if she's good, they won't let any harm come to her.'

'But Eliza, look what happened to you!'

The girl closed her eyes momentarily. 'It wasn't them that did this to me, was it?' She raised her hand to her destroyed face, but did not touch it. 'No. She'll be safe there.'

'Safe where, Eliza? Where do you think Mairi is?'

The girl frowned at her as though she were a silly child. 'Beneath the earth, of course.'

Audrey felt her stomach sink. 'Beneath the earth where?'

'In the land of love and light,' Eliza said. 'Where there's no sun or moon. By the water.' She spoke with the radiance of the right.

Audrey felt tears come again. The girl had lost her mind.

★

The next two days passed without incident, Audrey attempting to keep up the appearance of industry and attentiveness but her mind spinning, thinking of the swarming birds, the scribblings in Mairi's notebook, the grey dress, her father's words. Even the landscape, stripped now of heather and leaves, seemed more barren, more traumatised. As she walked alone back from the crofting townships, she tried to comfort herself again with the words Mairi had taught her: *druid* – starling; *caorann* – the clusters of rowan berries that shone scarlet against the pale blue sky.

She told the Buchanans that she wanted to visit Portree to buy clothes for the winter. This was not a lie. The days had shrunk and the winds blew colder; she was in need of a woollen walking dress and a sturdier pair of boots. But more than that, she needed to do something to help Mairi and to help herself, to stop her mind from turning and turning like a mouse on a wheel.

She travelled by boat, taking the steamer from Broadford and arriving at Portree quay by late morning. The land that rose to the left of the pier was covered in trees and shrubs, and on a hill to her right she saw a stream of sheep contracting and expanding like mercury. Her heart sank as she looked at the place, pretty though it was: there were two rows of houses, white as pearls, but it was hardly a metropolis.

The police station was a whitewashed building adjoining the gaol house in Somerled Square. She had feared that she would see Constable Norris there, but only two people

were about the place: a thin young man and an older officer
who sat by a fire writing something in a book. 'How may
we help you, young lady?' he asked as she entered the room.

Audrey gave her best attempt at a friendly smile. 'I
wondered if I might speak with the senior officer here.'

The man closed his book. 'Well, that'll be me. I'm the
inspector. Come this way.' He ushered her into a small
room sparsely furnished with a table and two chairs. 'Sit
you down,' he said, taking the seat on the other side of the
table. 'What's all this then?'

Keeping her voice as steady as she could, she told him of
Isbeil's death, Mairi's disappearance, Eliza's return.

As she spoke, the inspector knocked the old tobacco out
of his pipe onto the table and refilled it, his expression
implacable. 'Oh aye,' he said, when she mentioned Mairi,
'I know of the servant girl. Officer Norris has been looking
into it.'

'He hasn't found her?'

'Not yet, no. But then he's been kept busy: there are
many vagrants to be dealing with, you see.'

Vagrants, Audrey thought. He meant people who had
been evicted from their crofts and had nowhere to go. She
watched as he lit the pipe and took several quick puffs on it
to get it started.

'And you know about Eliza Fraser also?'

'Oh indeed. The folk that harmed her are biding in the
gaol here, waiting for the trial.' He looked at her through a
cloud of smoke. 'I knew nothing about the dead lass,
though. I wasn't informed.'

'It wasn't reported. The men present decided that it wasn't suspicious, that she'd drowned herself.'

'But you didn't agree with them?'

'The girl had an injury to her head. And there was something wrong with her hand. I'm not a doctor, of course . . .'

'No, you're not. Which doctor was it that looked at her then? McGilvray?'

'Yes.'

'Ah well, he's a good man, McGilvray. A good doctor. He'd ha' told me if he thought we needed to be looking at it.'

Audrey felt hopelessness seep through her. She had come here thinking that away from Broadford people might look at the case differently. But here again they knew one another. Here again she was the outsider, the Sassenach who should keep her nose out of their affairs. She pressed on.

'But do you not see, Inspector, that these incidents may be linked? That it's possible that someone is taking the girls?'

The inspector seemed to reassess her, taking in her silk dress and smooth hands. 'This is quite a claim to be making.'

'I realise that. I wouldn't have come here today if I didn't think there was something in it. I'm very worried about Mairi and what may have happened to her.'

The man drew again on his pipe.

Audrey continued. 'I heard that some years ago people

were abducted from the island and sold into slavery in America.'

The inspector nodded. 'That was a long time since. The Macleods it was.'

'Yes. Isn't it possible that something similar is happening now? Or that they've been abducted for some other purpose?' She thought momentarily of showing him the bird pendant, of telling him her suspicions that Isbeil had sold herself for silver. But when he spoke, a coldness had crept into his voice that stopped her.

'Abducted and returned?'

'Well, perhaps Eliza escaped but is too frightened to report what happened to her.'

The inspector looked at her. 'As I said, we have the folk who hurt Eliza Fraser here at the gaol.'

Audrey waited.

'We spoke to them only this last week about what it was they were doing to the girl. Seems they were trying to get her to admit what she really was.'

'Yes, I know that.'

'And they said, miss, that when they were burning her, she told them that she'd taken herself off to have a bairn.'

'I'm sorry?'

'Aye. That's the truth of it. She said that she'd been after hiding herself away in a cave to have the child so that no one would know of her shame.'

Audrey felt fear touch her throat. 'But that can't be true. No one knew her to be pregnant, did they? And she talks now only of fairies and of being kept underground.'

The inspector shrugged. 'I'm only reporting back on what they said. My wife has had five bairns now herself. I should think having one on her own in a cave would drive a young lass fair out of her mind.'

No. Surely that was wrong. That was not what Eliza had told her. But then, Audrey thought, Eliza had every reason *not* to tell. For a moment she had a vision of a cold dark cavern, a girl screaming within it. It could not be true.

'But what if she was lying, Inspector? What if she was too afraid to admit that someone had taken her? By not investigating, you're leaving other girls vulnerable. It could happen again.'

The man narrowed his eyes. 'I think perhaps, miss, that I am better placed than you to know what goes on here on this island. Miss Hart, is it?'

'Yes.'

'Well, Miss Hart, maybe things are different in London, but it's a great sin here for a woman to be having a bairn out of wedlock. I've known lasses go to great lengths to hide themselves and their situation. Now, was there anything else I can be helping you with?'

Audrey hesitated. 'Yes,' she said at length. 'There was one thing. I wondered if you might know anything or have any record of my mother's death. She died on Skye in May, 1843.'

'Oh aye. Where?'

'She fell from the Quiraing.'

The man gave a low whistle. 'Oh yes, I remember that. Two people, wasn't it?'

'I don't think so. Just my mother.'

'Maybe I'm getting things confused. There have been quite a few deaths: a woman fell from Port Neath a couple of years ago. And the Cuillins. People are forever falling from the Cuillins.'

'Might there be an investigation report, something like that?'

The inspector stood up, stretched his back and removed a large black book from a shelf. He took it over to the desk and began to thumb through it. 'Trotternish, then.' He turned over the pages slowly. 'No, there's no record of anything here, but there'll only be a report if there's been some sort of investigation. Probably there was none in your mother's case. The procurator in Trotternish will have a record of the death, but that'll be all.'

He closed the leather-bound book. 'Let me see you out.'

Audrey left the station building, her dejection deepening, and sat for a few minutes on a bench looking out onto the sheltered harbour, watching the sunlight on the water, the boats dipping on the swell. It was foolish to have thought that the police might be willing to help her, that the law would rally to her side. She remembered Dorothea's words in the week before she had left: *Little orphan girls against a wealthy man of status? It's not possible, Audrey, not in the world we live in now. We find other ways to win.*

She would just have to find one of those ways. She pushed herself up and walked along Church Street to the draper's shop, where she bought some good-quality brown fabric for a dress, a lace collar, and little white buttons made of shiny polished shell.

'You're staying for the black months, are you?' the woman at the counter asked her. She was a stout woman with a kindly, open face.

'I suppose I am, yes.' She thought again of her father's letter – of his insistence that she return home.

'Well, you're wise to be buying in warmer clothes. You might want to be getting another of these as well,' she said, feeling the fabric of Audrey's shawl with her short fingers. 'There's a woman on Wentworth Street who sells good thick ones that they make up at the woollen manufactory.'

'Thank you. I might do that.'

Audrey thought of Isbeil, and of the thinness of her shoulders as she covered them with the shawl. She shivered.

'Is there a jeweller's shop in Portree?' she asked. 'A silversmith?'

'Nothing like that, I'm afraid. Something for yourself, is it?'

'No. For someone else.'

She looked at the woman's round, honest face. 'I don't suppose . . .' She removed the silver bird from her pocket and held it out. 'Do you recognise this hallmark?'

The woman leant over the counter and peered at the pendant. 'I can't say I do, but then fabrics, those I know, silver not so much. My father might recognise it, mind. He travelled a fair bit in his youth. Wait you here now.'

She walked from the room and Audrey heard footsteps on stairs and a call.

After a minute or so the woman returned, a man with her, bent over with age. 'You show him what you showed me.'

Audrey held out her hand. He took the silver bird from her and brought it close to his eyes. 'That's a fine bit of craftsmanship, that is. A dove, is it?'

'I suppose it could be. I wondered about the mark here.' Audrey pointed. 'Is that a hallmark, do you think?'

The man squinted. 'Could be. Is it a tree there?'

'Yes. And it looks like there's a fish across it.'

'Well now, it could be Glasgow.'

'Glasgow?' she said sharply. 'Why do you say that?'

'The coat of arms for the city is having a tree and a fish in the shield, I think. I bided there awhile.'

Hadn't the minister said he was from Glasgow? But anyone could have brought the pendant to the island. The man held out the silver bird to hand it back to her. She took it.

'Of course it could be something else,' he suggested. 'It could be some pagan sign. Difficult to say.'

'Yes, thank you,' Audrey said, remembering her manners. 'I'm grateful to you both.' She looked at the woman. She was no longer smiling.

Audrey returned to Broadford in time for dinner. The new kitchen girl was helping Effy to serve. At first glance, she could almost have been Mairi – the same dark hair and narrow shoulders – but she did not have her grace, nor her strength of character. She visibly cowered before Effy, who blustered about the dining room, her skirts rustling. Audrey could not help but resent the new girl's presence. Mairi could not so easily be replaced.

'Did you get what you wanted in Portree?' Lord Buchanan asked as they took their seats.

Audrey glanced at him, wondering how much he knew. 'Yes thank you. I needed some clothing for the colder months.'

He curved his mouth into a smile. 'You're staying for the winter then? I admire your fortitude. I had rather thought all this business' – he gestured in the air – 'might have sent you running back to the warmer climes of London.'

Audrey met his eye. 'Well, I agreed to undertake the work. I intend to do so.'

'Very good, very good. Admirable resolve.'

There was a note of irritation in his voice. As Audrey watched him tuck his napkin into his collar, she was quite certain that he wanted her gone.

After dinner she walked along the library shelves, brushing her fingers over the gilded spines of the finely bound books, trying to find the volume she needed. She had looked in the encyclopedia before for hallmarks, but never for heraldic arms. The cat, Vinegar, sat on the sofa watching her. At last she found the one she sought and leafed through it to find the correct page. And there it was: a shield framed by two fishes, rings in both their mouths. Within the shield were a fish, a tree, a bird and a bell. The civic arms of Glasgow.

Here is the bird that never flew
Here is the tree that never grew
Here is the bell that never rang
Here is the fish that never swam

It was not the same as the silver bird's hallmark, but there were similarities. Could it signify Glasgow? There might be other coats of arms with trees and birds. Maybe the tree and the fish meant something else altogether: a fish out of water. A stranger.

She read through the journal for some time, but became increasingly unable to concentrate. There was a sound intruding at the edge of her consciousness. She watched Vinegar, who sat upright on the sofa, alert. He could hear it too – a rustling. She put down her book and moved over to the glass display cases. Nothing moved. For a few seconds she stood still, and then the sound came again, so faint she could not at first detect where it was coming from. Could it be a mouse? A rat? But then surely the cat would be there in an instant, and yet he still sat watching her. The rustling was louder now, somehow familiar, and Audrey felt sickness rising in her stomach as she made her way over to the other side of the room.

As she reached the display case containing the moths, the noise grew more distinct and her eye caught upon the source of the sound. One of the large death's-head hawkmoths was beating its wings furiously against the glass. Its body thrashed and writhed, and from the case came a high screaming sound. How could it be alive? It had been in the case for weeks. Ashamed of her own fear, Audrey backed away, stumbling into one of the shelves and sending books flying to the floor. She knew she had to try to help the thing get out, vile though it was. It seemed at that moment that the only thing to do was to break the glass, and rushing to the table, she picked up one of the polished hag stones.

She had meant merely to tap the glass to try to dislodge it from its frame, but she found she could not bear to look at the thrashing creature any longer, nor to be anywhere near it. For wasn't it after all a harbinger of death? She took the stone in her hands and threw it with all the force she could muster. There was a split second before it hit the glass where she saw that the moth was not moving at all, but was dead, still, pinned to the paper behind. There was a shattering, then a running of feet. Then silence.

By the following morning Audrey was calmer, but she could not dislodge the feeling that evil was descending. Even the day was dark and dank. Lamps had been lit throughout the house and the fire sputtered and choked against the damp air. Like the bird, the moth seemed to be an indication of misfortune to come: a warning. To Miss Buchanan, however, it meant something entirely different.

'I'm concerned about you, Audrey. I fear that you've become rather suggestible. You assured me when you first came here that you were reliable, resilient. Yet only eight weeks later you're throwing stones at glass cases in the belief that a moth has come alive and is going to harm you in some way.'

Audrey pressed her lips together. 'I'm sorry, Miss Buchanan, I will pay for the damage caused.'

Miss Buchanan waved the comment away. 'That is not my concern. I am worried about your state of mind, and about my work. It's important that it's done properly and quickly and by someone sufficiently detached from the superstitions to note them in an academic fashion.' Moving over to one of the cabinets, she removed a small reddish-brown object.

'We're all impressionable to some degree, especially when we spend time with those who believe the mystical to be real, and in times of stress. Even I have fallen into a superstitious mindset, when I was younger. When things were difficult.'

Audrey looked up at her.

'It is not easy to accept, Miss Hart, that you will never find companionship. Never run, never dance. Nor is it easy for others to accept. And when one is left on one's own with too much of one's own thoughts, they can turn inwards, can't they?'

Audrey nodded, unable to bring herself to say anything, for she was seized with shame that she was so easily readable, so obviously alone.

Miss Buchanan placed the object in her hand. It was flat-sided, smooth and light. 'A hundred years or so ago, people found these on the shores amongst the seaweed and believed them to be fairy eggs. They kept them beneath their pillows and wore them as amulets to ward off the evil eye. They carved them into boxes and ground them into powder, to make medicine.' She paused. 'But of course they're not fairy eggs. They're the seeds of a tree from the West Indies, which made their way to our shores. They are proof not of the existence of fairies, but of the Gulf Stream.' She gave Audrey a strange smile. 'We must make sure that we analyse what we see, what we hear – that we understand its true significance. We must remain logical even in the face of the uncanny. We must remain strong. We must search out the answers. Everything can be explained.' She nodded and walked from the room, Vinegar padding behind.

Audrey remained seated, the egg that was not an egg still in her hands. A few months ago she would have smiled at the notion that people once believed such a thing to be enchanted, but it was easy to dismiss the supernatural in the cold, swirling mass of London society, in the dining rooms and drawing rooms of the rich; even in her own pink-papered bedroom. Somehow things were different here. Somehow *she* was different. It was as though the beliefs that she had pushed down for years, the beliefs that she had been repeatedly told were the preserve of the uneducated, were resurfacing, had never really gone away. She was more frightened now, but she was also more determined. She would speak to the minister, however difficult that might be. She would find Mairi. She would not fail again.

★

By late morning, Audrey knew she was becoming ill. Her skin was cold but clammy; her heart struggled too hard to beat. Outside, the skies scowled and spat, but she wrapped herself in her travelling cloak and set off towards the manse. She would show the minister the silver bird with its Glasgow hallmark and watch how he reacted. She would ask him for the truth.

She walked down the track to the sea, the rain slanting against her face. As she neared the towpath, she saw Murdo, a dark shape in his hand. Occasionally he glanced about him, as though fearful of being watched. Keeping some distance behind, she followed him up the path through the trees, copper-coloured pine needles lining the glistening road. He came to the tree in the clearing that she had seen before, the bird corpses even more bedraggled in the rain, and began to nail the dark object into the wooden board. She crept closer, hoping that the snapping of twigs, the whisper of leaves would be drowned out by the drumming of the rain and the tapping of the hammer. As she neared the tree, she saw that he was nailing up what seemed to be a large crow.

Only it was not a crow.

Closer up, she saw that it was a creature with wings, half-bat half-bird, skin stretched taut over sinew. The face was unlike that of any animal she had ever seen. There was no beak, just a flat expanse of pale flesh studded with dull, dead eyes.

She heard again the rushing noise: the beating of wings and the whisper of voices. She felt the acid rising in her throat, and doubling over, she retched onto the ground, onto the pine cones and fallen leaves.

'Miss Hart? Miss Hart, are you all right?'

She heard his footsteps fast over the leaves, then his breath. When she lifted her head, she saw that the creature was gone and Murdo was staring at her with concern.

She was ill. She needed to return to the house.

For an entire day Audrey kept to her room, drinking only the tea and broth that the new kitchen girl brought her. Outside, winds raged in from the Atlantic and hail battered at the windows. Lying on her bed, she listened to the far-off roar of the waves as they raced towards Lanerly then smashed themselves on the rocks before it. She insisted that she did not wish for the doctor to be called, certainly not during a storm. She had no fever. She simply needed to rest.

When she slept, however, the dreams that took her were strange: vivid and dense and dark. She dreamt of an enchanted fairy cave of diamonds and golden shells – the grotto, made magical – which twisted all at once into a charnel house, grey and grim, the fairies' faces the grinning skulls of the dead. She saw her mother atop the Quiraing, birds that were not birds screeching in the sky about her, diving at her, tearing at her hair, jabbing at her eyes.

When she woke, shivering, she lay in the darkened room listening to the echoing boom of the waves and the shriek of the wind, telling herself over and over that none of it was real: it was only the nightmares that came with sickness.

These assurances didn't work, however – any more than telling people that their beliefs were a nonsense helped rid them of them. And when she tried to push aside visions of her mother and Mairi and the cloud of birds, the only thing that remained was Samuel and whatever it was that he had said to her father. *You are to return home immediately. I am afraid for you there.*

Towards the evening, she was woken from sleep by a rap on her door.

'May I come in?' It was Alec's voice. 'I've brought your supper.'

He entered the room and rested a tray on the little table: a pot of tea, cheese, some bannocks and a jar of rowan jelly, translucent orange-pink.

'I intercepted the maid on her way up. I wanted to talk to you.' He took the chair next to the bed.

Rain thrummed against the window, but the winds, Audrey noticed, had died down.

'I have to go to Edinburgh tomorrow morning, if the weather clears. I have a meeting with the publisher I told you about: he seems eager to print my work but he wants to discuss it with me.' His face was strained.

'Well, that's good, isn't it?'

'It is, yes. But Audrey,' he stretched his lips into a smile, 'I'm worried about you.'

'Oh Alec, I merely have a cold.' Even to her own ears her voice sounded high-pitched, brittle.

'You're unwell. You are not yourself.' He did not look at her.

'I'm merely over-tired, I think, but I will be up and about in no time.'

He lifted his eyes to hers now, seeming to try to read her. 'You must rest properly. We've all of us been strained these past weeks. You must not let my aunt push you, and you must not push yourself. You can't help anyone in this state.'

'I need to continue with my work, Alec. I need to find out what's going on.'

He put his hand over hers. 'I fear, Audrey, that this island is not good, not healthy for you. I wish I didn't have to go, not now. Will you promise me that you'll stay in the house while I'm away? That you'll leave any further work until I return?'

'Then it may be too late. What if Mairi is alive but trapped somewhere?'

A shadow crossed his face. Did he think her insane? 'I admire you, Audrey. Truly I do. But I also worry for you.'

'Well you needn't. I'm used to looking after myself.'

But she had always had her mother somewhere, protecting her, guiding her. She understood now that with her ring, her mother had gone. She had left her to face this all alone.

The sick feeling returned as soon as Alec left, and Audrey gripped the bedclothes to stop herself from shaking. For a moment she even considered calling after him to beg him to stay. No matter how much she tried to remain rational, she could feel things closing in, growing nearer. The day after tomorrow, Samhain would begin, the festival that marked the beginning of the dark months. It was the liminal time, the people said, the time when the boundary between this world and the other-world could more easily be crossed. Maybe that was why she felt this stifling, this tightening. She pushed the thought aside – she must rely on reason, not her fears.

She swallowed some water, trying to stop the nausea rising in her stomach. She prepared herself for bed, her hands still shaking: washing her face, applying her cream, untying her hair, combing it through – trying to find comfort in her everyday rituals, the safety of the habitual. Nothing, however, was normal. She could feel a constriction about her chest and throat, and though she loosened the strings on her nightdress, it was as if she could not breathe. She fought with the clasps on the window and threw it open, leaning out into the driving rain and drawing in gasping breaths, the coldness of it stinging her lungs.

It took a moment for her to understand what she saw. A white light hovered above the black water to the east of the bay. It seemed to waver in the night sky like a flame, burning from nothing. And then, before her eyes, it burnt out entirely and there was only the water – pulsing, dark.

Chapter 11

In the land of the fairies, Bainne begin to pine. She worried so much for her younger sister that she ceased to dance, and refused to eat. 'You must forget what the crow told you,' the fairies said. 'It was a trick to fool you. Nothing but lies.' But still she would not eat. Still she would not smile. And after three days and nights the fairies agreed to take her to their ruler.

The fairy king was a tall young man with auburn hair, skin like snow, and a cloak of emerald and gold. Bainne told him what the crow had said: of how she must return, of how she must find a way.

For a moment the king looked thoughtful, then he beckoned Bainne to him, and the bells on his fingers tinkled like stars.

'It is I who saved you from your parents,' he said. 'It is I who sent the little man. I will help your sister, as I helped you, but only on the condition that you will never after try to leave the fairy world. You must both stay here forever, where you are safe. And you must promise that, whatever happens, and whatever we do, you will not try to stop us.'

Bainne was eager to help her sister at once, so she agreed to what the fairy king asked.

Then he turned to his fairy servants and bade them prepare a chariot with four white horses as fast as the wind. 'It is time,' he said, 'to go above the earth.'

All day the people had been preparing. The livestock were driven down from the shielings and into the townships. Some of the animals were slaughtered, some driven into pens. In the crofts, cakes and scones were baking and boys were blackening their faces with peats and filling the basins for apple-dooking. At sunset, Samhain would begin. Audrey had forced herself out of bed and spent the day reading and at her notes. At five o'clock, the first of the bonfires was lit upon the hillside. From her window she could see the spots of light springing up around the countryside: tongues of flame to ward off the spirits. The people were taking precautions in the only way they knew. A few weeks ago she would have found it fascinating. Now she felt hollow with fear.

'It would be a very good time to go and observe the crofters,' Miss Buchanan said at dinner. 'Listen to what stories they relate, watch what practices they carry out. With the vanishing of the girls, they are no doubt in particularly superstitious mood. I would very much like to go myself.' She shook her head. 'In any event, they won't talk to me.' She looked grey with tiredness, Audrey thought, or perhaps with pain.

'Then I will go.'

'You're feeling strong enough?'

'I think so.'

Miss Buchanan looked at her unsurely. 'Nevertheless, I will ask Murdo to accompany you.'

'No,' Audrey said quickly. 'No thank you. I can go alone.'

Miss Buchanan raised her eyebrows. 'Is that wise? If you were to become sick . . .'

'They don't like him, Miss Buchanan,' she said quietly. 'They seem afraid of him.'

'Yes. Take his boy, then. Or the kitchen girl.'

Audrey shook her head. 'I would prefer not to.'

'Well, go alone if you insist. I'll be interested to hear of what you see. But don't over-tire yourself. We don't want you getting ill again.'

Audrey drank her coffee, bitter and rich, then went to her room to collect her notebook, gloves, hat and cloak. It was foolish to be afraid. Foolish.

Outside, the night sky was punctuated by flares from fires and the wind brought snatches of song to Audrey's ears. She wrapped her cloak tighter about her as she walked along the path towards Broadford. In the darkness the landscape had grown unfamiliar, pools of rainwater shimmering blackly. Across the bay she could see points of light in a circle and as she crossed the bridge she heard the chanting more clearly.

Nuair bhios mo chàirdean 'nan cad-al,
Air an leabaidh gu sàmh-ach,
'S ann bhios mis' anns an oidh-che fo an
choill' aig mo nàmh-aid.
While my kindred sleep peacefully in bed,
I shall be at night, hiding from my enemy.

Once she had passed the pier, she saw that people had assembled along the shore at Broadford in considerable numbers. They must have come from townships miles around. The points of light were, she now saw, torches, held high by the crofters. This was an age-old tradition, she reminded herself – nothing peculiar, nothing new.

As she drew closer, she made out faces she recognised, lit by the flames' flicker: Mackenzie, the storyteller from the ceilidh, was there, and some girls she had seen at the kirk. She tried to draw comfort from their familiarity. A group of men stood clustered together in conversation, and as she drew closer, she realised with a surge of revulsion that one of them was Angus Steele, the man who had tortured Eliza. Why was he not locked up? Surely he could not have been acquitted after what he had done. She backed away into the shadows, fear swarming over her skin. More and more people were joining the group, some carrying torches, which they lit from the others' flames, some bearing rods, caschroms and pitchforks, like an army assembled to fight an unseen enemy. Audrey could not fully understand what they were chanting, but she could make out a few words: '*Tha an t-àm air tighinn.*' The time is come.

With a start, she became aware of a woman standing close by her, with her cloak pulled up over her chin. It was the thin-faced woman from the ceilidh, she who had told of the changeling in a grave. 'Are you all right, miss?'

'Yes. I was just wondering what happened here at Samhain. I wanted to see the festival.'

The woman nodded towards the torch-bearers. 'They're after keeping the spirits away from Broadford with the fire and the steel.'

'And this is what happens every year, is it?' Audrey said, trying to keep her voice level.

'People are saying there's evil here.'

'Evil?'

'It's here that the lights have been seen. It's here that the girl drowned. It's from here that Mairi vanished. Folk think that tonight they'll come again.'

'For who?'

The woman looked at her strangely. 'We don't know that, miss.'

Audrey watched the ring of people, the moving row of lights. The crofters' faces were grave, unsmiling, and all at once terror seized her, closing its icy fingers over her throat. What if it was her who was next? What if this was what they had been building towards? First leaving her the body, then showing her Eliza, then taking Mairi. It was too much to be a coincidence. They'd come for the mother; now they would come for the daughter. But no, that was ridiculous. Her mother had fallen, simply fallen. And the other victims – Eliza, Isbeil, Mairi: they were young, without family, poor. She was entirely different. It was not her they wanted. It couldn't be.

She tried to stop her mind from running on like this. There were no spirits, no Host, only birds. She had to remain logical, just as Miss Buchanan had said. It was all superstition and nonsense, as her father and Dorothea had told her. But even her father had said he was afraid for her here. He must know something she did not, something her mother had told him many years ago.

The people were moving now, further along the road, and the wavering flames from their torches became fingers of light streaking through the darkness.

'Come this way,' the thin-faced woman said, walking ahead to join the throng.

Audrey tried to follow her, but everyone surged forward at the same time and, still weak from her illness, she found it impossible to keep up. She left the crowded path to run alongside, but the muddy ground sucked at her boots and she grew ever more confused. Shadows loomed at her, lights flashed. The chanting had become singing and a group of children sped past her, shrieking, playing some game she could not fathom. Then, at the edge of the group, she made out a face she knew.

'Mrs Campbell!'

The woman's pale eyes alighted on her. She did not smile, but reached out a hand. 'You shouldn't be here, *m'eudail*. Go home. Lock the doors. Cover the looking-glass. It's a bad time, Miss Hart. It's a bad time for you to be out.'

A younger, taller woman was at Mrs Campbell's side. She cast a nervous glance at Audrey.

'Have you seen anything?' Audrey's voice emerged broken and queer. 'Do you think Mairi will return, as Eliza did?'

Mrs Campbell shook her head. 'I don't know, I still don't know.'

'But you see things, you predict things . . .'

'I know more than I'm wanting to, but it's not always helpful. I see deaths before they come to pass, sometimes I see those returning home before they arrive, but when I try to see where Mairi is . . .'

'What do you see?'

'I don't see enough to know.'

'What do you see?' Audrey grabbed the woman's arm.

'She is below ground. That's what I see. I see that she is below ground, where the water is watching. That is all.'

Below ground, by the water. It was what Eliza had said.

'Is she still alive?'

'Something is alive, but whether it's her or something else, I don't know. There's nothing you can do, lass. There's no armour against fate.'

'We must go now,' the taller woman said, looking uncertainly at Audrey. 'We mustn't stay here.'

Audrey stood back to let them pass.

Mrs Campbell looked back at her. 'Away home now, Miss Hart.'

Below ground, where the water is watching.

★

The crowd surged on, to the north of Broadford. Children called and ran, people shouted to one another, others sang. As they passed yew trees running with water, it suddenly came to her. *Below ground, where the water is watching*: it meant in the kirkyard by the sea. Mairi was with Isbeil.

Audrey left the people and ran along the path towards the graveyard. It had begun to rain and the air was filled with humming, though whether it was the chanting of the people or the sound of the wind she no longer knew. As she moved away from the crowd, the darkness grew denser, thicker, seeming to press upon her and drag her down. Mud wrenched at her boots and branches clawed at her face. By the time she reached the kirkyard, she could barely see where she was going and had to feel her way along the wall, past weed-covered mounds and the dark, uneven shapes of the gravestones, to reach the spot where they had held Isbeil's paltry burial ceremony.

Closer now to the plot of land, Audrey knew that something about the ground was different. Where they had stood to scatter rowan branches there was now a mound of soil. With a surge of nausea, she understood that the grave where Isbeil's coffin should have lain was empty, dug out. In that instant she was a child again, standing by her mother's coffin, believing it an empty box. Only this grave was not entirely vacant. As she stood staring down into the hole, lit only by a faint glimmer of moonlight, she made out the edge of something, a white shape emerging from the earth. Not giving herself time to think further, she sat on the edge of the grave, then jumped down into it, her boots sinking into the mud. The sound was all around her now: the humming, the soaring of the wind, the raindrops on the earth. *Below ground, where the water is watching.*

She felt for the object she had seen from the surface and struggled to wrench it free from the mud.

'What in God's name are you doing?'

Audrey started back. A tall figure stood above her, a rush lamp in his hand, his features hidden beneath a wide-brimmed hat. It was the minister. In the glare of the lamp, she could see what she was holding: a clay doll.

'What is this?' she shouted at him. 'What have you done with Isbeil?'

The minister stared at her, then at the clay figure.

'You must come out of there.' Setting down the lamp, he lay on the ground, reached forward to take her arms, and dragged her from the pit. Then he shone the light into the grave.

'The coffin is gone. They must have taken it to higher ground.'

'They?' Audrey stood at the side of the grave, clutching the clay doll.

'The fishermen. They believe that suicides scare away the herring.'

She gave a high laugh. 'You expect me to believe that? Where is she? What have you done with her? Where is Mairi?'

The minister looked at her intently, taking in her mud-covered clothing and tear-streaked face. 'What are you doing out here, Miss Hart?'

'I am trying to find out the truth.' She must not cry.

'What's that in your hand?'

'You tell me.'

He reached to take it from her, but Audrey stepped backwards.

'I think we'd better be taking you back to Lanerly. Here, have this.' He removed his coat and placed it over her shoulders. 'Come with me. Quickly. Out of the rain.'

Audrey stood shaking, clasping the clay figure in her hands. 'There's something here,' she said brokenly. 'Something that will lead us to Mairi, I know it.'

The minister shook his head. 'There's nothing here but mud, Miss Hart. Let's get you home.'

Audrey did not know quite how they got back to Lanerly. Things had begun to drift into one another – phrases, faces, light and dark. She was aware that they were in the back parlour, where a bright fire blazed. The kitchen girl had placed a blanket over her and tried to feed her some hot broth, but she had no desire to eat. She wanted only to know what was happening to her.

The minister placed a cold palm to her forehead. 'As I thought, she's feverish. It was fortunate I saw her when I was coming back to the manse.'

Miss Buchanan was staring at her. 'I ought not to have sent her out. It was a mistake.'

'It was important that I went.' Audrey tried to tell the older woman with her eyes that they could not speak with the minister present, but Miss Buchanan only frowned at her.

'What are you holding?' She stretched out her hand, but Audrey kept the figure tight in her grasp.

'It's one of those clay figurines the fishermen make,' the minister said.

'It was in Isbeil's grave,' Audrey whispered. 'The body is gone.'

'As I tried to explain to Miss Hart, they must have moved it to higher ground so as not to scare off the fish.' The minister sighed. 'This is the madness we must contend with.'

Miss Buchanan was still studying Audrey. 'You are very unwell, I think. Minister, please fetch Dr McGilvray. Quickly.'

Audrey gazed into the fire, figures seeming to leap within it. She became aware that Miss Buchanan had placed her hand on her arm. It was the first time she had ever touched her. 'I should never have kept you here. It was selfish of me. I should have seen how impressionable you were. I think perhaps it's time for you to go home.'

'No! I must find Mairi. I must know what has happened to her.' She lowered her voice. 'The minister.'

'What of him?'

Audrey looked into Miss Buchanan's face. Her skin was parchment-white and her pupils were so large that her eyes seemed almost black. She could see the wavering flames reflected within them.

'What about the minister, Miss Hart?'

Audrey looked away, wondering if she could tell Miss Buchanan what she believed. But then what *did* she believe? She had thought he was somehow involved, that maybe they all were. Perhaps, however, this was nothing to do with the minister or with Murdo, but with forces far less comprehensible.

'I don't know,' she said eventually. 'I fear that Mairi has been taken somewhere she doesn't want to be. I've seen things, things I can't explain. I'm afraid. I'm so afraid.' She put her hands to her face.

'What things have you seen, Audrey?'

'Birds that are maybe not birds. Lights in the bay. Noises in the sky, within the house. Surely you've heard them too.'

Miss Buchanan narrowed her eyes. 'Noises. What sort of noises?'

'There's something here, Miss Buchanan. Something evil. The crofters know it.'

'Miss Hart, the crofters believe all sorts of things – incredible, fantastical things.'

'And maybe some of them are real.'

The older woman shook her head. 'I've been living too much among the dead, among my papers and letters and stories. I failed to see what was happening to you. I have failed to look after you.'

Audrey was looking into the fire again when she became aware that the minister had returned, Dr McGilvray with him.

'I hear you're not too well, Miss Hart.' The doctor stood

before her. She could smell the damp rising from his coat.

'There's nothing wrong with me.'

'Miss Hart believes there's something evil here,' Miss Buchanan said. 'I fear the fever may have gone to her brain.'

Audrey felt the darkness of their shadows, felt the weight of their presence pushing down on her. She tried to stand up. 'I'm not delusional,' she said, as forcefully as she could manage. 'Someone or something is taking girls, and no one is doing anything.'

'Miss Hart,' the minister said. 'You've had a bit of a time this evening. You need some sleep.'

'You think I can sleep when there's danger all about us?'

'The only danger is in your own mind.' His tone was soothing, but there was something hard within it.

'Let's get you upstairs, shall we?' The doctor stepped forward.

'No!' Audrey knew suddenly and violently that she must not be alone with him. She clutched at Miss Buchanan's arm. 'I'm not ill. That's not what's happening.'

The doctor moved closer to her, a vial in his hand.

'Get away from me!'

All at once the minister was holding Audrey by the shoulders and the doctor had placed his hand on her jaw, using his other hand to force the liquid into her mouth. She tried to fight but she had no strength, and as they stepped away from her, she fell back into the chair. 'What have you done? Have you poisoned me?'

Miss Buchanan was standing with her back to the fire: a dark form silhouetted against the flames. 'No, Audrey, they have not poisoned you. Dr McGilvray is merely trying to calm you. We are helping you, my dear.'

She reached forward and took the clay figure from Audrey's hand, and Audrey realised that she could no longer grip with her fingers. All her strength seemed to have sapped away and a cold heaviness was spreading through her body. As she slipped from consciousness, she stared at Miss Buchanan, who was still watching her, unblinking. Her eyes seemed even darker now: black as jet, black as night.

Part Three

Chapter 12

When a month and a day had come and gane,
Kilmeny sought the green-wood wene;
There laid her down on the leaves sae green,
And Kilmeny on earth was never mair seen . . .
She left this world of sorrow and pain,
And return'd to the land of thought again.

A blade of silver sunlight woke her, slicing through a window high up in the wall. She was not at Lanerly. She struggled to a sitting position, her head swimming. Her mouth felt sticky and vile, her limbs stiff and sore. The room was circular, with whitewashed walls that seemed to spin. She saw a stool, a small wooden table and, hanging on one of the walls, a tapestry. There was only one window and a small fire, unlit. The room was freezing cold.

She lowered herself out of the bed, but the ground slanted away from her and she had to clutch the iron frame to stop herself from falling. She stood for a moment while the room straightened itself and saw that she was wearing a white nightdress and a cotton shift. Her heart gave a shudder as she wondered who had changed her.

She pushed the stool up to the wall and climbed carefully atop it so that she could see through the narrow window. They were right on the coast, the bay curving around to a lighthouse. Was she still on Skye? She started at the sound of the door opening.

'I thought I was hearing you moving about. See will you get down from there?' It was the wide-set nurse who had guarded Eliza, her small eyes like currants in her doughy face.

'What is this place?'

The nurse carried a pair of dirty-looking slippers and a bundle of clothing. She dumped them on the bed and walked from the room, her hips swaying. 'You're to be putting them on.'

'Wait!' Audrey rushed after her, but was met by the clang of the door closing. As she fell against it, she heard the scrape of the key in the lock. She slid to the floor and stared at her surroundings as they shifted before her. The tapestry was an intricate design of knights in battle. This was not a hospital or an asylum. It must be someone's home. She stood up and walked unsteadily back to the window so that she could see out, but there was only the lighthouse, mountains whose forms she did not recognise, and the sea, miles and miles of sea, pinpricks of light glittering upon it coldly, like crystals. She moved over to the bed and with shaking hands put on the clothing the woman had left for her: a brown gown, far too large, greyish petticoats, and white stockings, torn at the heel. There was no looking-glass, but she could guess at what she must look like: a lunatic.

The nurse returned some time later with a tray containing a hunk of bread, some thin broth and a cup of tea. Audrey felt a little steadier by now, but still strange and remote.

'Please will you tell me where I am? Whose house this is?'

The woman's black eyes darted towards her. 'You're where we can be keeping a watch on you.'

'Who is "we"?'

'You eat your food now.'

The nurse left, shutting the door again. The room filled quickly with the foul smell of the soup. Audrey sipped at the tea, but it tasted strange and bitter. She thought of Mairi and had a sudden image of her alive, screaming. She had to get to her. She went to the door and began to bang on it with her fists. 'Open this door!'

She pounded until her knuckles ached and then stepped back, cradling her hands. A moment later, the door opened. It was not the nurse.

'You'll be doing yourself an injury banging on the door like that, miss.'

'Effy!' Audrey's chest flooded with relief. The girl had never been friendly, but she was at least a more familiar face. 'You must tell me: what is this place? Why have I been brought here? *Who* has brought me here?'

'Will you step back, Miss Hart?'

Audrey felt her stomach drop as she saw the look in Effy's eyes: hatred, unsheathed like a cat's claw.

'I'm not mad,' she said quietly, 'if that is what they think.'

'Aye. So that digging up graves, that was a bit of fun, was it just?'

'I thought . . . I thought . . .' What had she thought?

'Shouldn't have been playing Miss Buchanan's games, should you? Shouldn't have come here in the first place, meddling with our beliefs for a bit of fun. You English are all the same.'

'Was it Miss Buchanan who sent me here? Or was it the minister?'

No answer.

'What did he tell you? That I was to be locked up for my own safety? That I was insane?'

Effy folded her arms. 'You're to be kept here till arrangements are made for you to be taken away.'

'Taken away where?'

'You're a danger to yourself and others.'

'According to whom?'

'According to them that knows.' She looked at the tray. 'Have you anything against your food? You've barely eaten any. You'll not grow strong like that, will you?'

'Who is looking after the house while you're here, Effy? Or are we close enough to Lanerly for you to be able to carry out your duties there as well?'

Effy's mouth was a thin line. 'Kind of you to be

concerned, Miss Hart, but we're managing. You worry
about getting yourself better.' She moved swiftly from the
room, slamming the door shut behind her.

'Effy!'

Audrey heard the key turn in the lock, then the cold clip
of the girl's footsteps moving off along a corridor and down
a flight of stairs.

For a minute or so she sat on her chair trying to fathom
how she might escape, but it seemed impossible. Even if
she were to find a way out, she had no money, no proper
clothes and no shoes. She did not even know where she
was.

After a time, she returned to her bed and covered her
face with her aching hands, suddenly overcome with a
great weariness and hopelessness. She lay back down on
the cold sheets. She slept.

The next day Audrey's mind was clearer, as though the
sediment was falling to the bottom of the glass. She was
still unsteady on her feet, but her thoughts were less
disordered, and the feeling of darkness and constriction
was lifting. At first she wondered if it was because she was
away from Lanerly and whatever evil was there, but as her
thoughts grew calmer it occurred to her that it might be
something far simpler: someone had been poisoning her.

She had much time to think in her white-walled room.
The nurse left a few books for her, old travel memoirs and
medical manuals that she must have found in the house,
some with the inscription *Ex Librum Mathieson* on the title

page. She could not focus on the text, however. She thought of who had brought her here, and why. Effy had said that she was to be kept here until she could be taken away. Where? It was possible, she supposed, that they intended to return her to London, to be locked in an asylum. Or maybe she would be sent somewhere else, where she would never be found.

She ran her fingers over the embossed lettering on the spines of the books and thought of Samuel and the beautifully bound volumes he had once brought to her classroom as offerings. Tricks. She felt the rage grow within her, against him, against Miss Hodge and all of them at the orphanage, against Dorothea and her father. Against whoever it was that sought to detain her here now. It struck her that she had been wasting her time feeling guilty and ashamed when she should have been angry. She should have been furious from the first. A man had abused his trust and duped the vulnerable, and all anyone could do when Audrey tried to speak about it was to shush her as though she was a naughty child.

For hours she watched the gannets as they drew back their wings and plunged with astonishing speed into the frothing sea. Her mind ran back over her conversations with Miss Buchanan – about the abductions, about how girls were taken to bear the spirits' children. What had Effy meant by 'Miss Buchanan's games'? Could it be possible that the woman was playing out some strange folkloric fantasy, and that the minister and the doctor were helping her? Or perhaps she was stirring things up to test the crofters, teasing them, goading them, taking their beliefs as far as they would go. She thought of Miss Buchanan's glass-blue eyes and how they lit up when Audrey had spoken of Eliza Fraser. *Has there been any more talk of abductions?* She thought too of what Mr Shawfield had said about Miss Buchanan: how sad it was that she was confined to the house, unable to meet with the crofters and hear their tales.

There was no clock in Audrey's room, nothing to mark the passing of time save for the height of the sun, the lengthening of shadows against the wall, the gradual fading of the light. As dusk descended on that second day, it came to Audrey: somehow Miss Buchanan was bringing the girls to her. She was collecting them, just as she gathered the stories. Mairi was in the house.

When the nurse came for her the following morning, Audrey was ready. Hearing footsteps on the stairs, she rushed to the doorway, her fist balled, and as the door opened, she hit the woman as hard as she could, then ran past her along the hallway and down a narrow winding staircase – her legs, as though in a dream, not moving fast enough. She could hear the woman behind her, but she was heavy and slow and winded by her fall.

'Stop, you dirty scut!'

Audrey raced faster, running her hand along the banister to stop herself from tripping. At the bottom of the staircase was a white door, which she pulled at but which was shut fast. She fled into a dark corridor that seemed to go on forever, but which finally emerged onto a landing, and then she was at another door, which she opened, her breath ragged as she raced down another flight of stone stairs. She found herself in a wide hallway with a high ceiling and could see what must be the front door before her, but as she reached it, it was opened from the other side and Dr McGilvray stood before her, his expression flat.

'Going for a walk, were you, Miss Hart?'

Audrey stepped backwards, shaking, her breath coming in gasps.

The doctor closed the door heavily behind him and she heard the slow tread of footsteps approaching from another corridor. Effy emerged, and behind her came the nurse, her eye already swelling shut.

'Good day to you, sir,' the maid said. 'You'll see we've been having a wee bit of trouble with our charge. There's tea for you in the kitchen.'

The doctor nodded and walked from the hallway without looking again at Audrey.

The nurse hit her then, full in the mouth, and she felt her lip split, the blood bloom. She struck again and Audrey crumpled, the ceiling above her seeming to shatter. She was dimly aware that they were hauling her back to her room, her ankles dragging on the stairs, until she was being pushed face first onto the bed and she felt cold leather on her wrists as they strapped her down.

When she tried to pull herself up, the nurse was on her in an instant. 'You just lie there. Or are we going to have to get the good doctor to come and give you some more medicine, eh?'

Audrey tried to shake her head, but it would not move.

For some time there was silence, save for the crackle of flames and the quiet movement of the women, and Audrey felt herself drifting from consciousness, sinking. All at once there was a blazing heat by her cheek: a firebrand was inches from her face.

'You try that again and we'll burn you,' the nurse said. 'Just like Eliza Fraser was burnt.'

Eliza's destroyed face flashed before her and Audrey felt sick with fear. She was quite sure that they would do it; they would brand her as a farmer might mark a calf.

Then the heat faded. The fire iron clattered in the grate. The door closed and the women's footsteps retreated, their voices echoing in the passageway. Audrey lay on the bed, the straps cutting into her flesh, her face and head throbbing, a terrible tiredness upon her.

She closed her eyes, and her mother was there. Audrey felt no surprise, only relief, washing over her like a gentle tide. Even without the ring, her mother had returned. She smoothed Audrey's hair as she had done when she was little, on the nights when she was sick or sleepless or sad. It would be all right, she murmured. There was always a way out. It just might not be the way you thought.

On the fourth day, a visitor came.

'A visitor?'

'Aye,' the nurse said. 'Come to see how you are.'

Audrey's stomach gave a flip. It must be the minister, or maybe Murdo sent to report back on her.

'Who is it?'

The nurse stared at her coldly. 'Walk behind me. You know what'll happen if you try anything.'

When she entered the corridor, Audrey saw Effy standing against the wall. She followed close after Audrey so that she was hemmed in between the two women. They rounded a corner and came upon a white door, which the nurse unlocked. Audrey was sweating now, her hands clammy. They would have told the minister of her attempt to escape, and perhaps that in itself had decided her fate.

But it was not the minister at all.

'Alec!'

His eyes opened wide when he saw her. 'Good God. What's happened to you?' He stepped forward as if to touch her, but the nurse stood before him. 'Best to be keeping back, sir. She's a temper on her.'

Alec's expression darkened. 'You've hurt her.'

Audrey put her hand up to her cheek, acutely conscious of what a fright she must look with her odd garments, her strangely pinned hair and her swollen mouth.

'She has only herself to be blaming for that,' the nurse said.

Alec's eyes were still on Audrey's face. 'Oh indeed? Please leave us.'

'The doctor said—'

'The doctor be damned.'

The nurse and Effy exchanged a look. 'Very well, sir. You can have a few minutes, if you feel that strong on it.'

They left the room, but Audrey could tell from the cessation of footsteps that they were standing just outside, listening.

'How did you find me?' she whispered. 'Where are we?'

'Murdo's boy told me you were here. We're in Kyleakin, close to the mainland.' Alec shook his head. 'I'm so sorry: this is my fault. If I hadn't left you . . .'

'It isn't your fault, Alec.'

'I knew you were ill and confused. I should have stayed.'

'I'm not confused any more.'

She could see him taking in her matted hair, her changed appearance.

'It's true, Alec. Honestly. My thinking is clearer than it has been for days, weeks even.'

'And do you still believe that the Sluagh have been taking people?'

'I believe that I've been put here to keep me away from the truth, and from Mairi.'

'Mairi.' He was watching her closely, tenderly. He was not really listening. 'What did they do to you here, Audrey? Did they beat you?' He reached out his hand and touched her cheek. She thought for a moment that she might cry, but there was no time for that.

'Alec, do you know who ordered me to be kept here?'

He shook his head. 'No. I couldn't get anything out of my aunt: she would only say that you'd grown very unwell and that you'd been taken somewhere you wouldn't be a danger to yourself.'

'I'm not unwell, Alec. If I was unwell it was because I was being made so.'

She saw doubt flicker in his eyes. 'By whom? Who do you think was making you unwell?'

'I'm not sure. Perhaps the minister. Perhaps Murdo. Perhaps . . .' She stopped herself: she could not lay any blame on his aunt. 'I know it sounds mad. I know it does, but something strange has been happening; something that others don't want me to know about. I need to get out of this place.'

He was silent for a moment. There was just the soft sound of his breathing. Audrey leant forward and held his arm. 'You have to help me, Alec.'

'Enough of that now.' The nurse had returned. 'Let go of him, Miss Hart.'

Audrey moved closer, so close that she could smell the sea in his hair.

'They're keeping me in the tower at the front of the house,' she whispered. 'Please help me.'

The nurse pulled her back. 'You let him be now, miss. Don't be vexing yourself. Best that you go now, Master Buchanan.'

Alec's eyes were still on hers. Did he think her insane, or was there some gentleness there?

He turned to the nurse. 'Miss Hart is evidently unwell. No matter what her conduct, you will treat her with care.' His words were clipped and hard. He stared at Effy, who had followed the nurse into the room. 'I fancy you'll not keep your position at Lanerly if Miss Hart is further injured. Nor will you receive any reference. Make sure she's well looked after.'

Taking his hat under his arm, he walked towards the door. He turned back for a moment to look at Audrey, but his expression was unreadable.

For many hours that night Audrey lay awake listening to the wind whining and whirling around the tower. She tried to picture Alec's face, to remember his expression. He had seemed concerned, he had seemed to care for her, but she had thought that of Samuel, and she had been entirely wrong. She had been wrong about so much.

She was lapsing into sleep when she heard a thud, as of something hitting the outside wall. She wondered if it had been part of a dream, but after a minute she heard the noise again, closer this time. She threw back the blanket, ran to the window and opened it. As she pushed the chair up to the window, she heard a clunk: something had landed by her feet. She bent down and, in the moonlight, saw the shine of flint. It was a rock, and attached to it, a piece of string.

She picked up the rock, climbed onto the chair and looked down. She could see a dark form by the tree a short distance from the house, the arms outstretched, making a movement of hauling in a rope. After a moment's hesitation, she pulled on the string, the tension growing until she found that it was attached to a coil of rope. She tied the rope around the base of the bed, pulled on her slippers and then, taking the rope in one hand, began squeezing herself through the small window. Her head and shoulders went through easily enough, but even after days of barely eating, her hips stuck and she had to pull herself through the opening, the stone scraping her flesh, until she was sitting on the narrow sill beneath. Slowly she turned, then lowered herself down, finding footholds as best she could on the rough stone wall. As she descended, the rope began to tighten and she could hear the screeching of the bed as it was dragged across the floor. She descended faster, her feet slipping, imagining the noise alerting the nurse and Effy, their footsteps on the stairs as they raced to her room.

Sure enough, within a minute she heard shouting, but from the ground floor: they had not yet made it to her room. She slid down the last few feet, the rope tearing at her hands. And then someone was behind her. She turned.

'You.'

Alec led her over the wet grass to his boat, pulling her by the hand. The moon was high and draped everything in silver: the ground, the waves, the little boat that waited for them. He had brought a cloak, which Audrey wrapped about herself while he slipped the mooring lines. They could hear shouting from the tower: Effy and the nurse knew now that she had escaped, and would be running down the stairs towards the door. Alec pushed the boat off and began to row across the water fast and strong, his head down against the wind.

After ten minutes or so, he stopped, his shoulders heaving, and sat back. He pointed at a large leather bag, too breathless to speak. Audrey opened it and drew out some of her own clothing: a dress and shawl, her leather boots.

She pulled off her torn, grass-stained slippers and began lacing up the boots. When she looked up, she saw Alec was watching her.

'We must go to the mainland and get you back to London.'

'No. I can't do that. I need to find Mairi.' And, Audrey thought, I know where she is.

'Maybe so, but you can't return to Broadford. I can't protect you there. I don't know what they'll do.'

'Alec, I'm not asking for your protection. I'm asking you to trust me. I'm asking you to take me back there. I have my reasons.'

'What reasons, Audrey? At least tell me why we must go back.'

'I would tell you if I could. Please, just do as I ask.'

He leant forward suddenly, took her face in his hands, and kissed her so that she could taste the salt on his lips. 'As you once said, brave or foolhardy.'

He picked up the oars and again they pushed on swiftly over the dark water. After a time he gripped the halyard and hoisted the mainsail. It filled quickly, catching the breeze, and the little skid surged ahead, the rigging humming, spray bursting around the bow. Audrey held herself tensed against the wind, watching the dark waves streaked with white, salt-hardened strands of hair whipping her face, the taste of Alec's lips still on hers.

Within the hour they reached Broadford Bay and she could see lights at the pier. Alec dropped the sails, and took up the oars again, guiding the boat slowly and almost silently towards Lanerly, the only sounds the steady creak of the rowlocks, the wash of the waves. When they were close to the pier, Audrey crouched down in the boat to avoid being seen.

'Here,' Alec whispered, passing her a blanket. 'Lie down. Cover yourself with this. There are men on the pier.'

As they neared the shore, the voices grew louder and Audrey, lying in the bottom of the boat, shivered as she recognised Murdo's amongst them.

'Not long now,' Alec muttered to her. She could feel the change in the boat's motion as he slowed to pick up the buoy, and the gentle swing with the bow turning head to wind as he hauled in the line. Then he was by her again, lifting the blanket, touching her shoulder. 'It's all right.'

'Did anyone see you?'

'I don't think so. We need to go and talk to my aunt now. Tell her what you think is going on.'

Audrey felt her throat constrict. She could not tell him she suspected even Miss Buchanan, not without evidence.

'Tomorrow. We'll speak to her tomorrow. I don't yet want her to know I'm here. I'll stay at the inn.'

Alec frowned at her. 'You can't. You're soaked through. And how will you get there? You'll be seen.'

'I'll manage.' She attempted in vain to stop herself from shaking.

'Audrey, the men at the inn may report your arrival back to Murdo, to the minister. I have no idea what they'll do. We need to get you back into Lanerly. I know my aunt can seem cold and remote, but I believe she has an affection for you and that she'll protect you, especially when I speak for you.'

Audrey shook her head. If Miss Buchanan saw her before she found Mairi, everything would be lost. 'I can't risk being seen,' she insisted. 'By anyone.'

'Then we'll enter through the servants' tunnel. We should be able to get you up to your room unnoticed.'

'I don't know, Alec.' Her teeth were chattering now, through cold and exhaustion. Maybe he was right. Maybe it was the only option.

'Come on. Take my hand.' He helped her out of the boat and up the steps to the side of the house. 'This way.'

Audrey saw the tunnel, then – a dark mouth in the side of the hill – and she stopped, seized with terror. She could not go in there.

Alec, however, was already in the entrance, brushing things out of the way with his hands, and Audrey forced herself to follow him, for she did not want to be left alone in the darkness. Inside, the place smelt dank, of rotten leaves and rust. She could hear water dripping from overhead and feel moisture from the ground seeping through her shoes. Once she had taken a few steps into the tunnel she could see almost nothing, but felt with her hands along the damp wall. She walked into something and almost screamed, but it was only Alec, standing entirely still. 'What is it?'

'I heard a noise,' he whispered.

'What?'

'Listen.'

After a moment, she could hear it too. A low keening sound. 'What is that?'

'I don't know,' he breathed. 'I don't know.'

He went forward faster now, almost running, and Audrey tried as best she could to keep up with him. It was slippery underfoot, and more than once she stumbled to the ground and had to pull herself up again. The keening grew louder as they got closer. It was a girl's voice. The tunnel opened out and Alec was running now, his feet splashing in puddles of water. Audrey followed, trying to summon what strength she still had, until all at once the ground seemed to give way, a door clanged, and she was lying on her back in utter blackness. The wailing had stopped.

Chapter 13

They rode through the night to Bainne's home, where they found her little sister in the cupboard beneath the stairs, bruised and afraid. Bainne took her in her arms and they ran through the house as quickly as they could. As they reached the door, however, Bainne's parents awoke and saw them, and her father took up his pistol and gave chase.

The fairy king seized a peat from the still-glowing fire and, as they left, threw an ember from the peat upon the thatch. The ember took spark and the house took light. Bainne kept running, but she should hear the crackle and roar of the fire as it tore through the little wooden house. She heard the screams of her parents. She heard the screech of the crow, and when she looked up, she saw it zigzagging through the night sky, its tail alight, its wings scorched. But she kept running, running, back to her true home, back beneath the ground. She did not look back, not once.

Audrey was aware of a strong animal smell, of urine. Of bodies. Then came the sound of metal on flint: a tinderbox. First there were just a few gold sparks in the darkness, and then the flying flames of the lighted charcloth. The room flickered into light, the oil lamp throwing shadows onto the ceiling, showing a pattern of shells. They were no longer in the tunnel, but a room, with empty bookcases lining the walls.

'Alec?' she whispered. 'Are you there?'

'Yes. Yes, I'm here.'

'What is this place?'

'It was my study, once upon a time.'

As she pushed herself up to sitting, she saw damp wallpaper peeling from the walls, boxes stacked on a large wooden desk. On the other side of the room a movement in the shadows caught her eye. Her heart squeezed tight. She made out a large animal cage, its bars black against the grey walls. Within it were two white forms. She pressed her hand over her mouth to stop herself from crying out.

A girl moved to the front of the cage and took hold of the bars. Her face emerged gaunt and colourless in the glow of the lamp. She was dressed entirely in white and her dark hair fell dankly about her shoulders.

'Mairi,' Audrey said weakly as she stood up.

Alec was lighting another lamp. As the flame burst into life, Audrey saw a second girl standing against the wall at the back of her cage, a girl she did not know.

She turned to Alec, who stood with his arms folded,

looking at the girls. His face expressed no surprise, no alarm, no distress, and she felt herself hollow, her insides scraped out.

'Alec, what have you done?'

'I have saved them,' he said calmly.

'Saved them?'

'Yes.'

She looked again at Mairi, blinking in the light like a newborn pup.

'You've been keeping them down here, in the dark.'

'No, not always in the dark,' Alec said defensively. 'Only sometimes. When it was necessary.'

'Which has been often.' It was the first time Mairi had spoken. Her voice was flat and dead.

Audrey wanted to go to her, but it would mean moving closer to Alec, and more than anything she needed to escape – to get help. She looked about her. The shelves were all empty, save for a few jars. Beyond Alec was a door, shut.

She spoke slowly, trying to keep the panic from her voice. 'Why have you been keeping them here, Alec? What are you saving them from?'

'I had hoped, Audrey, that you would have worked that out for yourself.'

She glanced behind her and saw another door, also closed. 'Spirits?' she asked. 'You think you're saving them from the Sluagh?'

Alec laughed. 'How far you've come from the London girl who joined us in September. There are no spirits here,

Audrey. The only evil that exists on this island takes the form of man. A man of the church.'

She felt an icy sickness sweep through her.

'Yes. You see it now, don't you? Well, I saw it months ago; saw him seeking out the weak and slithering into their lives, claiming he was carrying out the work of God. I saw what he truly was.'

Audrey's mind raced to rearrange the pieces. 'Isbeil.'

'I got to Isbeil too late. He'd already sullied her. She tried to get rid of the child with potions, but she made herself ill.'

She pictured Isbeil that first night on the boat to Skye, shivering and sick and afraid. 'You killed her because it was too late to save her?'

'I didn't kill her,' Alec snapped. 'What do you think I am? An ogre? No, it was a terrible accident. She tried to get out of the boat.'

The boat. He had been taking them all by boat. Audrey thought of Isbeil's face, her battered head. She backed slowly towards the door. A few more steps and she would be able to reach the handle. 'Why didn't you just report the minister?'

'You of all people ask me that? And you needn't bother trying. It's locked.'

Audrey stopped. She looked at Mairi, shrouded in grubby white. The girl's eyes were still on her face. The other girl remained towards the back of the cage, but she could see that she too wore white, encrusted with dirt.

'The dresses,' she murmured. 'They were your sister's.'

She thought of the framed portrait: the fair-haired girl in a white gown, staring boldly out.

Alec's face tightened. 'They were, yes.' In the glow of the lamp, his skin was ghostly grey.

'He got to her too.'

He did not answer at once. 'You have no idea what it is like to watch your own sister turn from bright young girl to silent victim. She lost her confidence, her colour. Her body swelled with it, like a tumour.'

Flora had been pregnant, then. That was why she had drowned herself. That was why they never spoke of it.

'She wouldn't say who it was. She stopped talking, even to me. Maybe she thought I should have known, that I should have guessed. But I didn't. I didn't work it out until I saw him do it again, to Christy.'

Christy. It took a moment for Audrey to understand. Christy Maclean. Murdo's daughter.

At her name, the other girl had begun to cry. Audrey put her hands to her face. How long had Christy been down here, in this close, dank cell? Months, she thought. It must be months. Much of it alone in the darkness. And all that time her parents had lived only yards away, in anger and silence, resenting everyone around them, blaming each other for driving her away.

'I understood, you see, when I saw the charm.'

'The silver bird,' Audrey breathed.

'Yes. They found it after Flora drowned herself and assumed it was a gift from her lover. Which in a way it was. The dove of peace.' He gave a short laugh.

Audrey pictured the small silver bird, its wings out-stretched. *Keep me as the apple of your eye; hide me in the shadow of your wings*. It was nothing to do with the Sluagh; it was a bird of God.

'He used the same cheap trick with Christy. A poor little silver bird for a young girl's soul. I saw it on a bit of ribbon about her neck, and then I knew.'

Audrey stared at Christy. Though the girl was half hidden in shadows, Audrey could see she was as thin as a lath and caked in filth. Glancing to her right, she saw that there was a servants' call bell on the wall. 'Alec, why didn't you tell anyone? The police? The kirk?'

'You think they would believe me – a strange young man who writes fairy tales – over a man of the church?'

'But you are respected. Your father . . .'

He shook his head. 'My father is reviled, and I'm pitied at best, hated at worst. There was a time, you see, after my sister died, when I was unwell, full of the world's rage. My father had me shut away in the very place you were detained. For months. That's how I knew where you were. I didn't need Murdo's boy to tell me. No, Audrey. I am the laird's mad son. I'm surprised you didn't know that already. Against that, what evidence did I have? Only the silver birds. Only my perception of what he was, what he *is*.' He pointed at the cage. 'Even they wouldn't speak out about it, would you?'

Audrey looked at Mairi. 'Is it true?' she asked quietly.

'What difference would it have made?' Mairi said. 'Who would have believed it from a lass like me?'

Audrey felt the old nausea rising within her. *Girls like us . . . They think we're bad from birth.*

'Oh Mairi. I would have believed it.'

That was why Mairi had suspected the minister, why she had come to Audrey in her room that evening – because he had started on her.

'It's not why Alec took me anyway. He took me because I saw him.' Mairi pointed at Alec. 'That evening I was to go to the manse through the servants' tunnel, I saw him coming up from the basement carrying a tray. That was why he brought me here: he knew I'd tell. It was nothing to do with protecting me.'

Alec's face was hard, his jaw set. 'The minister would have ruined you just as he did Isbeil. Be grateful that I saved you before he did.'

'Grateful!' Mairi coughed. She was ill, Audrey realised. Of course she was, living down here in this airless, stench-filled room.

'They wouldn't have spoken out against him,' Alec continued. 'And even if they had, it would have fallen on deaf ears. A man of the kirk? No. I waited and I watched, and he carried on and on. I decided that the only way to save these girls was to hide them deep underground. Like Kilmeny.'

'The poem.' Audrey's eyes were still on Mairi, who was motioning with her head towards the other side of the room. Audrey followed her gaze and saw that beyond the cage was a curtain.

'But they're not safe here, Alec. They're not healthy. They are so thin.'

'That's because they won't eat their food.'

'Because you poison it!' Christy shouted suddenly. 'And then you whisper to us, don't you? Telling us your sick little stories. When we eat the food, the spirits come.'

The spirits come. He was drugging them. He was quite insane. She pictured Eliza – her vacant eyes, her nonsensical words. He had been drugging them and murmuring his fairy stories to them, down here in this deathly cell.

'You were doing the same to Eliza, weren't you, Alec? What happened? Why did you let her go?'

'As I said, Audrey, I am not an ogre. She became very ill. I decided I couldn't care for her here, as hard as I tried.'

'You took her out barefoot in a rainstorm and made her walk back to Broadford. And you threatened her.'

'I couldn't take the risk that she'd be traced back to Lanerly, or that she'd say something, that my work here would be stopped. I merely encouraged her to believe that it would be dangerous for her to speak out against the fairies. It always is.'

Audrey saw again Eliza's destroyed face, her empty eyes. 'You mean you drove her to such a state of fear and delusion that she didn't speak out even when the crofters lit a fire beneath her.'

Alec looked away. 'I couldn't have known they would do that,' he said quietly. 'I'm not responsible for their actions.'

Audrey stared at him, disbelieving. 'You've been drugging them, and me too. What with? Your aunt's opium?'

Still he did not look at her, and she was suddenly not afraid but furious. 'Answer me!'

'No, not opium. *Amanita muscaria.*' He looked at her at last. 'Fly agaric.'

'The toadstools?' She pictured the red and white spotted mushrooms of his fairy painting.

'Yes. I dry them. I've taken them myself. They aren't harmful.'

She remembered the musty smell of the shrouded room, and felt her stomach rise in memory of the acid. 'They harmed me.'

'You're perfectly well.'

'I was hallucinating. I was terrified.'

'You were getting too close to the truth. You had heard things; you had worked out that the vanishings were connected. It was important that you began to doubt your own conclusions.'

'Well you achieved that. I thought I was losing my reason. I *was* losing my reason. And you've done this to Eliza and Mairi and Christy when they were down here in the dark, alone.'

Christy had begun again to cry.

Alec gave Audrey a look of distaste. 'I thought that you of all people would understand.'

'Why? What on earth do you mean?'

'Do you think we didn't do our research, Audrey? That we didn't enquire as to what you'd been up to in London?'

Audrey's stomach dropped. *We.*

'My aunt wrote to that orphanage. You should have seen the response.'

She felt the blood leach from her face.

'But she understood it as well as I did, I think. You tried to protect those girls, didn't you? And what happened? Did the villain end up behind bars? Have the girls achieved their happy-ever-after?'

'No,' Audrey said quietly. 'It was never reported.'

'No, of course not. And still the man threatens you.'

She did not reply. He had been reading her letters, then. It was he who had moved the things on her desk.

He smiled. 'And yet you think that the authorities here on Skye would intervene in the case of a man of the church?'

She met his eye. 'But this, Alec. This is not the answer.'

'It's my answer.'

'You could have told me what you were doing.'

'I tried. You merely mocked me.'

'When?' But as soon as she had spoken the words, she knew. It was that afternoon in the grotto when she realised she had said something wrong. She saw again the light flickering on the walls, picking out the colours of the rocks, the iridescent shells. *For Kilmeny had been she knew not where, And Kilmeny had seen what she could not declare.* He had been testing her, and she had failed.

'I wasn't mocking you, Alec. I just didn't understand what you were trying to tell me.' *I have brought her away frae the snares of men.* 'You were telling me you were protecting them.'

'I had to help them, for no one else would.'

It was how she had felt about the orphanage girls, only warped into something monstrous. She looked again at Mairi. She had to get them out.

Alec was still talking. 'Even my aunt wouldn't stand up for Flora, did you know that? Even she, who'd fought all her life against the judgements and ignorance of others, couldn't bring herself to defend a girl ruined.' He looked at Audrey and laughed. 'You didn't know, did you? No, my aunt likes to give the impression that she's above all such matters – that she lives here alone, removed from the world out of choice. But like the rest of us mortals, she once wanted to be loved and adored. Just not by a man.' He smiled. 'Her parents still held out hopes of finding her one, but then came the accident. No one wanted a crippled wife. So she shut herself away here, out of sight. And what did she have left then but her stories, her precious stories?'

Audrey thought of Miss Buchanan's shrunken frame, her bright eyes. How unfair the world was, how cruel. Chewing people up and spitting them out, unwanted.

But the stories. The stories came from something. 'The birds,' she said. 'There were always the birds.'

Alec smiled in the half-darkness. 'Yes, I heard the stories about the black birds flying about above Eliza's house and that gave me the idea of stirring up the rooks just after you found Isbeil. It was easy, really.'

Audrey felt strange and sick. He had done that to her. He had made her think that it was something more than murder. 'And the starlings after you took Mairi. How did you do that?'

He shrugged. 'They often fly at this time of year. I needed to divert people's attention. They, and you, were only too willing to believe something mystical was involved.'

Audrey closed her eyes and thought of the swirling mass of birds. Was that really mere coincidence?

She opened her eyes, looked at Mairi. 'The story in Mairi's book about the woman disappearing on the Quiraing. You wrote that, didn't you? Just as you wrote the letter Christy supposedly sent Murdo?'

No answer.

'What letter?' It was Christy's voice, broken and low. 'What letter? What have you said?'

Audrey took a step closer to Alec. 'You can't save all the girls. You can't do this on your own. Why don't we go to the procurator fiscal in Portree? Or the county sheriff? I will speak for you.'

Alec narrowed his eyes. 'That won't work, Audrey.'

'No? Why not?' She took another step.

'If I let them go, they will accuse me of abducting them. They don't understand my purpose.'

'Oh, we understand,' Mairi said.

Audrey was moving slowly towards him, closer to the bell and the curtain. 'You can't keep them down here, Alec. They will grow ill, as Eliza did, or they will die, like Isbeil. You're a good man; you don't want that to happen. You don't want them to be down here all alone.'

'They will not be alone.'

She was close to him now, only a few steps away.

He met her eye and his gaze was frank, almost kind. 'They will have you.'

She ran then, pulling the servants' bell, pushing aside the curtain, opening the door behind it and streaking blindly into the blackness of the corridor. She flew down the passage into the deepening darkness, made it to the end of a long corridor and pulled open another door, but she heard his footsteps, then his breath, and her head was snapped back, his hand over her mouth. She bit, shouted, kicked and struggled, but his grip was strong and he pulled her back along the corridor and into the room, slamming the door shut.

He thrust her onto her front and stood on her back, hard, pushing her into the floor. Audrey could smell the chloroform as soon as he opened the bottle, and she could hear the girls screaming at him. She tried with all her remaining energy to twist herself up, but his hand was on her mouth again and the fumes were more than she could bear.

And then came a tapping. The sound of a stick on tiles.

'Stop that now.' The voice was loud, but level.

Audrey felt Alec relax his grip on her. She twisted her head round and saw Miss Buchanan, leaning on her silver cane.

'Well.' The woman was looking about the place, taking in the girls in the cage, the whole hideous truth of it.

Audrey could hear Alec's footsteps as he moved away from her towards his aunt. She crawled to her knees.

'So this is your story, is it, Alec? This is how you've been occupying yourself.'

Alec's voice was cold. 'How did you get down here so quickly?'

'I saw you and Audrey arrive in the bay. When you didn't appear, I gathered you must have entered via the servants' tunnel. I knew then that you had been up to something down here. And as I made my way down the stairs, I heard the bell, the bell that hasn't rung for three years.'

Audrey stood up slowly, her neck and back on fire with pain.

'You will let Mairi and Christy out of there,' Miss Buchanan told Alec. 'They're not animals. And then you will come with us upstairs and we will sit down and discuss this.'

'Of course. With tea,' Alec said. 'We will not do that. It's far too late.'

'It is never too late.'

'It was too late years ago, Aunt Buchanan.' His voice was oddly calm. 'It was too late as soon as Flora was dead.'

'Flora would not have wanted this, Alec.'

'How would you know? You barely listened to her. You did nothing to defend her against Father.'

'That's not true, Alec. You know how dear Flora was to me. I tried as best I could to reason with him, but as you are all too aware, my brother thinks very little of me or my opinion. I did what I could to help her.'

'You did not do enough!' He was moving towards her, his hand on his waistcoat.

For a moment Audrey stood frozen by fear, unable to believe he really meant to harm his own flesh and blood, or that it had to be her who stopped him. But as he came within a few paces of Miss Buchanan, he drew a knife from his waistcoat, and in that instant she ceased to think. She grabbed the lamp from the table beside her and rushed forward, bringing it down on the back of his head. With a sickening crash, the lamp splintered and Alec's hands were at his forehead. There came a high, strange screaming, which at first Audrey thought was Mairi or Christy, but it was Alec: the flames from the lamp had spread to his shirt and he was pulling at it, the fire moving from his shirt to his hair. Audrey saw Miss Buchanan's face lit with horror, but within moments she had removed her shawl and flung it over her nephew, pushing him to the ground, beating at the flames until they were burnt out and black and the room was silent save for their breathing.

She sat back from her nephew and looked at Audrey. 'The keys to the cage.'

'He has them,' Mairi said. 'They're in his waistcoat.'

Alec lay on his back, motionless, perhaps overcome by the fumes. Audrey walked carefully over to him. There was a hideous smell of burnt flesh, and of the blood that ran down his face and neck, pooling on the floor beside him. With shaking hands she felt along his chest for his pocket and slid her hand inside, feeling the metal, warm to the touch. She drew out a bunch of keys, then pulled away

from him. As she did so, his body gave a shudder and a
scream escaped from her lips, the keys falling to the ground
beside his head. She stooped to collect them and they were
wet against her hands, but she rushed over to the cage,
floundering in the semi-dark until at last she found the one
that fitted. The key turned in the lock. The door opened.

Chapter 14

And from that day on, that was where they lived, Bainne and her little sister, growing fat on cherries and apples and cow's milk and cream. They had no desire to see the world or its people, for the fairies were the only ones who had ever been kind to them.

Once in a while, they would be joined by a new friend – another child that the fairy king had saved. And sometimes, of a silver-mooned eve, he would take them all above the ground to stare at the sky, asparkle with stars.

Alec Buchanan

Mrs Campbell was the first of the crofters to visit Lanerly. It was the third week of November by then, and trails of fieldfares and redwings chattered across the sky, descending onto rowan trees to feast on the scarlet fruit before moving on again to the south. Mrs Campbell arrived just after three o'clock dressed in her best black gown and bonnet, peat-reek flowing from her skirts.

Audrey showed her through to the library and to Miss Buchanan, who sat straight-backed, nervous, Vinegar at her side.

When Audrey had first suggested to Miss Buchanan that she meet the crofters, she had been sceptical. 'These people will not want to see me, nor tell me their tales. They never have, and they certainly won't now.'

Audrey, however, had persisted. 'They've been telling Mairi and me that they want to see you. You're the woman who's collected their tales, who saved their daughters.'

'I hardly did that.'

'That's what they believe. And think, Miss Buchanan – you would hear the tales yourself, first-hand. The original language; the true magic.' Eventually she had agreed.

It was strange to see the two women together. Audrey supposed they must be about the same age, but whereas Mrs Campbell had the parched, leathery skin of a woman who had worked most of her life in the fields, Miss Buchanan was merely faded and wrinkled, like an old leaf.

'I didn't imagine that you would want to talk to me directly. Not given my nephew's actions, and my brother's.'

Mrs Campbell stared at her with her pale grey eyes. 'It was you that was calling the sheriff in, though, wasn't it? You who stopped Master Buchanan? No matter what your brother's done over the years, we won't be forgetting that.'

Lord Buchanan had left the island over a week ago, not intending to return. The minister too had disappeared, presumed to have left in the dead of night, terrified of the crofters and of Murdo Maclean. Then Murdo himself had gone, saying only that he was taking his family far away. In his place, a new agent had been employed to sell off the land, turning the inhabitants out for deer forest and sheep farms. The money was needed, Lord Buchanan had said, presumably to pay the bribes to keep Alec out of the courts and move him into an asylum in Inverness. Even Lanerly itself was to be sold.

Miss Buchanan raised her eyes to Mrs Campbell's. 'I understand that you have the gift – the second sight. Tell me about how it came to you. When did you first know?'

Audrey stayed in the library, supposedly to assist, but Miss Buchanan's Gaelic was far better than her own and the two women spoke so quickly and urgently that she did not understand everything that was said. Her thoughts strayed to Alec, the grief-broken boy who had grown warped and twisted like a hazel tree in the sea wind; the storyteller lost in his own story. She had wondered at first if she should have known, if she should have guessed what he was about. But she would not play that game again. She was not responsible for Alec, nor Samuel; their actions were their own.

And she was a little surer of her path now. Miss Buchanan had secured an agreement with a publisher: *The Stories of Skye* would be published in the New Year and Audrey would receive a percentage of the profits. Her own name would appear on the book. Shawfield too had written to her, asking if she might assist him with his work. The Isle of Skye might not be her home, but it was the closest she'd found to one and she wanted to stay. She would carve out a place, just as everyone did.

Mrs Campbell glanced up, met Audrey's eye. 'We should be going, Miss Hart. They'll be gathering at five, and we don't want to be late.'

They were all there this time: Mackenzie and the guests from his ceilidh, twenty or more crofters from the townships around. A watery sun shone in the sky as they waited at the graveyard beside the shore. Mairi stood between Audrey and Mrs Campbell, her face pearl-pale, her eyes dark pools. She was stronger now, but not well enough to be here; she had nevertheless been insistent that she come. For this was the burial Isbeil should have had to start with, albeit not within the kirkyard walls.

The fishermen were here now, in their dark blue jackets, carrying the wooden coffin on their shoulders. The minister had been right about that – they had moved her away from the sea believing a suicide would scare away the fish, and it was the money from the fish that kept their families alive. But of course Isbeil was no suicide; Audrey had never believed she was.

As the men moved to the place where the girl had first been buried, two others dug out the soil that had since been filled in. Mrs Campbell began the singing and it was the same song that Audrey remembered from before, only this time enriched by many voices and sung in the daylight rather than under the cover of dark.

It was the daylight that enabled them to see the ground.

It was the daylight that led one of the men to shout out, and the others to run to the graveside, and a girl to shriek, and the rest of them to walk forward and stare in silent horror at what lay before them. The grave had not been empty but had been filled in for a reason. And now the earth had been uncovered to reveal the form of a man: the minister, shrouded in soil.

The procurator fiscal was a tall, white-haired man with sunken cheeks and quick, intelligent eyes. 'It's important, you see, Miss Hart, that we don't set folks blethering away. Unlike in England, investigations of this kind are kept private.'

'I understand, sir.' Audrey looked about the sunless room above Broadford Inn that the procurator had made his office. The sheriff of Portree had commissioned an inquiry and the procurator was now at work interviewing witnesses.

'You know Inspector McMann, I believe.'

Audrey nodded at the inspector from Portree police station. He seemed smaller seated next to the procurator, less robust.

'We meet again, Miss Hart. I should have listened better to you last time, eh?'

Audrey gave a weak smile.

'I'm grateful to you for coming to see me,' the procurator said. 'It's not a pleasant matter, of course, but there aren't many who can be telling us about events at Lanerly. Alec Buchanan is, I understand, confined to a private institution.

Some believed he should face trial for abduction, but it seems our sheriff has been persuaded to think differently. And Mairi Finlayson is still in a poor way, is she?'

'She's much better than she was, but remains weak. And she prefers not to speak of what happened.'

'Of course. There's no need for us to be bothering her.' He opened a folder of papers and dipped his pen into his inkwell.

'You know where they found the Reverend Carlisle's body.' He looked at Audrey. 'And you don't need me to be telling you that he was not getting there by himself. What I want to know is whether you ever saw or heard of anything said against the minister that we ought to know about.'

Audrey twisted the ring on her finger. 'No, I don't think so.'

'Not even by Christy Maclean's father, Murdo? I can imagine he would have had a fair few things to say.'

'Perhaps, but I didn't hear them said. Murdo left Skye very quickly, taking his daughter and his wife with him. He didn't explain where they were going.'

'When was it that they left, would you say?'

'I think it was two days after I found Christy and Mairi. On the sixth of November. The day after Alec was arrested.'

The procurator glanced at the inspector before writing a note on a sheet of paper.

'Were you able to tell when the minister died?' Audrey asked.

'It's not an exact science now.' He looked up at her. 'But we would say probably around that time.'

Audrey looked at her hands. 'Yes.'

'And you've no idea where it was that Mr Maclean went?'

'None. He merely said that he was leaving. We've heard nothing from him since. But I think he's originally from Lewis.'

'Aye, we heard that.'

Audrey hesitated. 'Sir, did the post-mortem on the minister's body reveal a cause of death?'

The procurator coughed. 'The report was not conclusive, Miss Hart.'

'May I ask what it showed?'

A pause. 'The pathologist found a quantity of soil on the minister's lungs.'

Audrey met his eye and the procurator gave a slight nod. She shivered and looked away.

'Well, thank you, Miss Hart. You've been a great help.' The procurator closed his file of papers. 'As I said, I'd be grateful if you'd keep a still tongue in your head about all this. And now I think the inspector has some information for you.'

The policeman removed a piece of paper from his pocket and Audrey felt her stomach turn to water. It was a letter from the police in London, or a letter from the courts containing accusations of lies, slander, libel, insanity.

'We received a telegram via Dunvegan from a Mrs Kingsmere.'

It was a mistake. He meant Mr Kingsmere.

'Here you go.' He passed her the paper, which in her confusion Audrey almost dropped.

Dear Miss Hart,

Forgive the imposition, but I write to you urgently regarding forthcoming divorce proceedings. Your stepmother informs me that you have some information of which the court should be aware, namely about my husband's conduct at the Westminster Asylum. I would be much obliged if you could wire at once indicating whether you would be willing to provide my solicitor with a statement.

I believe we could help one another, and perhaps also others.

Yours very respectfully,
Viola Kingsmere

Despite herself, Audrey smiled; felt laughter rising uncontrolled in her throat. Dorothea had known the authorities would never touch a man of Samuel's standing. No jury would convict. In the new court, however, his name could be ruined, and his fortune depleted. *We find other ways to win.*

'Do you have a reply?' The policeman was watching her curiously.

'Yes,' Audrey said at length. 'Please write and tell Mrs Kingsmere that I would be happy to assist. And that my statement will follow in the next week.'

'Aye, very well.' He coughed, stood up. 'I'll show you back through the inn, Miss Hart. It's not a place for a lady.'

★

Miss Buchanan was in the hallway when she returned, standing at the window waiting.

'Well? What happened?'

'I'm not supposed to speak of it.'

'No, I'm sure you're not.' She ushered Audrey into the parlour and poured tea while questioning her on what the procurator had said.

'And then?'

'That was all he asked me.'

'But there is something else,' Miss Buchanan said, sitting back. 'Something else you're not telling me.'

Audrey twisted her hand in the fabric of her skirt. 'Yes, but it's nothing to do with the minister. It's about the orphanage at which I taught. You know about that, I think.' She removed the telegram from her pocket, unfolded it and handed it across to Miss Buchanan.

The older woman put on her spectacles and read the message, raised her eyebrows. 'Well. The law has not even been commenced and already the lawyers circle. What do you intend to do?'

'To give a statement, of course.'

'You know the man may accuse you of slander.'

'He might, I suppose. But it will be too late, won't it? It will already have been read in open court. The damage will have been done.'

Miss Buchanan smiled. 'Sometimes you are very much like your mother.'

Audrey stared at her. 'You knew my mother?'

Miss Buchanan's smile faded, her face slackened and

she looked briefly defeated. 'A long time ago, yes.'

'How?' she whispered. 'Why did you not tell me?'

Miss Buchanan pressed her fingertips together. 'I met Matilda when she was working at the kelp-making on the Buchanan estate. I used to go to the ceilidhs in those days, you see. Not often, but occasionally. She agreed to tell me her tales from home.' She looked at Audrey. 'She was captivating. Warm. Beautiful. She was much younger than me, and very different, of course, but we became friends.' She paused. 'When the work came to an end, she moved back to her parents in Ullapool. And then of course she married your father and had you.' She spoke briskly, as though it were of no consequence.

'But she kept returning to Skye.'

'She did. When she could. We had only a little time together, but that was the way it was.'

Audrey watched her, understanding. 'I came here too, didn't I, as a child?'

'Yes. A few times when you were very young. I confess I rather resented you.' She laughed: the sound of splintering wood.

'Why on earth didn't you say all this before, Miss Buchanan? Why didn't you mention it when I first wrote to you?'

The woman's lips twitched. 'I hadn't spoken about your mother for many years. When I received your letter, it was a shock. I thought you must have known. That it was the reason you'd contacted me. I decided it would be better to wait until I met you, find out what you knew. But when we spoke, I realised that you knew nothing.'

'No, I didn't.' Audrey breathed out. 'You could have told me. It would have been a kindness.'

'I intended to, but it just didn't seem possible. You are so like her, you see. The same expressions, the same determined way of going about things. And then, well it was too late to say anything.'

As she spoke, the layers of defence Miss Buchanan had built up over the years were peeled back, and Audrey saw for a moment the loneliness of decades.

'In any event, I didn't want you to think that I'd chosen you because of your mother. I didn't, in fact, want to speak about her at all.'

Miss Buchanan was just the same as her father, then. They did not wish to speak of their sadness, their disappointments, and so she must be lied to and kept in the dark. Well, she did not accept that any more. She deserved answers. 'What do you know of her death?'

Miss Buchanan glanced up at her, pained. 'What do you mean?'

'I was told very little about it. Only that there was a collapse; that she slipped and fell. You must have heard something of it. You must yourself have asked.'

Miss Buchanan looked very pale, suddenly tired. 'I was there, Audrey. We both fell.'

For a moment it was as though Audrey was looking at the scene from the outside: two women, one old, one young, seated at a parlour table, talking. 'But my father told me that he was with her. He said she had wandered apart from him and fallen.'

Miss Buchanan shook her head. 'No. He was not there. I was. That's why I walk with this silver stick, why I live with constant pain.' She stood up and moved to her bureau, unlocking a little drawer and taking out an envelope. Her movements seemed strangely, unbearably slow. She returned to Audrey and placed the envelope in her hands, then took the seat beside her.

From the envelope Audrey removed a newspaper cutting, faded pale by time and touch. It was a report from the *Inverness Journal*.

Fatal Accident at Staffin

We regret to announce the occurrence on 5th May of a most melancholy accident at the Quiraing. Miss Charlotte Buchanan of Broadford, Skye, was out walking with a Mrs Matilda Hart, a friend visiting from Aberfeldy, when part of a cliff gave way and both fell from considerable height. The descent from the cliff edge is some forty feet and jagged rocks protrude at regular intervals.

Mrs Hart was killed. Miss Charlotte Buchanan, whose fall was broken by a rock, was severely injured. She is being treated in Portree for various fractures and it is believed and hoped that she will recover. The deplorable event has occasioned a general expression of sympathy and regret towards the families of both women.

Beneath the article were two pictures: on the left was a print of the image that Audrey had looked at so often, of herself standing with her mother, her mother's arm around her. On the right was a picture of a tall, upright woman in a riding habit, a crop in her hand, her fair hair gathered back into a chignon.

She looked at Miss Buchanan, her eyes swimming. 'Why would my father lie? Why would he say he was there?'

'I suppose because to tell the truth would involve him explaining to people why he was not on that mountain with your mother; why I was. Maybe he didn't want you to do your own investigating when you were older and find out about me. That is what I assume, Audrey, but you would have to ask him.'

Audrey felt sapped entirely of energy. 'Did she die immediately?'

'She did. She did not suffer.'

'You did.'

'Yes. I did.'

'You are "L".'

'Yes. Lotty. She called me Lotty. A ridiculous name, one that no one else has ever called me.'

As Audrey stared at her, she felt the facts upon which she had built her life disintegrating. 'Why are you only telling me all this now?'

'Because I'm a weak old woman who finds it easier to collect other people's stories than tell her own. Because I've spent my life hiding from others so that they might not judge me. They say in the townships that I'm a witch – I know that. But I've never turned into a cat, or upturned eggshells to make ships sink. I've merely stayed here in this house and made my life among the stories and artefacts of other people's lives. I'm sorry. I've failed you both.'

Audrey closed her eyes. She thought of her father telling her the story of her mother's death. It was just that: a story. One that made things easier for him. She thought too of his letter summoning her home. He had known she would find out. He was not afraid for her. He was afraid for himself.

Miss Buchanan had pulled her chair up closer to Audrey. She was placing a book in her hands. 'Here. Your mother's stories. You see, I already had them. She copied them down for me long ago. It was she, in fact, who first had the idea that I should make a formal collection.'

And there was her mother's neat, curled handwriting and the stories that Audrey knew so well – 'The Harvest Maiden', 'The Little Bird' – but with many more that she had never seen before, and she felt a sob rising in her throat because there was so much of her mother that she had known nothing about, so much that her mother had concealed because she felt she had no choice.

'I have more that I can show you, in time,' Miss Buchanan said.

Audrey turned over the pages, feeling the paper beneath her fingers, but her eyes were too clouded to read. All this time she had been searching for her mother, and she had been right here, at Lanerly.

★

The sea that morning was the grey of gunmetal and the ground was hard with frost. In the sky above, a gull shrieked and turned, its wing a flash of silver. Audrey, standing on the pier, thought of the starlings that had appeared the day after Mairi vanished, of the strange light above the bay. Were those mere coincidences? Mirages? *Everything can be explained*, Miss Buchanan had said. But even she could not account for it all.

She watched the boat approach, the figure of the foreman as he raised his hand.

Mairi stepped forward and took Miss Buchanan's arm. 'It's here, miss.'

'Yes, girl, I am not altogether blind.'

The little boat came in next to the pier and a man moved to help the boatmen bring it alongside the landing jetty, throwing the mooring lines and securing it with springs.

'If I'm to travel at all,' Miss Buchanan had said, 'it will be by boat, not by some wretched coach. Yes, I know it's not the season for it, but my broken old bones can't be doing with the bumps and jolts. And in any event, I like to see the sea.'

The men helped them climb into the vessel, two stepping forward to help Miss Buchanan embark. Mairi and Audrey handed up the bags full of clothing and journals and books.

They were going to Trotternish once again, to stay with John Shawfield. He was keen to assist with *The Stories of Skye* and it would, Audrey pointed out, be far quicker and easier for them to meet in person. Miss Buchanan had resisted initially, of course. It would be the first time she had returned to the area since the accident; the first time she had left the house in years.

'But you could show me the places you visited with my mother. I think you owe me that, at least.'

And so now they were seated, all three of them, swathed in shawls, in a boat that bobbed upon the pewter-grey sea. Looking at Mairi, swaddled in wool, Audrey thought of Isbeil in her damp blue dress, of placing her shawl across her shoulders as she tried to help her that very first day.

It's just the sea, that's all it is. I never liked the sea.

As they pulled forward and rounded Irishman's Point, Audrey looked back at Lanerly, a dark form outlined against the pale winter sky, Beinn Na Cailleach rising behind it, a giantess protecting the land.

A breeze filled the sail and the boat moved faster, the cold spray bursting around the bow, the rigging humming, the wind on their faces, and the open sea ahead.

Historical Note

The idea for this book came from a real case from the 1880s, the West Ham Vanishings, in which a series of children and young adults disappeared from the East End of London. It is said that one of them, Eliza Carter, returned briefly before her final disappearance to tell her friends that the fairies had kidnapped her and forbidden her to return home. Her blue dress was later found in West Ham Park, its buttons missing, but she was never seen again.

The folk tales related in the book are mainly adaptations of stories found in *Superstitions of the Highlands and Islands of Scotland* by John Gregorson Campbell (1862), *Popular Tales of the West Highlands* by J. F. Campbell (1890), *Fairy Faith in Celtic Countries* by Walter Evans-Wentz (1911), and *Folklore of the Isle of Skye* by Mary Julia MacCulloch [in *Folklore*, 72 (3), 509–19, and *Folklore*, 33 (2), 201–14 (1922)].

If you would like to read further about the Clearances in Skye and what followed I recommend *Martyrs: Glendale and the Revolution in Skye* by Roger Hutchinson (2015).

Thank you for reading this book. I love to hear from readers so do get in touch on social media, or via my website, which was designed by the brilliant Faith Tilleray.

http://annamazzola.com

https://twitter.com/Anna_Mazz

https://www.facebook.com/AnnaMazzolaWriter/

https://www.instagram.com/annamazzolawriter/

Acknowledgements

My mother, Elizabeth, has long had a fascination with fairies and fairy tales. This book is partly her fault. Worse still, she helped look after my children so that I could write it.

Thank you to my husband, Jake, and to all my family for supporting me and my writing. Not everyone is as lucky.

Thank you to my agent, Juliet Mushens, the Wonder Woman of the literary world (if Wonder Woman wore leopard skin prints).

Thanks to my brilliant editor, Imogen Taylor, and all the lovely Tinder Press team.

Thank you to all my writer friends for keeping me sane, and to North London Writers, South London Writers and Mary Chamberlain, who helped me make this a better book.

And thank you to all those who generously gave their time to assist me with my research, in particular Alison Beaton and Anne Macdonald at the Skye and Lochalsh

Archive Centre, Professor Louise A. Jackson at the University of Edinburgh, Hannah McDiarmid, Carolyn Emerick, Professor Chris French, Will Francis (boat adviser), Dr Tom Wedgwood (medical adviser) and Jake Wetherall (technical consultant and husband).

Lastly, thank you to the Folklore Thursday community on Twitter for all their help, in particular to G. H. Finn for coming up with the name Vinegar for Miss Buchanan's cat.